Death at the Orange Locks

Anja de Jager

CONSTABLE

CONSTABLE

First published in Great Britain in 2020 by Constable

This edition published in 2021 by Constable

1 3 5 7 9 10 8 6 4 2

A CIP catalogue record for this book
is available from the British Library.

ISBN: 978-1-47213-046-4

Typeset in Bembo by Photoprint, Torquay
Printed and bound in Great Britain by Clays Ltd, Elcograf S.p.A.

Papers used by Constable are from well-managed forests and other
responsible sources.

Constable
An imprint of
Little, Brown Book Group
Carmelite House
50 Victoria Embankment
London EC4Y 0DZ

An Hachette UK Company
www.hachette.co.uk

www.littlebrown.co.uk

Chapter 1

There was a noticeable chill in the air as Thomas Jansen and I stood on the northern bank of the IJ, close to the Orange Locks. He wore his thick jacket done up to under his chin and had his hands stuffed deep in his pockets. Earlier, when the sun had been out, there had been a hint of warmth in the air, but now the wind blew over the water and took the temperature down a couple of degrees.

This water was the source of Amsterdam's wealth. It was now a river but it still carried memories of when it had been part of the South Sea, many centuries ago. To my eyes, even today it still seemed like a sea, with massive cruise ships docking at the inland harbour and ships carrying freight. Across the wide expanse, the buildings of the port were clearly visible, shaped like massive whales, as if the captains needed that visible reminder to help them figure out exactly where they were supposed to dock. It would take a ferry more than five minutes to cross from the south bank to the north.

The Orange Locks were the border of where Amsterdam ended and the villages began. To the east, the IJ became the IJssel and then the IJsselmeer, a lake so large that early last century a small section of it was poldered to build a city, which now had over a hundred thousand inhabitants. Before the enormous Orange Locks had been built in the 1870s, that lake had been part of the sea.

The Dutch obsession with controlling our waterways had no limits. When we saw water, we could never just leave it be. There was always the question of what we could do with it: polder it and build a city on it, swim in it, dam it, build bridges over it, send boats across it.

Or, in the case of the man I was looking at, die in it.

The body lay on top of a plastic tarpaulin, and yellow tape cordoned off part of the road. Even though it was hard to judge someone's age after they'd been in the water for a long time, I was quite sure he was middle-aged. He was the right age to have been on one of the river cruise ships. I could only hope that wasn't the case, because it would be problematic. We could do without a boat holding thousands of people being stuck in Amsterdam's inland harbour, or having to track down someone who'd been on a ship that had already departed days ago.

'I've got to ask,' the female police officer in uniform said. 'You're Lotte Meerman, aren't you?' Her trousers were wet up to her knees. The fluorescent yellow of her jacket stood out against the dark grey of the water.

'Yes,' I said. 'That's right.'

She grinned from ear to ear. 'I thought I recognised you.' Her smile was nearly as bright as her jacket. She didn't look old enough to be a police officer. Her partner didn't look much older. That was clearly a sign of my own ageing.

'Why didn't you leave him in the water?' Thomas cut through the chat.

'I'm sorry.' Her smile rapidly disappeared. 'I know we're supposed to do that.'

That was standard procedure. For floaters, careful recovery was important. The water cooled the body down quickly but then kept it at that temperature. Especially at this time of year. It made it easier for forensics.

'If you knew that, why didn't you do it?' Thomas asked.

'We thought that maybe he was still alive,' her partner said.

I couldn't understand why they'd thought he could possibly have been alive. The body was bloated. This guy had been in the water for days. It was much more likely that they hadn't thought at all but had acted before their brains had kicked into gear.

'Right,' Thomas said. 'He was floating face down, wasn't he?'

'Yes, and as soon as we turned him over, we saw he was dead,' the female officer said.

We had been called in because there were cuts and bruising on the man's face. That didn't necessarily mean that he had been assaulted before he drowned. He had been floating in a body of water used by a number of large vessels and could have been hit by any of them postmortem. The forensics team would examine the body more closely to see what had happened. Death had not been that recent. If I'd had to guess, I would have said that he had died less than a week ago. Luckily, we didn't have to rely on my guesswork.

'Leave a floater in the water next time.' Thomas was right to pull them up on it. I would have let it go because it was chilly enough today that it didn't matter a great deal. Had it been the height of summer, it would have been a different story.

I wondered how long these two had been police officers. They'd carefully taped off the area around the body. Sure, we would want people to stay away from the corpse, but this wasn't the crime scene. Who knew where he'd actually entered the water. I wasn't sure it was even a crime. As the body was fully dressed, he could have just fallen in somewhere. It wouldn't be the first time that someone, possibly drunk, had toppled into a canal and died. The postmortem would tell us an awful lot more.

'We thought it would take a while before we'd get help out here,' the male officer said. 'That everybody would be at Centraal station.'

There had been a suspected terror alert at Amsterdam's main station this morning. Apparently a reliable source had given a warning of a large-scale impending attack and it had sparked a major operation. The station had been closed and the capital was on high alert. While most of our colleagues were involved with that, Thomas and I had to stand here at the water's edge and deal with a body. It was the icing on the cake that the first officers on the scene had already messed up. With a bit of luck it would turn out to be an accidental death.

'But at least we got to meet you,' the female officer said to me. 'I'm sorry we messed up.' She handed me a wallet. 'This was in his inside pocket. The other pockets were empty.' She paused for a second. 'I checked as soon as we'd pulled him ashore. That will help you identify him, won't it?' She was desperately keen to have done something right, bless her.

'He still had his wallet?'

'Yes, his coat was zipped up, so it hadn't fallen out.'

I opened the wallet. There were credit cards and a driving licence. They were heavily water-damaged but the plastic had done its job and the details were still readable. The dead man's name was Patrick van der Linde. His address placed him on the south side of the water, on the KNSM Island. He was a local, then.

'Have you notified his next of kin?' I asked.

'No, we waited for you.'

Thomas grimaced, but I would have waited too. Nobody liked having to tell someone that their husband, son or father had died.

The face of the male cop was starting to look as grey as the cloudy sky. 'Go and dry off,' I said. 'We'll take it from here.'

After they'd walked off, I went over to speak to the woman who'd first spotted the body. 'At what time did you see him?' I asked her.

'I called you as soon as I noticed him,' she said. 'It was just after nine, I think. I was out walking my dog.'

'You always walk your dog here?' Thomas asked.

'Yes, I always take the same route.' She smiled at him and ignored me. I guess he was attractive in the way of a man who had been cute when young and hadn't aged too badly. I bet he used more skin treatment products than I did. I didn't hold that against him. 'Twice a day: morning and evening.'

'The body wasn't here last night?' I asked.

The woman shrugged. 'I'm not sure. I don't think I would have seen it in the dark.' She was definitely less interested in answering my questions. *She* wasn't excited to meet me.

It did surprise me that nobody had spotted the body before that. There were always a lot of joggers and dog walkers using the path along the water's edge. Maybe someone had seen him but not called us, or maybe they'd thought it was only a mannequin or something. It was possible that he had floated closer to the middle of the shipping lane, less easy to see from the road. Over a hundred thousand boats a year went through the locks, and if it had been the height of summer, I would have expected one of them to have spotted him. How quickly drowned people were found all depended on where they'd entered the water and what the current was like, and of course whether we were searching for a body or not. If we were lucky, they would wash up at one of the banks quickly. With this man, it had taken days.

'He was face down,' the woman said. 'Otherwise I would have jumped in to try to save him, but he was floating, his arms stretched out. He wasn't moving.'

'He's been dead for days,' Thomas said.

'That's what I told them,' she pointed at the two cops in the distance, 'but they insisted on dragging him out. I don't think they really listened to me.'

I wondered if their minds had been on the attack at Centraal station that they had been excluded from rather than on the task at hand. Alternatively, maybe this was the first dead body they'd dealt with and adrenaline had kicked in and they'd acted instinctively.

I took the woman's details and told her to go home. We might have more questions for her later, but I doubted it. Forensics arrived. They bagged up the body and took it to the lab.

I held up the driving licence to Thomas. 'Better do this, hadn't we?' It would be unpleasant and we should get it out of the way.

Chapter 2

The KNSM Island had been created at the beginning of the twentieth century. The word 'island' always made me think of naturally shaped pieces of land, like Texel in the north of the Netherlands. This island wasn't like that at all. It displayed the Dutch liking for straight lines. The perfect edges screamed that this land was artificially made, but since that was the case with so much of the Netherlands anyway, it didn't stand out. A large part of the country had been reclaimed from the sea, and this island in the IJ was no different.

The KNSM – the Royal Dutch Shipping Company – had constructed the island to accommodate their factories and warehouses. Naming it after themselves was probably the ultimate in advertising; or perhaps the ultimate in hubris, because not long afterwards, they went bankrupt. After that, the land hadn't been used for decades, and squatters had moved in and made the place theirs. But twenty years ago, Amsterdam's relentless expansion had created a need to use every centimetre of land that could be found, and the island had been redeveloped. Right at Amsterdam's eastern edge, it was now a trendy and buzzing part of town.

The address on the driving licence was at the far end. Flats had been built in a large ring around a communal open space dotted with concrete benches and plants. Patrick's flat was on the twelfth floor. I pushed the button for the lift. Not many places in Amsterdam had lifts. If there was anything that identified the city — apart from the amount of water — it was the steepness and height of its stairs. In my place along the canal, I had to go up three vertiginous flights of steps before I reached my front door. I liked to think that they kept me fit, though if you had problems with your knees, there were better places to live. Here, we went up twelve floors without having to do any work at all.

I rang the doorbell. A woman with blonde highlights opened the door. From Patrick's driving licence, we knew he'd been in his late fifties. This woman looked about the same age. People would probably describe her as well preserved. She wore a string of pearls, and fake diamonds adorned the front of her black loafers. Her pink lipstick was perfectly applied.

'Yes?' she said. 'How can I help you?' She didn't seem distressed. This struck me as odd. The man we'd found had been dead for days. Surely she must have been worried about him, unless he was in the habit of leaving home for a week without contacting his wife.

'I'm Detective Lotte Meerman,' I said as I showed her my badge.

'Of course, I've heard of you,' she said, smiling widely. 'Come on in. I'm Margreet. Margreet van der Linde.'

I hadn't been surprised when my uniformed colleague had recognised my name, but the fact that members of

9

the public were now doing the same was disconcerting. Margreet's smile indicated that she was pleased I was here. That she'd been expecting me, almost.

It made me feel even worse about the news we had to give her.

It was always in moments like these that the professional defence, the ability to keep an emotional distance, melted away. I had no problems looking at a body, but death became reality in the face of the people who were left behind.

We followed her down a narrow corridor, past a glass door to the kitchen and into a living room with a circular table at one end and a sofa at the other. The windows gave an uninterrupted view over the water of the harbour and the houses on the other side. Margreet sat down on a large leather chair.

'I'm so sorry to have to give you bad news,' Thomas said. 'A man was found drowned this morning and we have reason to believe it's your husband.'

The smile on her face didn't disappear. 'No, no, that can't be right.' She waved her hands in front of her energetically, palms facing us, to indicate that we were clearly wrong and to ward off our negative words. 'Pat's a really good swimmer. Thanks for coming here, but it must be someone else.'

'We don't know exactly what happened yet,' I said, 'but we found this on the body.' I showed her the wallet and its contents. 'Is that his?'

She kept eye contact with me and didn't even glance down. 'I'm sorry you've had a wasted trip; it can't be him.'

'We would like you to formally identify him,' Thomas said. 'And once we know more about the cause of death, we may have more questions.'

She shook her head. 'I really don't see the need. It can't be him, he can't have drowned.'

'Is there someone who can go with you?' Thomas carried on as if she hadn't said anything. Margreet's unwillingness to even consider that the dead man was her husband was clearly annoying him.

I was equally convinced that the man found in the water had been the man whose photo was on the driving licence, but I also recognised her attitude for the self-preservation exercise it really was. The longer she could convince herself that her husband hadn't died, the longer she could keep smiling.

'It's important that we identify him,' Thomas said.

I looked out of the window and could see four people swimming in the water of the canal; dark shapes pulling orange buoys behind them. Not only did those floats alert boats to keep their distance, but they were also hollow and kept the swimmers' belongings dry and safe. I knew this because one of my friends had once persuaded me to go for an open-water swim in the canal with her. Even though it had been refreshing and fascinating to see the streets from down below, I still preferred to be on dry land. If I had to exercise, I would rather be on a bicycle. It was warmer, and less likely to give me a disease. The people I could see in the canal probably weren't taking in gulps of water. They swam like older ladies in a swimming pool, with their heads high, chatting as they propelled themselves forward.

'Or we can ask someone else instead,' Thomas persevered, 'if you don't feel up to it.'

'Well, you know my daughter.' Margreet looked at me. 'Should I get her to go? Even if there's really no point?'

I stopped looking at the swimmers. 'I know her?'

'Yes. My daughter and my son-in-law met with you two days ago. To tell you that my husband had gone missing. Surely you remember.'

For a moment I couldn't think who she was talking about. Then realisation hit like a ton of bricks. 'You mean Nadia? Nadia's your daughter?'

Thomas shot me a look that I could easily interpret. It said: is this something we need to talk about?

And yes, he was right, we needed to talk about it, but not here, not now. I'd tell him what had happened once we were outside.

To give myself a moment, I looked at the swimmers again as I remembered the moment the duty officer had contacted me and said there were two people waiting to see me.

I shouldn't have asked for their names. I should have gone downstairs and been confronted with them out of the blue. It would have been easier. Instead, I'd done the normal thing and asked who they were. As soon as the duty officer told me, my stomach churned as if someone had punched me.

'We reported my husband missing as soon as twenty-four hours passed and the police were finally willing to look into it,' Margreet said. 'They told you that, didn't they?'

I hadn't been the one they had reported him missing to. They had only come to see me to ask if I could expedite things. When I hadn't volunteered to take the case on – because why would I? – they hadn't told me his name. They hadn't shown me a photo. Nadia's surname wasn't van der Linde.

I hadn't connected the dots. If I had, I wouldn't have come here.

Chapter 3

Thomas managed to hold back from asking me questions until we were at a café on the south side of the island, overlooking the water where I'd seen the swimmers. They'd gone by the time we got there. Margreet had given him Nadia's number, and after we'd left the flat, he'd called her and asked her to do the formal identification instead of her mother. This was easier than persuading Margreet. I thought it was the right choice: Nadia was probably better capable of dealing with the traumatic strain the identification would cause. Charlie Schippers, our colleague and third team member, was going to accompany her. I assumed that her husband was going to come with her too. I didn't want to think about the two of them, but I knew a conversation about them was coming up.

Thomas had gone to order our coffees and I stared out of the window. He knew me well enough to understand that caffeine would make this upcoming chat a lot easier, but to be honest, I was expecting it to feel like an interrogation.

Nearby, a row of houseboats was moored in what had once been a working harbour. This area, Eastern Docklands, was made up of more man-made islands and harbours. The boat closest to me had washing dangling from a line strung where the sail would have been: three black T-shirts and a bunch of random socks. There was a single red sock, a lone striped one, one with dots and one that was solemn black. What had happened to their partners? Had they been twinned with other odd socks? On another line, some pairs of underpants, a tracksuit top and jogging bottoms flapped manically in the wind. The top was grey, the bottoms were blue. Whoever had done the laundry had washed a load of things that didn't go together. It was possible that they had hung them out to indicate that the boat was lived in; the equivalent of leaving the lights on when you went out in the evening.

'Fill me in.' Thomas's voice broke through my study of the ship. He put my cappuccino in front of me. 'How do you know the daughter?'

There was no point pretending, and I couldn't think of a smart way to escape the question. 'Nadia, Margreet's daughter, is my ex-husband's new wife. They came to the police station two days ago to ask if I could get involved in locating her missing father.'

'Seriously? Your ex-husband?' Thomas knew me well enough to have heard all the stories about Arjen and how we'd divorced less than a year after the death of our baby daughter, after he'd cheated on me and got his secretary pregnant. 'He's a brave man, coming to see you.'

'His wife's father was missing, so he thought he'd ask me for help.'

Thomas laughed. 'But to talk to you about that, it's . . . I don't even know what to call it. You of all people.'

I shrugged. When I'd heard they'd come to see me on Monday morning, I had thought they were certifiably insane. That thought had been immediately followed by the question of how desperate they must have been.

On my way down to meet them, I'd felt worry sitting in my stomach as heavy as a millstone. I didn't want to open the door and see the man I'd managed to avoid for four years. Amsterdam wasn't a big city, and a couple of times I'd thought I'd seen someone who looked like him and had crossed the road or turned into a side street to avoid a situation that was only going to give me pain. But now I was going to walk straight into it.

If you're a detective, it's hard to refuse to talk to someone who is visiting a police station. I didn't go to the ladies' first to check my hair and make-up, and I was proud of that. Instead, I went straight to the stairs and headed down.

Even as I pushed open the door to the small room, I thought I could still step back. But this was work, I told myself. They wouldn't have come to the police station if there wasn't an issue. Also, surely four years must have dulled the pain; this was a chance to find out how much it still hurt.

It's a surreal experience, seeing people in the wrong place. I couldn't remember a single time that Arjen had come to the police station before, not even when we were still married. I tried not to scan his face to check how he'd aged, but I couldn't help but think that behind the extra wrinkles, the receding hairline, I could still see the younger person, the one I remembered, the one I'd first fallen in love with and had ended up hating.

16

I wondered if he looked at me like that too, if he noticed the now dyed-dark hair, the short-cut bob. I wondered if he remembered our good times, or that the last time we'd met in person, I'd screamed at him.

If he'd come to talk about something serious, I hoped he saw a police detective and not his ex-wife. If I'd been him, I wouldn't have brought the new wife, not if he wanted to get in my good books. A visual reminder of how we'd ended things, and more importantly of *why* we'd ended things, was not going to help him.

'The duty officer told me you asked for me specifically,' I had said. 'I assume it's not a social call.'

'No, we need to talk to a police officer,' the woman had said.

Even now, two days later, I thought they would have been better off talking to any other officer than me. I picked up my coffee cup to give my hands something to do.

'Talking to me was audacious,' I said.

'That's putting it lightly,' Thomas replied. 'Still, I guess it was a while ago.'

'I hadn't seen him in four years, not since the divorce.'

'It's nice that you're friendly now.'

'Friendly? Hardly. I still hate his guts.'

'Oh. Okay. Does he know that?'

'I'm sure he does.'

'Maybe the wife put him up to it,' Thomas mused.

'I don't know if the mother actually knows what my connection to Arjen is,' I said.

'Still,' he said, 'there's no reason for you not to work on

17

the investigation.' Of course his thoughts had immediately gone to what it meant for the case.

'Officially, you're right. But it feels wrong to stay involved.'

'Why? Did you say anything to them when they talked to you?'

'It was by the book,' I said. And that was largely true.

There had only been one moment when I'd slipped.

Nadia had started telling me about why they'd come. She was impeccably dressed in a close-fitting navy-blue dress. I was wearing jeans, boots and a jumper over a T-shirt. You never quite know what you're going to get at the police station, and layers are the way to go. She crossed her legs and a shiny leather shoe bounced in the air.

Was she nervous about seeing me? Or was it whatever they had come here for that was making her uncomfortable. She smiled at me and I didn't return it.

I'd met her before I'd known she was screwing my husband, but I hadn't met her since. Arjen had kept her out of my way during the divorce proceedings, knowing full well that whatever words I was willing to share with her, they wouldn't be friendly.

I probably wouldn't have been violent; I liked to think that.

'It's my father,' she said. 'He's gone missing.'

Knowing that I couldn't compete with her, even if I'd wanted to, hurt. The fact that she'd destroyed my marriage hurt. Sure, it took two people to cheat and Arjen was just as guilty as Nadia, but if this woman hadn't become pregnant, I would have had a chance to fight. We could have tried again. Instead, the betrayal cut deep. She'd taken everything from me in one fell swoop.

I hated her. I hated him. I hated that she was young and beautiful.

'When did you last see your father?' Being professional was a useful tool in tough situations like these. The colleagues who'd taken the initial report would have asked all those questions, but I said it quickly to push my violent thoughts out of the air.

'Me?' Nadia asked. 'A couple of weeks ago.'

'No, not you personally.' At least I didn't give an exasperated sigh. 'When did anybody see him last, I meant.'

'There was a company do just around the corner from where he worked,' Arjen said. 'He didn't come home after that.'

'And this was last night?'

'No, Friday night. Two days ago,' Nadia said. 'My mother called me Saturday morning to ask if we'd heard from him. We hadn't, so we went to the police immediately, but they told us we had to wait twenty-four hours before we could report him. We did that yesterday – twenty-four hours later – but when we still hadn't heard anything today, I thought maybe we could talk to you.'

I shook my head. 'Not my department.'

Arjen jumped in. 'We know that. But I don't think they're taking it seriously, and if there's anything you could do to help, we would really appreciate it.'

I wasn't at all surprised that the team who had initially taken the statement had tried to reassure the family that it was quite likely the man would come back home. 'What did they say? That he was an adult who had probably just walked out?'

'Yes.' Nadia gave me a wry smile that again I didn't return. 'Almost exactly that.'

There were many reasons why people left home. Second families, bankrupt companies, boredom, desire for a different life had all featured in the cases of missing people I'd worked on. There had also been suicides, early-onset dementia, accidents and crimes, but these had been less frequent than the cases where the person came back a few days later claiming they'd just needed some time away from everything. Therefore the police's initial assumption would often be the latter, whereas the family could only imagine the worst. We'd act differently if there was a history of mental illness, or something that indicated that the missing person had been involved in criminal activities; was 'known to the police', as we so delicately called it.

'Are there any reasons to be concerned?' I said. 'Does he have health issues? Mental issues?'

'No, nothing like that. He's a healthy fifty-seven-year-old.'

Fifty-seven. My parents were in their seventies. I guessed if your husband was going to cheat on you with his secretary, it was always going to be a younger, prettier secretary.

'There's no way he would have just walked out on my mother,' Nadia said.

That was the moment of the slip. Instead of taking a note of what she'd said, I spoke before my brain had got into gear. 'Husbands walk out when you least expect it,' I said.

Arjen flinched as if I'd slapped him.

I wanted to take the words back as soon as they'd left my mouth.

'Can you tell us what to do?' Nadia continued as if I hadn't said anything out of the ordinary. 'How to look for him?'

'I'm sure the case is in good hands,' I said. 'But have you checked the hospitals? Have you tried tracing his phone?'

'Checked the hospitals?' Nadia exchanged a glance with Arjen. 'We haven't done that yet.'

'Start with the ones close to where he lives. Maybe he's been in an accident. It's worth asking.'

'We'll do that,' Arjen said. 'If we find him, we'll let you know.'

'No need to tell me,' I said. 'Contact the person who initially took your details. That's who you need to keep informed.' I had known that this was why they'd come, but it still hurt that he was here purely to ask for a favour, even though I could only imagine how pissed off I would have been if he'd said he was here for a chat.

'But if we need to talk to you, can we get in touch?' Nadia said. For some reason she was keen to keep me involved. She must think that four years was long enough to let bygones be bygones.

'Sure,' I said.

'Have you still got the same number?' Arjen asked.

I nodded. I did well to stay quiet and say nothing. It was a painful reminder of all those years together, the fact that he knew my mobile number by heart and that I knew his.

So yes, Margreet van der Linde had been right. Nadia had come to see me two days ago to report her father missing, and I hadn't done anything.

Now I knew the man had died. And I still wasn't going to do anything.

'It was by the book,' I said again. 'I told them to keep in touch with the team they'd reported it to. That's all.'

'Then what's the problem?' Thomas said. 'It's not as if these people are members of your family.'

The problem was that if I got involved in the case, I would have to spend time with my ex-husband. I would have to talk to him and his wife. I would end up seeing his kid. I wanted to stay as far away from that as possible. I didn't want all those feelings of pain and hurt to flood over me again.

This was about securing my sanity rather than any police regulations.

'Are you worried your ex might be involved in the death?' Thomas asked.

'Oh God, no.' The answer came immediately; I didn't even have to think about it. 'He might be a cheating bastard, but he's not a killer.'

Thomas laughed. 'It's great to see that you can be objective about this.'

'You think it's funny, but it really isn't.'

'I'll run the investigation,' he said. 'You can help me out.'

When I'd seen Arjen two days ago, it had filled me with anger. I didn't like feeling like that. Doing this job was stressful enough without having to meet on a regular basis with someone I'd once loved and who had betrayed me.

'I think we should take this case, especially with so many people tied up with the Centraal station terror alert,' Thomas said.

'If only the body had been on the other side of the Orange Locks,' I said. 'That way it wouldn't have been an Amsterdam issue.'

'Well, dead bodies have problems getting through locks,' Thomas pointed out. 'Finding him where we did means he went into the water on the Amsterdam side. It's very much our issue.'

If the locks hadn't been there, he might have floated out to Schellingwoude and left Amsterdam's territory.

'Your ex-husband's new father-in-law is not a family member,' he continued. 'You don't have an ulterior motive, no bias. Your ex isn't someone you're trying to protect, so I really can't see any conflict of interest.'

'They'll feel uncomfortable with me there,' I said.

'But they came to you. They asked for your support. If they hadn't done that, I might have agreed with you.' He smiled. 'Though who cares what I think anyway?'

'Why are you so keen?'

'Why not?'

Getting out of this wasn't going to be as easy as I'd thought. If only Arjen and that woman hadn't come to see me.

Chapter 4

Back at the police station, I started typing up the report on Patrick van der Linde's case. It was best to keep things tidy so that I could hand it over to someone else quickly. I was working my way through my notes on the meeting with Margreet and the missing persons report filed two days ago when someone kicked my chair.

Our office had four L-shaped desks, pushed together to form a plus sign. My desk was by the window. Charlie sat next to Thomas, diagonally opposite me. He was out, dealing with the identification of the dead body. I was sitting with my back towards the door, and I'd been so focused on describing where we'd found the body that I hadn't heard someone come in. I looked up and saw Stefanie Dekkers, a detective inspector in the financial fraud department.

'Hello, fellow outcasts,' she said. She wore a pair of stiletto-heeled red shoes. They screamed that she never walked anywhere. Her black suit was livened up by a shirt the same colour as the shoes. If I'd worn an outfit like that two days ago, I would have felt at less of a disadvantage in my meeting with Nadia. Clothes can be like armour. Unfortunately, the way Stefanie dressed wasn't my style. We'd worked together on a case before, and I'd found out then that her way of working wasn't my style either.

She pulled out the chair at the desk next to me. 'It feels as if we're the only ones left in the entire police station.' She took something out of her handbag. 'I wanted to show you this,' she said. It was an economics magazine. 'I'm on page twenty-three. Not as good as your front page, but still pretty decent.'

I could of course have told her that she was crazy to want that kind of public recognition, but I also knew how much this meant to her. As I'd once pointed out to her, I might have got my photo in the papers, but she was a detective inspector and I wasn't. Much of what Stefanie thought of as my success had resulted in clashes with the authorities that made promotion a pipe dream.

'Congratulations,' I said. 'Thanks for showing us.' The photos were nice. She looked competent but not strident. For a female police officer, that was often hard to get right. The article described some financial case that I wasn't interested in, but I scanned it for just long enough to be polite.

She shrugged. 'I wanted to show someone and you were the only ones here. I was surprised that you're not involved in the operation at Centraal.'

'It's not that we're outcasts,' Thomas said. 'We had a floater to look at.'

'I guess not everybody can be involved in the terror attack. Someone has to do the normal everyday crime too.'

'If this turns out to be natural causes, we might well get assigned to help them out,' he said. 'If they need it.' He looked at the article for no longer than I had and handed it back to her.

Now that she had achieved what she'd come for, Stefanie got up and headed for the door, carrying the magazine proudly, ready to show the article to anybody kind enough to ask about it.

Charlie Schippers came back in just as she was leaving. 'It was Patrick van der Linde,' he said, giving me a look like a spaniel trying to be angry at its owner for not taking it out for a walk. Having to do a formal identification with the family was nobody's favourite part of the job. 'The daughter and her husband recognised him immediately,' he added. 'Not a shadow of doubt.'

'That's good,' I said. I didn't mean that it was good that Patrick van der Linde was dead, of course, but at least we had a name to put to the body.

Charlie had joined our team not that long ago and already seemed to regret it. The traffic police, his previous department, would be right in the middle of today's events at Centraal. He must have been wishing he was still with them.

Thomas dropped a folder on my desk. He'd been meeting with the pathologist and knew I always started with the photos. I would normally have gone with him, but I'd stayed at my desk. It seemed important to make the point that I wasn't working on this case.

'The pathologist pretty much ruled out accidental death,' he said.

Well, that was one hope dashed. 'He was beaten up?' I said.

'The majority of the wounds were postmortem, according to the pathologist. Probably happened over the four or five days that he'd been dead. Floating in a busy shipping lane will do that.'

'Five days?'

'Or thereabouts.'

'It's astonishing that nobody saw him before,' Charlie said.

I thought about how the body had looked when we'd first seen it at the edge of the water. 'He was fully dressed. Thick coat, woollen jumper, shoes. Everything would have been soaked through. It might have been some time before he surfaced.'

Thomas took a photograph out of the folder. 'The pathologist said that only this one,' he pointed at a large wound on the back of the victim's head, 'was done when he was still alive. Something heavy with a straight sharp edge. She suggested that potentially a standard-size builder's brick would have done it.'

'A brick? Someone hit him over the head with a brick?' Charlie said. 'So he was dead before he hit the water?'

'No, there was water in his lungs. He drowned.'

'He fell into the water when he was hit?' Charlie frowned.

'Maybe,' I said. 'Or they pushed him in on purpose after they'd bashed him on the head.'

'Wouldn't he have come round once he was in the water? It's not that deep along the edges.'

'We don't know where he went in,' Thomas said. 'For all we know, he was dumped in the middle of the IJ, where it's deep. He might as well have been dropped at sea if it was there.'

'Then he would have had to have been on a boat,' I said. It seemed overelaborate to smash someone on the head and then take him out into the middle of the lake. No, the assault must have happened on a boat. Maybe on one of the ferries – but then surely someone would have seen it happen. 'Do you think it was significant that we found him right by the Orange Locks? Anybody leaving Amsterdam by water would have to go through there to get to the North Sea Canal or the IJsselmeer.'

'Either way, it wasn't robbery,' Charlie said. 'He still had his wallet in his inside pocket.'

'Could it have been an accident?' I really wanted it to be an accident. 'What if he fell and hit his head on a sharp edge?'

'And rolled himself into the water afterwards? I don't think so. Also, looking at the shape of the wound, the lower edge is deeper than the top edge. The pathologist said that an object was brought down on his head with force. That's why she ruled out an accident. He was hit with a downward motion.'

That made sense. If he'd fallen onto something, it would have been the other way around. 'Okay. Someone bashed his head in and he ended up in the water. What about the timing?'

'The pathologist said that it would be very hard to establish an exact time of death. The water was cold, so that would have slowed decomposition down, but there's a temperature difference between the deep water in the centre and the shallow sides. We don't know how long he'd been floating there for, so she was reluctant to give us anything more precise than that he was killed between Friday evening and Saturday morning. If we need a tighter timescale, she can do some flotation tests.'

Some of the stream patterns of the river were carefully documented to help the ships navigate the shipping lane into Amsterdam's inland harbours. If we needed more certainty, we would have to first find out exactly where Patrick had hit the water, then track the pattern to where we had found him. The only way to get exact timings would be to follow a pig's carcass across the water, and the cruise ships didn't like it when we did things like that. Our forensics scientists might find it a fun experiment, but we would only do it if it was absolutely crucial to our investigation.

There were easier ways to make the window smaller. 'He was at a company dinner on Friday evening and didn't come home after that. It was close to his place of work,' I said, remembering what Arjen and Nadia had told me. 'It's in the missing persons report.' I still had it open on my screen. 'According to this, the do finished around ten p.m. We could check out any CCTV in the area, see what we can find. Maybe one of the cameras picked him up, though there aren't that many of them around there. It's going to be tricky to find out where it actually happened.'

'You hate it, don't you,' Thomas said, 'that this is now a murder case.'

'I don't care,' I said, 'but with everybody so busy, we could do without a tricky murder with no obvious crime scene.'

'What's going on?' Charlie asked.

'Oh, Lotte doesn't want to work on this case.'

'Why? Did you know him?' Charlie asked.

'Of course not,' I said. It was true. I didn't know Patrick; I'd never met him. But it would have been horrible if I'd had to do the identification with Nadia and Arjen. A shiver ran down my spine at the thought of it.

At that moment, my phone rang. It was my mother. She had a real knack for calling me at inconvenient times. 'Hi, Mum,' I said. 'I'm a bit busy right now.' It felt as though I was always saying that to her.

'Don't forget you're coming to mine for dinner tonight.'

'Of course. I know that.' We always met on Wednesday nights, so I didn't understand why she felt the need to confirm.

'Don't be late.'

I looked at my watch. 'I'll be here for a bit longer. A couple of hours maybe?' I should round things off neatly.

'Can't you come earlier?'

'Earlier?' I looked at Thomas. 'Hold on.'

'You can head off home if you want to,' he said. 'Charlie and I can take it from here.'

'Are you sure?'

He nodded.

'I'll make it up to you tomorrow,' I said.

But that was a lie. He'd be annoyed with me tomorrow, because I was going to ask the chief inspector to take us off this case.

Chapter 5

My mother was busy in the kitchen, and all her bustling about made me nervous. She wasn't a great cook and I wished she'd just ordered a Chinese takeaway instead of trying to make pasta for us. I wasn't all that good at cooking either, but I was trying to fix that with Mark's help. My boyfriend was fantastic at preparing wonderful meals without it taking any effort whatsoever. Even the kitchen would remain clean. My mum and I both just about managed to make something that was barely edible whilst making it look as hard as cooking a seven-course gourmet dinner.

Some things obviously ran in the family.

She put the dried pasta in the pan, set the timer going and added the water from the kettle.

'You should start timing it when the water is actually boiling,' I said.

'Look here.' She showed me the back of the package. 'Add boiling water and cook for ten minutes. That's what I've done.'

I peered into the pan. The water wasn't boiling any more after having hit the cold metal. 'Mark always says you have to wait until the bubbles come back.'

'Mark says, Mark says. As if that guy is the only one who knows anything about cooking.'

I was taken aback. She liked Mark. She normally kept going on and on at me about not messing up this relationship. She'd snapped at me out of nerves, I was sure. What was she nervous about, though? Just about what the food was going to taste like?

She added two minutes to the oven clock. It would probably take a couple of minutes before the water would come back to the boil, so that sorted out that problem. I decided not to say anything else.

'I bought some wine,' she said. 'Can you open it?'

'Wine? What's the occasion?'

'Why should there be an occasion? Can't we just have a glass of wine with dinner?'

This might not have been a matter of concern for other people, but as we usually had our weekly Chinese takeaway with glasses of tap water, I eyed up the bottle with the kind of suspicion I normally kept for the suspect in a murder case. As I opened it, I scanned the kitchen for any sign of what might be going on. The bottle had a screw top. I was disappointed, because I liked easing the cork out. There was something satisfying about the sound of the pop as it was released from the neck of the bottle. Mark once told me that natural cork shrinks when pressure is applied to it. Perfect for hammering into the tops of bottles, and the pop is the sound it makes when it expands again after being released from its prison. I wondered who the first person had been to figure that out. I pictured a man hitting all kinds of material with a hammer until he found the one that contracted.

My inspection of the kitchen didn't find anything out of the ordinary. My mother had laid the table with two plates and two sets of cutlery, so this wine wasn't about finally introducing me to the mysterious other person in her life.

I told myself off for overthinking things. Just because she was acting differently from normal didn't mean something was up. Sometimes I thought that being a police detective made me too suspicious of everything. There were cases where people did something new for no reason whatsoever. Maybe Mum had been on a cooking course, or watched a cooking programme on TV and thought it would be fun to try something like that herself. Or – much more likely – maybe she'd got into an argument with the owner of the takeaway place and no longer wanted to go there.

See, there were lots of innocent explanations for what she was doing.

Still, it put me on edge. I felt that I was waiting for something to happen; that there was a bomb in the corner of the room that I couldn't see but that could explode at any minute. Time was ticking away slowly, like the timer on that oven clock.

I poured the wine into the two glasses my mother had put out, then took a large gulp. Better to be partially sedated for what was coming. You didn't make it to this age without knowing when something was up with your parents. It was no different from Pippi knowing that a trip to the vet was coming up whenever I got the cat carrier out.

33

I felt as antsy as Pippi and couldn't take it any longer. 'Just tell me,' I said.

'Tell you what?'

'Whatever it is you're going to say. Whatever this is.' I gestured at the food and the wine.

My mother sighed. 'Lotte, there isn't always a conspiracy. It's your job that makes you distrustful.'

Just because I'd thought the same thing a few minutes ago didn't mean I was going to agree with her. 'It's the fact that you're cooking for us and that there's wine that makes me worried. It's got nothing to do with my job.'

The oven clock beeped. There was no way the pasta had been cooking for ten minutes yet.

'How much time did you put on the clock?' I asked.

'Ten minutes. Plus whatever you wanted me to add.'

I looked into the pan. 'That doesn't look cooked yet.'

'It's cooked.' She switched off the gas. 'The clock beeped, so it's cooked.'

I grabbed a fork and stuck it into a piece of pasta. It was still half raw. I turned the gas back on. 'Give it five more minutes.'

'Then it will be totally ruined.'

'It will definitely be disgusting if we eat it now.'

My mother looked at the back of the packet again. I could see that she thought the instructions must be wrong. I wondered if she'd deducted time when she altered the clock, instead of adding it. I was getting better at cooking, I thought, if I could actually judge how much longer something needed before it was edible. In the land of the blind, the one-eyed man was king. I might be a lousy cook, but I wasn't as bad as her.

If it was possible to stir food with an annoyed attitude, that was what my mother was doing. Why listen to your daughter if you knew so much better yourself how to do something? There was clearly no reason to thank me for my intervention.

Parents and ex-husbands were put on this world to try us.

We waited in silence until the clocked beeped again. My mother drained the water from the pan and put the pasta on a plate. She dolloped red sauce on top.

I carried both glasses of wine through to the table, which was too large for the front room, and put them on the coasters my mother always used.

'How's work?' she asked.

'It's fine.' I took a sip of wine. 'Arjen and his new wife came to see me the other day.' My mother was still in touch with them, so she would want to know about that.

'Nadia? You shouldn't call her the new wife. They've been married for years.'

'You still call Dad's wife his new wife and they've been married for decades.'

'That's different.' It was what she always said. She forked up some pasta but didn't raise it to her mouth. Instead she said, 'Is she nice?'

'Who? Nadia?'

'No, your father's wife. Do you like her?'

I shrugged. 'Maaike's okay. She and Dad get on well. That's all that matters.'

'That's good to hear.'

If I hadn't been suspicious before, I definitely was now. 'What's brought this on? Why do you want to hear about Maaike?'

'What is it like when a parent remarries?'

I put my fork down. 'What's going on?'

'Richard asked me to marry him.'

'What?' Luckily I had no food in my mouth, or I would probably have spluttered it all over the table.

'And I said yes.'

This was insane. 'You've known this guy how long?'

'We've been going out for longer than you and Mark.'

Going out. If this wasn't my mother, it might have been cute. If I'd known and liked this Richard, I might have been happy for them. 'Mum, you haven't even introduced him to me.'

'I didn't want to.' She looked down at her food. 'I was worried.'

'In case I didn't like him?'

'And in case he didn't like you. I didn't want you to dislike each other at first sight.'

'Why get married? You're both in your seventies.'

'We want to live together. There are legal reasons why it makes more sense. If something happened to either one of us, the other wouldn't be able to make any decisions unless we were married or had signed a civil partnership document.'

'If something happens to you, you want him to make the decisions, not me?'

'And it's the same for him.'

'He has kids?'

36

'Two. A son and a daughter. We thought the first step should be that we all meet.'

'I . . . I don't know what to say. We should have done the meeting first.'

'I wanted to tell you as soon as we decided. I want to be able to wear my engagement ring without you being all eagle-eyed and weird about it.' She got up and walked to the cupboard. She got a little red box out and opened it to reveal a plain gold band that she slipped onto the ring finger of her left hand.

It wasn't that I hadn't known she was seeing someone. When she'd told me she'd met Richard's family last December, I had known how serious it was. That would have been the perfect time to ask her to introduce Richard to me. She had probably wanted me to ask her.

'Are you going to wear a white dress?' I asked with a hint of a joke in my voice. Getting angry or upset wasn't going to do anybody any good.

'Don't be so silly,' she said. But she was smiling as she glanced down at her shiny new ring.

The chandelier in the communal hallway was comfortingly familiar when I got home, shining as if nothing momentous had been announced tonight. I slowly took the stairs up to my floor. When I unlocked my front door, Pippi greeted me with a loud meow. I bent down to scratch my little black and white cat behind her ear.

'Are you hungry, sweetie? I'm sorry. Would you like some food?'

Pippi dashed into the kitchen and I followed her. She was staring longingly at the cupboard that held the Felix. The Felix cat looked just like Pippi but without my cat's cute black nose. I tore open a packet and emptied it into her bowl.

Cat fed, I sat in my front room and called Mark. 'Well, my mother landed a total bombshell on me,' I said. 'She's going to get married.'

'But you haven't even met the guy.'

'She met his kids and grandchildren a few months ago. Do you think she's ashamed of me?'

'Don't be silly.' There was something about the complete certainty in Mark's voice that soothed me. 'She was probably worried you wouldn't like him, or maybe you were busy.'

'She wants us all to meet.'

'That's a good idea. Tell me when it is.' As always, his calm felt like a security blanket. Maybe this didn't sound very romantic, but he was the normality in my otherwise crazy life. He was so grounded that he stopped me from spiralling out of control. I considered telling him about the drowned man we'd found this morning, but decided not to.

I was always careful not to overload him with what had happened to me during the day. It would be so easy to talk about cases and murders and all the bad stuff I saw, but that would be unfair on him. He would listen to me and he would be calm but I knew that he would soak it all up and it would change him as it had changed me. It would damage his view of the world and make it as cynical as mine. Sometimes not talking about something was the way to protect people from what was going on. It wasn't to shut them out; it was for their own good. Not taking him into my confidence meant not taking him into the darkness of my job. Talking to Mark always reminded me that there was a world out there that wasn't obsessed with crime, where people didn't get divided into either victims or perpetrators, where the majority of those you met were happy, law-abiding citizens going on with their lives, with their own little worries and concerns.

Why would I destroy his world view when I was getting so much solace from it? It was better to talk about an upcoming wedding than about death and violence.

'I'll ask my mother for some dates,' I said. 'We could all have dinner together.'

'Do you want me to come?'

'God, I *need* you to come,' I said.

He laughed, but I hadn't been joking.

Chapter 6

The next morning, I went to talk to Chief Inspector Moerdijk without stopping off at my desk first. I had to tell him about the relationship between me and the dead man. Well, there wasn't a relationship as such, but I was sure that if I explained the situation, he would probably remove me from the case. I'd worked for him for a while now and he knew me well enough to appreciate that I didn't often ask to be excused from something.

Moerdijk had changed since our new commissaris joined us a few months ago. Having to report to someone younger than him had driven it home that he was never going to be the chief of police in Amsterdam. His aspirations would now only be fulfilled if he left to head up a smaller police station somewhere else. He wouldn't make that move. His edge seemed to have dulled.

For another middle-aged man that might have caused him to let himself go and put on weight. Not so for Moerdijk. He seemed to have embraced his love of running even more. He'd told me that he was training for an Ironman next month. His extreme health regime bordered on the fanatical. The crazy amount of exercise he did made him too thin, and even though he was less than ten years older than me, his face was shot through with wrinkles.

I could see his running gear lying behind his desk. If I was going to psychoanalyse him, I would suggest that exercise was a part of his life that he could control, unlike his career. Of course I wouldn't mention anything like this to Moerdijk. He wouldn't appreciate it.

He gestured at me as soon as he saw me, indicating that I should come in. 'I was waiting for you to talk to me,' he said. 'Thomas told me yesterday.'

'Told you?'

'Yes, he came to see me yesterday evening and explained it all. The dead man is your ex-husband's father-in-law?'

'Yes, and I would prefer not to work on the case.'

'That's not an option, I'm afraid. We're really short at the moment because of the attack at Centraal station. There are no other teams available. Just do your best. Thomas said he would lead the investigation; that he'd talked to you about that and you were fine with it.' He raised his eyebrows.

I shouldn't have gone home early yesterday to have dinner with my mother; I should have talked to the boss. Now I was left with no other solution than to agree that this was what I'd said to Thomas. 'That's right.'

'I'm surprised. It's not like you not to want to be involved. Not without a solid reason, anyway.'

It was a solid enough reason for me. 'I prefer to stay far away from this case. That's what I wanted to say.'

The CI tapped his pen on his notebook thoughtfully. For a few seconds everything hung in the balance. 'Normally I might have agreed with you,' he said finally, 'but I don't have that luxury at the moment. There isn't much manpower available, and because this wasn't an accidental death, I'm left with no room for manoeuvre. Thomas is willing to take the lead. He was very keen to do so, I should say.'

'He's welcome to it,' I said. 'I'm good with him running the investigation.' I could take holiday or stay in the office and type up reports.

'Come and talk to me again if you change your mind,' the CI said.

My mobile rang before I'd even reached my desk. It was the duty officer. There was a visitor for me: Margreet van der Linde. Like her daughter, she clearly liked calling on people without giving them any notice. It was easiest to tell her straight away that I couldn't be her point of contact. I should get that out of the way, so I turned around and went back downstairs.

'I wanted to talk to you,' she said, 'rather than the guy who came with you yesterday. He's fine – don't get me wrong, I don't have a problem dealing with him – but I think it's easier to talk to you, as you're a friend of my daughter.'

'A friend?' I had wondered if Margreet knew who I was, and how I was connected to her daughter and son-in-law, and here was my answer: obviously not.

'Because of the connection, I'm actually going to be less involved,' I said, being deliberately vague. 'If you have information, you should talk to Thomas Jansen. He's leading the investigation.'

'Oh,' Margreet said. 'I didn't know about that. My mistake.' Her face fell.

She wore the same shoes as she'd had on last time – leather, with sparkling stones on the toes – but her socks didn't match. The left one was blue, the right black. It reminded me of the washing on the line on that moored ship. I immediately felt sorry for her. Whatever I had said to the CI about not wanting to get involved, and however much I wanted to stay away from this case, I couldn't find it in me to just send her away. But neither did I want to become her go-to point of contact. This was a fine balance to walk.

Even though she was indoors, she shivered. Grief or lack of sleep had caused that, not the temperature in the police station. Also, she was wearing a thick coat, buttoned up all the way to the top, and a scarf tied around her neck. She wasn't a small woman, but she seemed shrunken inside her clothes, like a child swaddled in too many layers. I should probably ask her to go, tell her to come back later when Thomas got in, but my eyes fell on those mismatched socks again and I just couldn't do it. Things couldn't be easy for her.

'Can I get you a coffee? Or a cup of tea?' Doing that would make me feel less of an evil person. After all, there was no reason to dislike the mother of a woman I hated. I could be kind. 'What did you want to talk about?'

'I want to make sure there was no mistake.'

'A mistake?'

'I still don't think it's possible that it's him. My daughter must have been wrong.'

'She went with her husband. They were certain, my colleague told me.'

'Do you think I could talk to your colleague? I didn't sleep all night. There must have been a mix-up somewhere. She must have misidentified him.'

I remembered grief. I remembered only too well how hard it was just to get dressed in the morning, how you tried to keep up appearances but failed. You tried to pretend that you were dealing with everything well and then you put on mismatched socks.

Margreet was doing her utmost to convince herself that her husband hadn't died. She didn't want to accept it. I didn't think talking to Charlie would make her believe that this was real.

'There's a café really close,' I said. 'Let's get out of here.'

She smiled in gratitude. 'That would be nice,' she said, as if this was a friendly chat and not a meeting with the detective investigating her husband's murder. It *would* only be a friendly chat, I corrected myself; I was going to have nothing more to do with the case. 'Wait here for a minute; I'll just pop up to get some things.' The photos of the post-mortem were still on my desk. I could bring them with me.

When I got into our office, I was pleasantly surprised to see that Charlie was already here. This might work out well. 'The identification yesterday,' I said. 'Were there any issues?'

'Issues?'

'They were certain, weren't they?'

'Oh yes, absolutely. She saw immediately that it was her father. I mean, the guy's face was bruised and swollen, but not so much as to make him hard to recognise.'

I nodded. That made sense. After all, I had recognised him straight away from the photo on his driver's licence. I scanned through the photographs on my desk but quickly realised that many of them were too graphic to show Margreet. I chose a couple that only showed his face. That weren't too horrific.

In the back of my mind, I hoped it wouldn't be necessary to show them to her. I didn't think she actually doubted her husband was dead. She just wasn't ready to accept it yet.

The little café wasn't busy. Only a couple of tables were occupied. A young man who looked rather bleary-eyed was obviously trying to wake himself up with caffeine but seemed to still be struggling. I picked a table far enough away from the other people that nobody could overhear us.

'I don't know what Nadia told you,' Margreet said, 'but Patrick was such a loving man.'

I managed not to choke on my cappuccino. 'We've never talked about her father,' I said, entirely truthfully. That she used the past tense told me enough. This chat wasn't about wondering if her husband was still alive; it was because she needed to talk to someone. I was happy enough to be used as a sounding board by a woman coming to terms with her loss. It would have been easy to object – I wasn't a social worker; having this conversation wasn't part of my job – but there had been enough situations where a chat just like this one had given me useful information. In a way, it was part of the investigation.

Not that I would stay on the case for long, of course, but if there was anything relevant, I could pass it on to Thomas.

'Today people look at it differently; they think fathers should spend time with their children. I totally get that, but it was different when Nadia was a child. Patrick always worked hard to provide for his family.'

She made it sound as if Patrick had been eighty instead of in his late fifties. It was odd, but I could read between the lines: Patrick had been a workaholic and Margreet was concerned that Nadia had complained about him. She was getting her defence of him in first. I tried not to do the maths to figure out if I was closer to Margreet's age or her daughter's.

'Because of his work, because of the money he made,' she continued, 'I could afford to stay at home. That's how we did things. That worked for us. I told Nadia she can make her own mistakes.'

'Her own mistakes? Has something happened between you and your daughter?'

'We had a bit of an argument last night. Nothing serious.'

'What did she say?'

'Oh, it's nothing. I just know that you and Nadia know each other from before, and . . . well, I don't know what she said, but I don't want you to have the wrong idea about Patrick. That's why I wanted to talk to you, really. He was a good father and a good husband. I want to make sure you know that.'

Was she worried that we wouldn't investigate his death properly if we thought he wasn't a good man? If that were the case, the police's workload would be hugely reduced. I could just imagine families having to fill out a questionnaire about the habits of the deceased, and us using it to decide how many man hours we were going to dedicate. It didn't work like that. If someone had been murdered, sure, we helped the family get justice through the courts, but it was much more about stopping a murderer.

'Are you sure she identified my husband correctly? It's what I wanted to check with the other detective.' She took off her scarf and coat, revealing more signs of how much she was struggling. She was wearing her blouse inside out; I could see the reverse stitching on the seams. I suspected she would be appalled if I pointed it out to her; it would be even more embarrassing than telling someone their fly was undone.

I took a sip of my coffee. 'It really was him. Your daughter identified him but I could tell from the photo on his driving licence too. There was no mistake.' I said it kindly. 'I understand it's hard to accept.'

'It's my own fault; I should have gone to identify him instead.'

'You can see him if you want to.'

She shook her head. 'I trust my daughter. Was it murder?'

'We don't know for sure yet,' I said. 'We know he drowned, but we don't know why he fell in the water.'

'He didn't kill himself,' Margreet said. 'He wasn't the type.'

You never knew, I could have told her that. People tried to kill themselves for a number of reasons, many of which the family didn't know about. But in this case, I tended to agree with her. That he still had his wallet on him, and all his clothes on, ruled out a mugging, and the head injuries were the wrong shape for a suicide. I nodded.

'It could have been an accident,' she said. 'He could have just fallen in.'

'What kind of work did your husband do?' If he'd been a builder, or someone working near the docks, an accident was much more likely.

'He ran his own company. That was why he worked so hard: he was responsible for all the people who worked for him too. They were his extended family in a way. That's what he always used to say. It's why he cared so much.'

Arjen had run his own company too. So Nadia had picked someone just like her father. Only ten years younger than her father, too. I hoped my coffee cup hid the grimace on my face. This was madness. This was why I shouldn't be involved in this case. Even a casual chat with the victim's widow reminded me of my cheating ex. In the past, it had often been sympathy for the victim's family that had driven me. Sympathy with the victim's daughter was in short supply in this case.

'What kind of company is it?'

'They design all kinds of speciality lights.'

'Outdoor lighting?' I was still thinking about something that could have made an accident more likely. He could have been struck from above by a fallen rig or something like that. 'Something that needed scaffolding?'

'No, nothing like that. It's small lighting to incorporate in cards and T-shirts. Maybe you've seen the T-shirts with the lights that blink in time with the beat? It's their bestseller. They sell a lot of them at gigs. Of course they do corporate gifts too, but working with bands and music was always Patrick's favourite.'

'Not really my thing,' I said. Maybe I should tell Margreet who I was and how I knew her daughter.

'I'm so glad I came to see you,' she said. 'I don't know who else to talk to about these things. My friends are ignoring me, or they don't understand. My swimming friends asked me where I was this morning. As if I could go swimming in that water. I felt really weird about it, so I cancelled. But that was good, because now I can have a coffee with you.'

There were many things I could have said, such as that it wasn't the police's duty to have coffee with people, or that I wouldn't be working this case for much longer. But as she turned round to catch the waitress's attention, I saw the label sticking out at the back of her blouse, and I couldn't get the words out.

Chapter 7

Thomas was standing by his desk, shuffling a pile of papers together, when I walked into our office.

'I'm going to talk to the daughter,' he said. 'We need to ask her if she has any idea why somebody would have wanted to murder her father. Do you want to come?'

His eyes challenged me, but I didn't respond. I didn't need to prove myself to him, though if I had even the slightest inclination to work on this case, I needed to prove something to myself. I hadn't completely changed my mind about wanting out of this investigation, but Margreet's efforts to cope, and the evidence that she was failing to do so, had moved me. I felt a connection with her. After all, I'd been there myself. I'd pretended everything was fine when really I'd been falling apart. Still, I had to make sure I could do this. However sorry I might feel for Patrick's widow, I wasn't going to stay involved if it hurt too much. It felt like stepping carefully onto the ice to check if it was going to hold your weight or if you were going to fall through. Had the ice around my pain grown thick enough over the last four years for it to hold firm under the onslaught of meeting Nadia again?

'If you don't want to, just tell me,' Thomas said. 'If you're that worried about seeing her, I can wait for Charlie to come back. Is she really pretty?'

He could be such a total git. 'If your wife ever cheats on you with someone,' I said, 'I'll make sure to check the guy out, because he'll be much nicer than you. And younger.'

Thomas grinned. 'I like the fighting spirit. I agreed to go to their house.'

'Where do they live?'

'You don't know? I thought you would have checked them out.'

'Very funny. No, I didn't want to see him ever again, so the last thing I would have done was sit outside his house watching him and that woman.'

'They're outside Amsterdam,' he said. 'They live in Haarlem.'

That was probably why I hadn't seen him around in four years. I knew my mother had stayed in touch with them. I didn't ask her about it and she didn't tell me. At the time, she and I had fallen out, and she had contacted Arjen for reasons that had seemed like revenge but that had probably been loneliness. That was one good thing about her getting married: she wouldn't need my ex for company if she and I were ever on bad terms again.

'Does he know you're seeing someone else?'

'Arjen? Why would he care about that?'

'He doesn't have to be so worried that you're going to beat him up.'

'How does that follow?' I couldn't immediately understand his train of thought. 'Are you saying that what someone has done to you matters less once you've moved on?'

'Something like that.'

'So if someone steals your car, you should forgive him because you've now got a nicer car anyway? A much better, more comfortable car?'

'Are you implying that men are like cars?'

'I think that if it's about something more important than that, you're even less likely to forgive.'

'You're not so angry these days,' Thomas said. 'You're calmer.'

I stretched out and reached with the palms of my hands towards the ceiling to release the tension from my shoulders. 'Life isn't bad at all.' I sounded smug even to myself and I had to stop smiling.

'New love's happiness. So cute.'

'It's nice. It's good.' It was great really. It was great to sleep in the arms of someone who loved you. Someone you liked and who made you laugh. I didn't think I could want anything else from a relationship other than to be with someone who made me a better, happier person.

'If it's all good,' Thomas said, 'then work on this with me. Stop asking the chief inspector to take you off the case.'

'He told you, then?'

'It wasn't anything I couldn't have figured out by myself. I know you well enough to guess that you were going to see him first thing this morning.'

I dropped my hands back down by my sides. 'We'll see how this goes,' I said. It would all depend on how much my current happiness protected me against past pain. 'I met with

Margreet earlier. She thinks I'm her daughter's friend.' I thought about her mismatched socks and her inside-out top. 'It was very sad. She told me she used to go swimming but can't any more because the husband she loved drowned in that water.'

I knew it was easier for her to talk to me than to my colleagues. I wanted to help her, and that meant working on her husband's murder case, if at all possible.

The house was twice the size of Margreet's flat. If I'd felt at all guilty for taking too much of my ex-husband's money after the divorce, which had paid for my very nice apartment along the canal, those feelings vanished as soon as I saw where he now lived. That money had been mine by rights; I'd put a lot of cash into his company when he first started it up. When it had become hugely successful, I'd deserved my chunk of the investment back. He'd obviously done well since then. He'd sold the firm not that long ago. Not that I'd kept tabs on what he'd been doing, of course, but it had made the front page of the business papers and it had been impossible to avoid.

Nadia opened the door to us. Her eyes opened wider when she saw me. What had she expected? That Thomas would be alone? That she and Arjen could appeal to me to look into her father's case when he was missing, but that I would drop it as soon as he'd been found dead? Or maybe she did not want me involved now that this might turn out to be a murder case.

'My mother just called me,' she said. 'Apparently she talked to you earlier.'

I grimaced. 'She thinks you approached me after your father had gone missing because I'm your friend. She had some questions for me. It was fine.'

'I'm sorry,' Nadia said. 'Come through. Arjen is here too.'

We followed her to the living room. I had once read somewhere that when women get together, they automatically rank themselves in terms of looks and attractiveness. That was probably a piece of research written by a man. It wasn't something I did all the time, but I did do it now, and there was no denying it: Nadia was prettier than me. She was younger than me. Plenty of women get plastic surgery after they divorce to show their ex that they're just as beautiful as the new girlfriend or the new wife. In my case, there would be no point. Nadia would always win hands-down. No amount of effort on my part, if I even wanted to make an effort, would change that fact. But I knew it wasn't really about that.

Pain stabbed my chest so deep that I had trouble breathing. Pain, or maybe grief.

What really hurt wasn't the fact that Nadia had taken Arjen away from me; it was the existence of the child. To tell the truth, it had always been about the child.

I couldn't help but think that if she hadn't died, my Poppy would have been two years older than the little girl playing on the floor of my ex-husband's house.

If she hadn't died, there would have been a point when Poppy would have been this big, with golden curls, a wide smile and blue eyes.

I swallowed. My legs felt weak and I was grateful for the sofa behind me. Even as I sat down, I realised that it would be far better to stand up again and walk out of here. Anything would be better than having to watch the little girl playing with her pony.

Arjen was looking at me and I couldn't decipher the look on his face. It could have been pity. Nadia's shock at seeing me could also have been the sudden realisation that their daughter was here. She might have felt sorry for me too.

'You saw Patrick on the night of the eleventh?' Thomas asked.

'Yes, I saw him the evening before he went missing,' Arjen said.

I took a deep breath and opened my notebook. Pity was good. Because I hated to be pitied, and hate was preferable to sadness in situations like this.

'There was a dinner to welcome me,' Arjen continued.

'You?' I said. 'Why?'

'I was going to help Patrick at the firm for a bit. He wanted to change strategy and I had time on my hands.'

'He got bored of being a house husband,' Nadia joked. She put her hand on Arjen's knee, then looked at me and took it away again.

'Were there any issues at work?' Thomas said.

'Not really sure,' Arjen said. 'I hadn't started there as such. But now I wonder what he did after the company do. Where he went and who he met.'

I glanced at the little girl. It wasn't a My Little Pony she was playing with, but one that was more anatomically accurate. It was delicate in her chubby fingers. She made it dance up and down, ready to clear the obstacles made out of other toys. She wore a red and blue striped top, thick dark blue tights and a corduroy skirt. Her golden hair bounced. It was the same colour as the pony's mane. Her smile was as bright as her hair. She was a happy child, looked after by two caring parents, with a father who spent time with her because he'd sold his company.

She looked like Arjen.

Poppy had looked like him too, whatever my mother had said to the contrary.

'Was that the last time anybody saw him?' Thomas asked.

'I don't know that, but I do know he didn't come home that night. Margreet called us at three or four in the morning. I was fast asleep. She asked if I was still with Patrick, but I'd been home for hours.'

Her grandparents must dote on her. I didn't think Arjen's parents had ever really liked me. They hadn't stayed in touch with me after the divorce. Why would they? I knew it could be hard on parents when their kids split up and they had less access to their grandchildren. In our case, that wasn't an issue. There had just been Arjen and me, and it had been easy enough to cut ties with me.

'You didn't all leave at the same time?' Thomas asked.

'I had to get back to Haarlem. Patrick lived a block away from where we had dinner. He wanted to stay behind to pay the bill too, without anybody seeing. He was always like that.'

I hadn't contacted Arjen's parents either. His mother had had a go at me after I'd miscarried the first time. I should never have told them about the pregnancy before the three-month point. She'd shouted at me that it had been reckless of me to keep working. She told me that I was insane to carry on doing this dangerous job.

It was probably the only thing that my mother-in-law and my own mother had ever agreed on.

'You're telling me you were the last one to see him?'

'No, someone at the restaurant must have seen him afterwards. The waiter, for example.'

Even though I was off work on maternity leave when Poppy died in an unexplained, unexplainable cot death, she'd blamed me for that too. She was the kind of woman who needed to apportion blame; she couldn't accept that some things just happened for no reason. I could see her point. I was sometimes like that too, but I'd never been able to talk to her calmly again after that. Whatever sympathy there had been between us was irrevocably destroyed when she'd piled guilt on top of whatever I was going through at the time. There was no word for my feelings. Calling it grief was putting it too lightly.

'Did anything happen at the dinner? What was the mood like?'

'I thought it was fine. I hadn't met any of them before, of course, so it might be harder to judge, but it all seemed amicable.' Arjen glanced at me again, even though Thomas was the one asking all the questions.

I could only imagine that his mother had done a little victory dance when Arjen had brought home his pregnant lover and dumped the careless wife who let her babies die. She'd once sent me a letter to say that I was a greedy bitch to take my share of the money after the divorce. She didn't say that I was wrong; she acknowledged that I had a legal

57

right to it but wrote that I should have walked away with nothing.

As if I was worth nothing.

As if my behaviour deserved nothing.

I dragged my gaze away from the playing child and looked down at the empty page of my notebook. I hadn't thought about any of this in over a year. Now it was all coming back.

What the hell was I doing here?

Suddenly I knew I had to get out.

'Excuse me,' I said. 'Where's your bathroom?' I sounded ridiculously polite, even to myself.

'You're really pale, Lotte, are you okay?' Thomas said.

'On the left, in the hallway.' Arjen answered my question.

I got there just in time to turn on the tap of the little basin to cover the sound of my sobs. I put my hands over my face so that I wouldn't have to see my ugly crying face in the mirror.

Self-pity was even more hateful than someone else's pity, I told myself sternly.

When I'd finally regained some control, I splashed water on my face. My efforts to keep my tears inside had given me hiccups.

This was just great.

I sat down on the toilet. How long could I hide in here? I heard the murmur of voices in the other room. I flushed the toilet I hadn't used, washed my hands, and dried my face with a soft blue hand towel that smelt of washing powder. Then I pushed my hair behind my ears and pulled my shoulders back, ready to face them all again.

I was happy. My life was great.

So why get pathetically upset over something that happened years ago? Why drag all of that up again?

I took a deep breath and opened the bathroom door. When I stepped back into the room, Thomas immediately got up. 'Thank you,' he said to Arjen and Nadia. 'I think that's all we need at the moment. If we have any further questions, we'll call you.'

'Sure,' Arjen said.

I noticed his eyes on me, but I turned away, opening the front door and leaving the house without saying anything. It must have seemed strange, but I didn't think I could get any sounds out, and I wasn't even going to try.

Thomas beeped open the car doors. I got in, grateful for the metal protection of the vehicle. He sat beside me.

'I'm sorry about that, Lotte,' he said. 'I shouldn't have asked you to come.'

The normal response would have been to say that it was okay, but I knew it wasn't. That the fault was as much mine as his — my hubris in thinking I could cope with coming here, seeing them — didn't make me feel any better.

I didn't think Thomas understood why I was so upset. He might have got the wrong idea. He didn't know that seeing Arjen made me think of those days again, when our beautiful little girl had died, when I'd gone back to work early from my maternity leave, because being at home only made me think of one thing. It was work that had rescued me, work that had allowed me to move on and the company of my colleagues that had restored my sanity. Having death and violence around me allowed me, at least for a few hours, to forget about the death in my own house. A death from

59

natural causes more heartbreaking than any that work served up.

I understood, of course, that this death had been worse for me because it had been my baby girl. That plenty of people would say that at least she'd gone peacefully in her sleep, which was infinitely better than being brutally murdered. I could never tell anyone that dealing with violence on a daily basis was the perfect displacement activity to stop me thinking about Poppy. My boss would probably have sent me home if he'd known, and with hindsight, I'd been very lucky that nothing bad had happened while I was walking around in a daze.

I knew I was wired up differently and I could never share those thoughts with anybody. They would make me seem crazy.

Not talking about stuff came naturally enough to me anyway. For most of my life I had been interested in the kind of things that other people would find morbid or unnatural. What would make them shiver with disgust, I found infinitely fascinating.

There comes a point when you stop trying to change yourself. I was lucky that my job allowed me to work in the area that interested me; that I had colleagues who were just as warped as I was. My mother would say that it was the job that had damaged me, but I knew that I'd been messed up from the start and that work had been my salvation. At least there was one place where I felt normal.

Now it seemed that the past I'd tried to think of as little as possible had come crashing into my work life. There was one obvious solution: don't get involved. Don't talk to Arjen, his wife, her family.

There was no official reason why I shouldn't investigate this case but I could try to fabricate one. Give it some time and I could surely come up with something. How hard could it be? I might have wanted to support Margreet, but it wasn't worth this much pain.

Chapter 8

When we got back to the office, I went straight to Chief Inspector Moerdijk's office. Thomas trailed me.

'This case is an issue,' I said to the CI.

'Grab a chair.' His smile was kind. We'd worked together for years, and now, like an old marriage, we were probably going to be together until one of us dropped dead. Well, until one of us retired. Still, if you had to work for a long time with anybody, CI Moerdijk was as good a boss as you were going to get.

'You need to take me off this case. I'm not working on it.'

He dropped the smile. 'You can't refuse,' he said. 'It's a murder case. It's important. We've been officially assigned.'

'I can take time off. I'll just go on holiday.'

'Until when? Until the investigation is finished? That could be two weeks, six weeks, never.'

'I'm hoping we'll close it quicker than never,' Thomas said.

'I can't meet with them again.' I turned to face Thomas. 'I can't go back to that house.'

'Then don't. We'll divide up the investigation in such a way that you have nothing to do with the family. You can look into his financial situation.'

'Is there anything to suggest the family is involved in the murder?' the CI said.

That I had to think about that question showed how little time I'd actually spent on the case so far. I'd been too tied up with the personal side to do any background research. 'We don't know that much yet,' I said, 'but at first glance, I would say not.'

'I agree,' Thomas said.

'If it was any other case, any other investigation, would you spend time with the family aside from victim support?'

'No, not really.'

'So why don't we add a family support officer to your team and then you'll never have to talk to them. It should be easy enough.'

'No need to add anybody,' Thomas said. 'Charlie and I can do that.'

I thought about Margreet wearing her clothes inside out and her socks that didn't match. She'd said she preferred talking to me.

'We can do this, Lotte,' Thomas said.

When Nadia had come to the station with Arjen when her father had been missing, I'd been okay. Her mother had been kind, even if she didn't know who I really was. I didn't necessarily feel that I owed them, but I could still help.

'Okay,' I said. 'Sure. I'll give Thomas support.'

'We can look into adding someone to your team, though. How about someone to work on the company's financial side? I'm sure Stefanie Dekkers from the financial fraud department could help out. They've just rounded off a big case.'

The one that was mentioned in the article she'd shown me. 'I don't need her help.' I spoke quickly, before Thomas could say that it was a good idea.

Anybody but her.

That evening, Mark and I arranged to meet for dinner in the small café we often went to on Thursday nights. He was already waiting at our usual table when I came in. I liked it when it was that way around, I enjoyed those seconds when I could watch him without him knowing. Observe him without being observed myself in return. I tried to see him the way other people did, a lanky man with messy dark hair and glasses, but the sum of him added up to so much more for me than it would for anybody else. It was the way he accepted me that made all the difference. Or maybe it was that we'd known each other since we were kids, even if my mother had been at pains to point out that she'd been with her fiancé for longer than Mark and I had been going out.

He looked up as if he knew that someone was watching him. I took a seat opposite him and he immediately turned around to get the waitress to come over.

'It must have been a shock,' he said. 'I know you need a drink. The usual?'

I could only nod. How did he know about the afternoon I'd had? Was the aftermath of my freak-out at Arjen's house still visible on my face?

'Who would have thought your mother would want to get married again?'

Ah, that. 'I know, right?' I said, but my mother announcing her engagement was no longer the worst thing that had happened to me in the last twenty-four hours. 'I never thought she'd do that. She said she'd not introduced me to him on purpose. Can you believe that?'

Mark ordered a glass of white wine for me and a beer for himself. As soon as the waitress had left, he reached out and took my hand. 'It doesn't mean she doesn't love you,' he said.

I rubbed my thumb over his palm. 'I know,' I said again. 'She loves me, she's just ashamed of me.' Being in his company calmed me down.

'You got close to your father again. It could be that she's worried about that.'

'Why?' I frowned.

'She might think you'd see her new marriage as a betrayal.'

'If that's what's on her mind, she's being silly. I'm happy she's seeing someone; I'm really happy she's no longer by herself and that I don't have to worry about her. I just don't get why she's getting married to this guy. At her age.'

'There are legal benefits.'

'They could sign a living-together document and that would be exactly the same.'

'They're not living together yet. Your mother is church-going. That could have something to do with it.'

'No sex before marriage, you mean?' I shuddered. 'I don't want to think about my mother having sex. Why did you have to bring that up?'

'Me? I didn't say a thing.' Mark laughed. 'You were the one who mentioned sex. It's all in your mind.'

The waitress came back with our drinks. I didn't let go of Mark's hand but lifted my glass with my left. I took a sip of the white wine; it was clear and crisp.

'If she was going to sign a living-together contract anyway, she probably thought they might as well get married.'

'He even gave her a ring.'

'It's quite romantic, don't you think? Not just practical.'

'I hope I like him. Can you imagine if he's terrible?'

'If he's terrible, you can say something. If he treats her badly, you can say something. If you just don't like him, you're going to be polite and make pleasant conversation.'

'He's got two children and a couple of grandchildren. My mother has met them already.'

'They're probably all scared of you.'

'Scared?' I sat back in my chair and smiled at Mark. 'But I'm such a nice person. And really easy to get on with.'

He grinned. 'They'll understand that after they've met you.'

'You'll come, won't you?'

'I wouldn't miss it for the world. Your mum is my biggest fan.'

'I know. She always tells me not to mess this up.' Having Mark there would make it so much more bearable. He had this uncanny ability to make me realise that things were actually funny when I thought they were annoying. He laughed at me and that allowed me to laugh at myself too. It was good. 'I'll call her to set up a time for us all to meet. And I'll behave. I promise. I won't embarrass her.'

I took another sip of wine. The alcohol was soothing and washed away any annoyance. If this was what my mother wanted, then who was I to judge? The longer I thought about it, the more normal it seemed. I had been surprised by the sudden announcement, that was all. I'd had no idea that marriage was on my mother's mind. In fact, I couldn't think of a single occasion when I'd talked to my mother about marriage as an institution.

When I was getting married to Arjen, my mother and I had rowed. There had been a difficult moment when I'd insisted that my father should be there too. They had divorced when I was five and I wasn't even close to my father at that point, but having both my parents at the ceremony had felt like the right thing to do. My mother had strongly disagreed. She'd told me that she'd been the one to raise me, so why did I want my father to walk me down the aisle? I couldn't answer that question; it had just been what I'd wanted. In my head, I'd had this image of what the perfect marriage was going to be like, and if my dad didn't walk me down the aisle, it was going to be doomed from the start.

In the end, it had been doomed anyway, but at least I couldn't blame a faulty ceremony for that.

I didn't know what my mother's views on marriage really were. I only knew that she'd always spoken disparagingly about her marriage to my father. It felt strange that I hadn't known she wanted to get married again. Maybe she had been dating other men in the decades since she and my father got divorced, only to find love again in her seventies.

I had to admit, if I put it like that, it was actually quite sweet. I shook my head. My mum would not like being thought of as sweet.

'How was your day otherwise?' Mark asked.

'Fine,' I said. 'We're working on a new murder case, but Thomas is taking the lead. I'm focusing on one particular angle. It's early stages still.' I hadn't talked to Mark about the murder since we'd found Patrick van der Linde's body. If we'd met yesterday, I might have mentioned it, but I wasn't going to tell him about seeing my ex-husband, his new wife and their child. I didn't want to talk about how much that had hurt.

He wouldn't ask more, I knew that. Even with other investigations, the normal ones, I would keep a lot of the details to myself. Not only because it wouldn't be right to share those with him from the point of view of the victim's family's privacy, but also because I didn't want to dump a whole load of graphic details on him every time we met. It might be normal for me to see a dead body with wounds all over it, but for a civilian, it definitely wasn't.

On top of that, I didn't want him to think that his job wasn't important compared to mine. Who would feel that it was appropriate to talk about building projects after he'd just been told that a man had been murdered and drowned in the IJ?

'Did you go to the Orange Locks as a kid?' I said.

'I don't think so. They're not particularly pretty.'

'They're fascinating,' I said, feeling defensive on behalf of one of Amsterdam's more functional bits of architecture.

'My mum would take me to watch the boats go through. It was fun.'

'Did you have a boat?'

'No, but watching the little boats in there, three abreast, and then sometimes a huge oil tanker, it was exciting. A real summer's day outing.'

'We didn't do that. We'd go to the zoo.'

You didn't have to pay to watch the boats clear the locks. That was probably why we went there instead of to the zoo.

'Do you want to go to the Locks for a day out? Is that why you're bringing them up?'

'God, no. I was thinking about it because we found a body near there yesterday.'

Mark burst out laughing. 'Of course you did. Silly me. I should have figured out how your brain works by now.'

I told him some of what was going on and held back on other bits. It was a tightrope between sharing my experiences with him and not overwhelming him. It wasn't an easy balance and I wasn't sure I always got it right, but I was trying my best.

'I'm surprised you had time for dinner,' he said. 'You'll be busy again.'

There was nothing like a murder case to have me running around like a headless chicken. Another balancing act: dividing my time between my work and my private life. Making time for other people while I was working a murder case was normally tough.

'Busy, but not crazy so.' I smiled. 'I'm only support for Thomas, so he can work all hours. It will do him good.'

'His wife won't be happy.'

'He's very keen to do it,' I said. 'But I'm not sure he discussed it with her beforehand.'

'He's hoping for the kind of publicity that you've been getting.'

'Really? Why would he want that?'

My previous cases had brought me more recognition and press coverage than I would have liked. I'd worked on some high-profile investigations and maybe the press were intrigued by the idea of a female police officer dealing with murderers. My photo had been on the front page of the newspapers a couple of times. I had hated it every time. The idea that Thomas could be jealous of that struck me as strange. But then people often coveted things they didn't actually want. I'd been like that: I'd thought I desperately wanted something that someone else had, only to appreciate how difficult it was once I had it. It was ironic that Thomas was jealous of recognition I'd rather not have, whereas I was envious of his stable marriage and his three kids, who, if the photos were anything to go by, were cute and well behaved. I wanted to tell him that he had the better side of that trade.

'People crave what they haven't got,' Mark said. 'They don't understand the value of holding on to what they already have.'

'You're wise beyond your years,' I said with a smile.

'I'm just older than I look.'

'What are you working on?' I asked, wanting to change the subject from my work to his.

He told me about the project to refurbish the inside of an office building. 'It was originally built in the seventies and the interior is really outdated. We have to put in ducts for cables and redo the walls. It's going from a place where everybody had their own office to entirely open-plan.'

I grimaced. 'Are the people who work there happy about that?'

'I'm not sure how much of a say the employees actually had in the decision. The company said it was to enable better communication, but in reality, it's because this way they can fit in ten per cent more people without having to move to new premises.'

'But how will they keep on using it if you're breaking everything down?'

'We're going section by section and the people who work in the bit we're converting are in temporary offices. It's a nightmare project. Not only do we have to keep everything tidy, and it's less efficient, but we're also under immense time pressure. I shouldn't have taken it on. The company doesn't have that much money, so we're having to cut corners every-where too, making do with solutions that will fail within ten years. They don't care, though.'

'But if they're growing, then there must be money.'

'It's all about cash flow. They might have plenty of capital and investments but not enough to pay the bills.'

I tried to pay attention to what Mark was saying as I surreptitiously glanced over his shoulder at the board on the wall to check what tonight's specials were.

'Do you know what you want to eat?' he asked.

'I'm sorry,' I said. He'd obviously caught me looking at the menu. 'I was listening to you.'

'You tune out when I talk about numbers and I tune out when you talk about gory details.' The way he said it made it obvious that it really was fine, rather than a passive-aggressive dig. 'I had a chance to look at the board as I was waiting for you. I'm going to have the chicken.'

'Same,' I said.

Mark allowed me to be myself and keep my sanity at the same time. I was lucky to have him.

Chapter 9

The offices of Patrick van der Linde's company were located within walking distance of where he'd lived, facing the water of the Ertshaven on the south side of the KNSM Island. It was just along from where Thomas and I had had our coffees two days ago. We hadn't known at that point that Patrick had worked so close by or we might have popped in for a chat then. We also hadn't known that it hadn't been an accidental death.

We still didn't know exactly where his body had gone into the water, but if it had been near here, it would have had to have floated around the island. I didn't have the current patterns of the IJ yet, and I wondered how the locks influenced the way the water moved. It seemed unlikely that he'd died here. Surely his body had been thrown into the water on the other side.

The office block was close to the Azartplein tram stop and near a white bridge that connected this artificial island to the next one down. In our typical literal naming style, the bridge was called Verbingingsdam. Connection Dam. The houseboats moored all the way along the water were more upmarket than the office. It was a slightly run-down two-storey building with garages on the ground floor that must function as a warehouse.

Charlie had come with me this morning. I wouldn't say that I'd had to drag him out, but I had seen some doubt on his face: should he go with the person who had got him the job in CID in the first place, or should he stay with the person who was leading the investigation? That was how quickly alliances changed as power shifted. To be fair to him, he obviously wanted to be at the centre of this investigation, and I had relegated myself to the sidelines. Who wouldn't want to be where the action was?

I felt aloof from the case. I was setting out in my own direction not because I was convinced that this was the right thing to do, as I'd done often enough in the past, but because I didn't want to talk to the family. I reminded myself that even with a normal investigation, we would have gone to the victim's place of work, especially if he was the owner of a company. I had to snap out of thinking like that. This *was* a normal investigation; the only thing not normal about it was my attitude. Just because the victim had been the father of the woman my ex had cheated with didn't mean that he didn't deserve just as much justice as any other citizen.

As soon as I saw the premises, I realised that this wasn't a big company. I could see about twenty people staring intently at their laptop screens. I wondered what it must be like for them to have lost their boss. I guessed that suddenly their jobs were at risk: who would run the company now? Would it be sold off? It was something I should look into. Somehow I couldn't picture Margreet running a business, but then I didn't know much about her background. It was of course very possible that she had started the company with her husband but had stopped working here at some point. It was possible that she would slip back into the role she had left behind.

We had arranged to meet with the company's lead designer, Nico Verhoef. I wasn't entirely sure what a lead designer did, but according to Margreet, he was the one who knew everything about the company. He was as good a place to start as any, and he'd been happy to make time for us this morning.

He turned out to be a tall man in his late thirties. All the features in his face were large, from his chin to his nose to his bulging forehead. Even for someone as tall as he was, they were out of proportion, more like those of a teenager who hadn't grown into his face yet. He showed us into a small office that seemed even smaller now that he was inside it. His awkward movements again reminded me of a teenager who wasn't yet used to his height or the length of his limbs.

'This used to be Patrick's office,' he said. 'No one's been in here since we heard he'd died. I don't know if it's appropriate to use it for this meeting.' He looked at me as if he expected me to have the answers to all things to do with death. 'But there's nowhere else private.'

The room was small. It had a table and two chairs at one end, and a desk at the other. The table was only just big enough for two coffee cups, and I had to rest my notebook on my knee. On the wall were framed certificates. They seemed old. I would have a closer look at them after I'd talked to Nico.

He took the chair from behind the desk and rolled it over to the table. It was higher than the other two chairs, and he loomed over Charlie and me.

'When did you last see Patrick?' I asked.

'It was the evening of the team dinner.'

I remembered what Arjen had said about that dinner. 'Was it a special occasion?'

'He introduced his son-in-law, who was going to start work here.'

'Is he here now?' It would be typical if I ended up having to deal with Arjen here as well.

'No, there was no point in him starting.'

'That's good,' I said without thinking.

Nico frowned.

'I mean it's good that you were all together the last time you saw him.'

'Did he die that evening? Is that our alibi?'

'We don't know yet. We still need to formally establish the time of death.'

'Okay.' Nico accepted my odd behaviour. 'What did you want to talk about? You said you needed information about the company.'

'Yes. Were there any problems?'

'Problems? Like what?'

'Anybody who didn't get on with Patrick?'

'As you can see, it's a small company. Everybody gets on.'

'Any problems in the past?'

'No, not really. None that I can think of.'

'And what is it that the company does?'

'We make lights. Advertising lighting, novelty items, those kinds of things.'

'Novelty items?' Charlie asked.

'We mainly do bespoke items like glow sticks for gigs, but with the band name. T-shirts with lights that blink to the beat.'

'Is there a big market for that?' Charlie followed up.

'The market was better a few years ago. When advertising budgets were bigger, we had more business. But we're still making a profit, can pay our staff.'

'Any suppliers you owe money to?' I asked.

'No, we pay all our bills on time.'

'Are you owed money?'

'Here and there, but no large amounts.'

'How many people does the company employ?'

'There are seventeen of us.'

'And what's going to happen now?'

Nico slumped on his chair. 'I'm not sure,' he said. 'I'm keeping things running until I hear otherwise. I guess his wife will inherit the company. Or his daughter. I don't know. But what can I do apart from make sure we keep going?'

'And you're in charge at the moment?'

'I don't know. I'll look after the products, the purchasing and manufacturing, and Karin is in charge of the finances.'

'Karin?'

'Karin Lems. She's our admin assistant really but she deals with the invoices and with payroll.'

'We'd better have a chat with her too.'

'Now?'

'Sure, why not?'

77

Nico got up from his chair, happy to be released. 'Let me fetch her. And if you have any further questions, give me a call.' He handed both me and Charlie one of his cards.

Karin was one of those women who would get invoices paid because everybody was too scared to ignore her. She looked like a retired drill sergeant, with short white hair cropped close to her skull and dangly triangular earrings. Even before she opened her mouth, I knew that her accent would be pure Amsterdam.

'I worked with Patrick for almost fifteen years,' she said without waiting for me to speak. 'He was a good boss and I don't know what you're doing here.'

'We're here because Patrick was murdered,' I replied calmly, 'and we have to investigate all areas of his life.'

'There isn't much to investigate here,' she said.

'Nico told me that you're in charge of all the finances.'

'I do the invoicing, payments and payroll. That's it. I'm not an accountant.'

'Was there anything out of the ordinary recently?'

'Like what?'

'Bills that were unpaid? Large invoices?'

'No, everything was normal. We pay all our bills. Sometimes our clients are a month or so late, but that's nothing unusual.'

'You said Patrick was a good boss?'

'Yes, otherwise I wouldn't have stayed here for years.'

'People here got on?' Charlie asked.

Karin's eyes swerved from mine to his. 'We got on. We still get on.'

'I believe there are seventeen employees?'

'That's right.'

I looked down at the business card in my hand. 'It says here that Nico is lead designer. What does that mean?'

'He designs the products. Creates the lights, draws what the clients want.'

'And then you make them?'

'Here? No, of course not.' Her voice indicated that I must be an idiot. 'We create the specs and then get them made in China. There's no way we could do it here. That would be far too expensive.'

'And then they get shipped back here from China?' Charlie said.

'That's right. Shipped here or directly to the client, depending on what the timescale is like. If it's a rush order, it goes straight to the client. We like for them to come here so that we can check them, but there's not always enough time for that.'

'So Patrick was . . . ?'

'He was the managing director.'

'What exactly did he do? On a day-to-day basis, I mean.'

'Talk to important clients, find new factories to build products for us.'

'What do the seventeen people here do?'

'Why didn't you ask Nico that?'

Because the more I heard about the company, the less I understood it. I thought it best not to tell Karin that. 'I'm asking you,' I said.

'Four people in sales, two in admin – including myself – three designers, two customer support consultants, one IT support.' She counted off on her fingers as she spoke. 'Two in outsourcing, one marketing manager and two account managers. That's it.'

'Account managers? What do they do?' It was a good thing I'd never worked in a commercial company. At least in the police force we mostly had job titles that made sense.

'They make sure the product arrives at the right place at the right time and that the client is happy with what they get.'

'Right.'

'Because we want them to order from us again.'

'Of course.' I felt out of my depth. 'Did you go to the company dinner last week?'

'No, that was for sales and designers only. Admin never get invited.'

'I thought you said Patrick was a good boss?'

'Not having to go to a company dinner is no hardship. I have better things to do with my evenings than spend them with my colleagues.'

'Didn't you say everybody got on?' Charlie said. I liked that he'd picked up on that. If nothing else, interviewing this woman would give him more experience. He was doing well, I thought.

'Getting on and wanting to spend your spare time with them as well are two different things.'

'Did you know Patrick's family?'

'I think his wife came here once. Or maybe twice. And then his son-in-law showed up the other day. Patrick introduced him to everybody.'

'That was before the company dinner?'

'That's right. The dinner was for the important people to get to know him better.'

The way Karin said 'important people' made it clear that she wasn't part of that group and was unhappy about it, whatever she might have claimed before. It made me wonder if calling Patrick a good boss wasn't purely a wish not to speak ill of the dead.

'Was Patrick in the office a lot?' I was asking random questions because I didn't have any idea what I was actually looking for. I could only hope that one of them would elicit some sort of proof that the company was entirely unrelated to the MD's death so that I could then do something else. Something to do with another investigation entirely.

'Yes, of course. He came in first thing and often left late. He worked hard, but it was tough. We had to do more and more bespoke projects and I know the margins aren't the same. The real money is in the projects where you can just tweak a design a bit and resell it, but there haven't been many of those.'

'What did people think about his son-in-law coming to work here?'

'If he could help us, then why not?'

'Nobody was annoyed about it?'

'Not that I heard.'

'Okay, so Patrick was a good boss, there are no money issues and everybody likes each other.' Charlie summed up.

'That's right.'

'What do you think is going to happen now?' I asked.

'Who's going to run the company, you mean?'

I nodded.

Karin laughed. 'How would I know? I'd be the last person to find that out.'

I brought the interview to a close. That had been utterly pointless. On the way out, I had a look at the other people working here. They were a mixed bunch in terms of age and gender. A pretty girl with long dark hair stood up. Karin gave a small shake of her head and the girl sat back down.

I addressed the room. 'If anybody has any information that might help us find Mr van der Linde's murderer, please get in touch. My name is Detective Lotte Meerman and this is my colleague Detective Charlie Schipper. I'll leave some cards here with our phone numbers. Please call us.' I put the cards down on the desk at the front. I had no expectation that anybody was going to call me.

Karin walked us out.

'Who was the woman who stood up?' Charlie asked. I wasn't surprised that he'd noticed her.

'Oh, Therese? She wanted to talk to me about invoicing. It's nothing.'

Chapter 10

'Can I get you a coffee?' Charlie said as we left the building and were walking along the water's edge back towards where the car was parked. 'I need to talk to you about something.'

'Of course,' I said. 'Coffee's always good.'

We went to the same place I'd been to yesterday with Thomas, but a day of sunshine had transformed it. Instead of only having the smallish indoor space, the café could now seat twice as many people, as they'd opened the terrace too.

'In or out?' Charlie asked.

'Oh, outside, of course.' Who knew how long this weather was going to last?

As he went inside to order the drinks, I chose the table closest to the café building so that we'd be sheltered from the wind. I had to keep my coat on, but I unzipped it and took my scarf off. I stared out over the water and watched the shifting cloud formations, forced together by the wind and then torn apart again. I had a feeling that Charlie wanted to talk to me about working more closely with Thomas. Only a few months ago, the two of them had been arch-enemies. Thomas hadn't been keen on Charlie joining our team and hadn't been shy about letting everybody know. But as Charlie had slowly proved himself to be a useful team member, the animosity between the two of them had diminished to the point where they were almost friendly. They were never going to be best mates, but they no longer disliked each other. For the atmosphere in the office, this was a big step up.

Charlie came back carrying our drinks. My cappuccino had chocolate sprinkled on the top. The good thing about having worked together for a few months was that he knew exactly how I liked my coffee. To be honest, as long as it had caffeine in it, I was happy to drink it. With my old boss, I had always discussed work at the coffee machine, and it seemed that I had passed this habit on to anybody who worked with me subsequently. Anybody who wanted to get on my good side, at least.

'They're forecasting eighteen degrees for tomorrow,' he said.

'Eighteen? In March? That's crazy. I want winter to feel like winter and spring to start later.' But I didn't mean that really. I enjoyed these early rays of sunshine as much as everybody else. It just felt precarious, as if at any moment the weather could turn again, snatch away those precious moments of spring and dump us back into winter's darkness. I was getting better at simply enjoying the sunshine when it was here instead of worrying about tomorrow's rain again, though that didn't mean I'd stop carrying the precautionary umbrella.

Charlie picked up his cup and looked out over the water. 'It's a bit awkward,' he said.

I wanted to tell him to get on with it. Being traded in by a work colleague for someone more useful was just like getting dumped. And like ending a relationship, it was best to do it quickly.

'I don't know who else to speak to. I could ask my mum, but that would be even more embarrassing than asking you.'

My coffee went down the wrong way and I coughed violently. 'You want to talk to me about something you can't even ask your mum?'

He blushed. 'I didn't mean it like that.' He put his cup down. 'I shouldn't have said anything. Forget it.'

'No,' I said with a grin in my voice. 'You can't stop there. You want some advice on something. I'm intrigued. Tell me more.'

'This was a bad idea.'

Yup, he was right. But there was no way I was going to let him off the hook now. 'You've come this far,' I said. 'You might as well tell me. You've bought me a coffee and that entitles you to . . .' I looked at my watch, 'exactly thirty-three minutes of female help with whatever issues you have.'

He stared at me, and I smiled sweetly back. 'You know that all women think in the same way,' I said, 'so how can I help? Do you have girlfriend problems? I'm sure I'm able to read her mind perfectly.'

'I should have asked my mum,' Charlie said. 'She would have been less sarcastic.'

'Yup. But you didn't. Tell me first, and if you don't like my response, you can always ask your mum for a second opinion.'

'My girlfriend wants us to move in together.'

I waited, but he didn't say anything else. 'That's it?'

'What do you mean?'

'You need to give me more details.' I realised I didn't know much about him at all. I wasn't someone to ask about people's private lives. For all I knew, Charlie could still be living with his mum and he wanted my advice on how to tell her that his girlfriend was moving in with them. Surely not, though. He was too old to be still living with his mum. He had to be thirty at least. He'd worked in the traffic department for almost a decade before joining us.

'What kind of details do you want?' he asked.

'You don't live with your parents, do you?'

'God, no!' He narrowed his eyes. 'How old do you think I am?'

'What does age have to do with it?' I said to avoid the question. 'Your parents could have a huge house and you could live in an annexe for all I know.'

'My parents live in Veere in a bungalow and I live in a flat here.'

This was going to take forever. 'Explain the problem to me.'

'Isn't it obvious?'

'No, not to me. Is your flat too small for the two of you?'

'It's not that. I'm not sure I want to live with her.'

'Ah, I see. It's too big a commitment?'

'No, I really love her and I want us to be together.'

If he didn't get on and tell me what the issue was, I thought I might explode. 'Just too soon?'

'No, we've been seeing each other for a couple of years.'

Then what? I wanted to scream. What is the problem? 'So why don't you want to live with her?'

He leaned forward and whispered, 'She's really tidy.'

I was impressed with myself for keeping a straight face. 'And I'm guessing you're not?'

'Right. She's only ever been to my place once, because it's a tip. And I'd hired a cleaner beforehand. She still thought it was a mess.'

I bit my lip to stop myself from laughing. 'It's a serious choice between your relationship and your lifestyle as a major slob. I understand now.'

'Are you laughing at me?'

I gave up any pretence and allowed my grin to show. 'Yes. Yes, I'm laughing at you. Sorry.'

'I should have asked my mum.'

'She would have told you to go tidy your room.'

'It's not funny.'

'It is funny. You're willing to risk your relationship because you don't want to clean your flat.'

'You don't understand. She's a total neat-freak. She bought this book by Marie Kondo and has colour-coordinated bookshelves. All her T-shirts are folded in exactly the same shape. She says I own too much junk and should throw out anything that doesn't give me joy. It drives me nuts!'

'She won't have many boxes to move into yours, then.'

'It's not the moving. It's the ongoing. I'd be okay throwing stuff out, but I don't know if I could live with equally folded T-shirts and necessary joyfulness all the time.'

'I get it.' I drank the rest of my coffee. 'I'll be serious for a moment and give you sensible advice. You need to decide what's easier to live without: your messy lifestyle or your girlfriend. That's the choice you're making. Now that she's brought up living together, there's no chance of things staying the way they are. You're either going to move in together or you're going to split up. You need to decide which one you prefer.'

'I knew I should have talked to my mum,' Charlie said. 'You're too logical.'

I was still grinning when my phone rang. It was Karin, the finance person. She wanted to talk to me. In private.

Chapter 11

'They asked me to speak to you,' Karin said. 'And I thought it would be best to do it without your colleague there. I'm not happy about this, but it's better that I do it than one of them. They said that if I didn't, they would.' She scratched at the grey stubble at the back of her head. 'They would exaggerate anyway.'

We were sitting at a table in a bar and restaurant close to their office called the Clipper. The place was large, and pretty much empty, and it was a good spot to have a chat. I had ordered a bitter lemon – there was a limit to how much coffee even I could drink – but Karin had said she needed something alcoholic to get her through this and had asked for a glass of white wine.

'I was so upset when I heard that Patrick had died. I'd worked with him for fifteen years. I was there in the early years, before Nico had even joined.' Her eyes glazed over with unshed tears that she pre-emptively rubbed away with the back of her hand. 'That's why I didn't want to talk to you about the rumours. I didn't think it was right. But they forced me to. They came to me after you'd left your card and asked me if it wasn't relevant. Well, I don't think it is, but I should tell you about it anyway.'

I got my notebook out. 'Tell me about what?'

'He was of a different generation. He didn't think there was anything wrong with putting an arm around someone's shoulders.'

I could tell where this one was going.

'Women these days are oversensitive,' Karin continued. 'They complain about anything. We never made a fuss about things like that.'

'Did he harass someone?'

'One of the sales girls complained last year. She left, but her figures were terrible anyway, so I think she was making it all up.'

'And he would put his arm around her?'

'I think she didn't like being touched. She had issues. You can't blame him for that.'

I wondered if Karin had been in love with him; she was defending him so earnestly. 'Is that what your colleagues asked you to tell me?' She had probably volunteered to talk to me, since the truth might well be nastier than what she was indicating.

'Yes. Well, kind of.' She pulled on one of her dangling earrings.

'There was something more recent,' I said. It wasn't even a question.

'This girl Therese, the one you saw in the office, she also works in sales. The other girl used to get upset, but Therese didn't mind. She flirted with him. I saw her do it, and he flirted back. That was all there was to it, until she started to go out with Fabrice, our IT guy. It wasn't Therese who was uncomfortable with Patrick, it was Fabrice.' She nodded energetically, her earrings rocking back and forth.

'Therese asked you to talk to me?'

'She didn't exactly ask me . . .'

'You wanted to be the one who told me this.'

'We'd spoken earlier anyway, and I thought it would make sense if I talked to you again.'

There must have been more to this. Something more recent than the flirting that the boyfriend was now unhappy about. 'Did something happen at the dinner? Before Patrick went missing?'

'I don't know, I wasn't there.'

'Were you the only one who didn't go?'

'As I said, it was only for sales and design.'

'Everybody from those departments went?'

'Yes, and that shows it, doesn't it? Therese didn't mind, otherwise she wouldn't have gone.'

'Didn't she have to go? If it was a work do?'

'If she was uncomfortable with how Patrick acted, she could have thought of an excuse.'

It was quite possible that it would have been more awkward to refuse the invitation than to endure Patrick's behaviour. 'Did Patrick act differently after he'd had a drink?'

'He was a bit more tactile, but not in a bad way. He was a nice man. A good boss.'

'I think you should give me Therese's surname and her details. I need to talk to her myself.' I recalled the pretty young woman with the dark hair. Uncalled for, a memory popped into my head of Margreet talking about her lovely

91

husband who had always been so good to her. 'Was that why she stood up when I asked if anybody had information? She didn't want to talk to you about invoicing. She wanted to speak to me about what Patrick got up to after he'd had a couple of drinks.'

Karin looked down at her glass of wine. 'I don't want this to be how he's remembered. He did a lot of good things. He helped me when I went through some tricky times financially. It's not fair that those girls want to damage his reputation.'

The waiter came across. He had dark hair tied back in a man bun. That was probably a requirement for going anywhere near the kitchen. 'Can I get you ladies another drink? One more glass of Pinot Grigio?'

'No,' I said. 'We're done. Just the bill, please.'

Karin finished the rest of her wine.

'Patrick was murdered,' I said after the waiter had walked away. 'This isn't about protecting his reputation any more.'

But part of me understood her reluctance to speak ill of the dead. I wouldn't want to tell Margreet about this either.

Chapter 12

I walked back with Karin to the office. It only took ten minutes to get there, to move from the north side to the south side of the thin strip of land, crossing the road that bisected it from east to west. She opened the door to the premises and I automatically went into Patrick's office again. As Nico had said, it was the only space that had any privacy. I was also reminded of the other thing Nico had said: that maybe it was wrong to use this space. I was here to talk about what Patrick might have done wrong, looking into his life. Digging up things about the victim's past was always a large part of any investigation. Even when it bordered on victim shaming — what had they done to get themselves killed? — it was essential. We had to find any leads we could.

I looked at the framed documents on the wall. They were evidence of the company's success: new clients and new partnerships announced to show this was a thriving firm. I looked at them closely as Karin fetched Therese, scanning the headlines and the articles.

They were successes from over a decade ago.

I was sure they were hung there to show prospective clients that this was a blossoming company that knew what it was doing, but the dates on the clippings spoke not so much of success as of recent failure. It was of course possible that Patrick hadn't been interested in hanging anything in his office recently, but it seemed odd that none of the articles were from less than ten years ago.

Ah no, here was a more recent one. A smiling Patrick van der Linde stood in front of the office building. *Lighting design firm Linde Lights signs with EnviroBuild for office refurbishment.* I'd heard of that company: they were Mark's main competitors in Amsterdam. The article was three years old.

Therese joined me as I was still studying the documents on the wall. 'Am I interrupting?' she asked, popping her head around the door.

'I was waiting for you,' I said. 'Take a seat.'

Therese was very beautiful. Her long dark hair was glossy and straight. She wore a white shirt tucked into a smart skirt, and even though the outfit was simple, on her it looked perfect. She was wearing make-up, but it was understated, only necessary to enhance what nature had provided her with. Not like mine, which was to hide the dark circles under my eyes.

It was easy to imagine that her clients loved her, but also that Karin of the short crop and triangle earrings hated her.

'I don't feel good about this,' she said. 'I mean, Patrick is dead. That's why I asked Karin to talk to you.'

That surprised me. I'd assumed that Karin had taken it on herself to tell the story. 'Why did you ask her?'

Therese shrugged. 'She'd known Patrick for a long time. It didn't seem so bad if she did it.'

'She implied that something happened at the company do. Tell me about that.'

'It was no big deal. Patrick was just drunk. Do I need to go into this now? It doesn't make a difference any more.'

'Your boss was murdered. The company dinner might have been the last time anybody saw him alive. It's crucially important that you tell me what happened.'

'His murder had nothing to do with me.'

'I never said it did,' I said to allay her worries, 'but it's important to establish Patrick's behaviour in general.'

'Behaviour? He was our boss. We cared about him. I don't like how you talk about his *behaviour*.' Her voice rose. 'As if he was a criminal. Someone killed him.'

I'd misread the situation. She wasn't keen to talk about this at all. Instead of a boss who'd been harassing her, it seemed that she had actually liked him. I was reminded of Karin telling me that they had been flirting at one point. I had seen him as a middle-aged man cheating on his wife by touching up his subordinates, but what if my distorted opinion of this family was influencing how I judged everything that had happened here?

I needed to backtrack to get Therese to talk to me openly.

'I'm sorry,' I said. 'That came out wrong. Can you tell me about that evening? We're not sure of the exact time Patrick died, but it could be that it was shortly after the dinner. It would be very useful for me to hear exactly what happened. Karin couldn't tell me that because she wasn't there.'

Whenever you interviewed a witness who had difficulty remembering a certain event or was reluctant to talk about it, going back to an earlier moment in the day and working up to the moment that you wanted them to talk about was a very useful method.

'Had the event been planned for a while?' I asked.

'No,' Therese said. 'It was a spur-of-the-moment thing. Patrick did that a lot.' She smiled. 'He would say: let's all go out, it's been a tough day. Not many bosses were like that, but he was generous.'

'So you were all working and then he said: let's go out?'

'He'd introduced his son-in-law, Arjen, to everybody and said that it would be good for us to talk to him in a less formal setting. That was what he called it. Less formal. As if this office was formal.' She looked at me. 'I think he thought that this way we could talk to the guy about things other than work. See what he was really like. Patrick thought that mattered, since this is only a small office. His second family, he called it.'

'Was it odd that only sales and design were invited?'

'No, not really. I guess he thought other people wouldn't have to work with Arjen as closely.'

Just like with any family, in this second family certain people were more important than others. I was getting a sense of where the lines had been drawn in Linde Lights.

'What time did you head out?'

'The others left at around five thirty, six. I still had a bit of work that I needed to finish. Someone has to get new accounts in.' She grinned. 'I arrived at the venue just before seven, I'd say.'

'What was the name of the place?' This company dinner seemed to be rather important.

'Didn't you meet Karin there? It was at the Clipper. She said she'd show you.'

'I see.' The place where she'd just had a glass of wine. 'She didn't mention that this was where you went the other night too.'

'Patrick went there a lot. It's close to the office.'

'You got there around seven,' I said to get the interview back on track. 'Then what happened?'

She shrugged. 'It was a normal evening. We talked about work until Patrick told us to change the subject.' Her eyes teared up. 'I can't believe he's dead. He was always so larger-than-life, a man with so much energy.' She wiped away her tears and blew her nose.

'Take your time,' I said. I'd seen this before too: something that might have been annoying at the time had turned into a lovely memory postmortem. Maybe the entire sales team had complained about these company events. I definitely wouldn't like it if CI Moerdijk, for example, told us with only a few minutes' warning that we had to all go out. I would probably have other plans I would have to rearrange or cancel. Therese might have been annoyed that everybody had headed out and left her alone in the office to get on with work. She might have wanted to go to the cinema that evening, or have an early night.

But whatever she'd wanted at the time, that annoyance had been erased and now it was a nice evening because it was the last evening her boss had been alive.

There was a reason why people didn't speak ill of the dead, and it wasn't purely because they could no longer defend themselves. It was because they could no longer take any action at all. They couldn't be annoying, funny, caring, hard-working or anything else, so why not think of them kindly? Why not remember the good things they had done and gloss over the bad?

It was normal behaviour but it wasn't very useful for a police investigation.

I needed to hear about the bad as well as the good. I needed to coax Therese into telling me what had happened that evening – the bit that she was so reluctant to discuss. The part that she preferred Karin tell me about instead.

'The rest of the group had been there for almost an hour when you joined,' I said. 'Was everybody eating?'

'Oh no, they'd waited for me, of course. They called me from the restaurant, asked what I wanted to eat.' She smiled. 'They were so caring; they wanted to make sure I was coming.'

'Who called you? Was it Patrick?'

'Yes, it was.' Her smile wavered only slightly. 'He was always the one to get the entire team there. He felt bad that I was still working after everybody had gone out.'

Perhaps she hadn't wanted to go but then her boss had called her and she'd had no choice. 'He called you, asked you what you wanted to eat and ordered for you?'

'Yes, wasn't that kind? That's exactly the sort of thing he did.'

It didn't come across to me as kind. It felt manipulative. My mother would say that I always saw the worst in people since I dealt with criminals and crime all the time. Maybe she would agree with Therese that it had been a kind gesture. But I doubt he paid overtime for the hours his employees were forced to spend having a company dinner.

'You arrived,' I said, 'and the food was served?'

'Yes, as soon as I got there.'

'The others had been drinking.'

'Of course.'

A solid hour of drinking time without eating anything.

'Tell me what happened then. You got there, the others had been drinking for a while, I guess it was pretty lively?'

'It wasn't for that long.' True to form, as soon as I asked about anything that could be seen as controversial, Therese stepped in to defend them. 'It was only an hour. It wasn't as if they were drunk or anything.'

I had to be careful how I asked these questions, so as to stop her retracting into her shell. 'Who were you sitting next to?'

'I was at the far end of the table. Frank was to my right and Paula opposite. I don't think you've met them. They're in sales too. They were in the middle of a conversation. I think it was about running – they both run marathons – but I'm not sure. That could have been a little later.'

'And Patrick?'

'Was at the other end of the table.'

'How many people were there?'

'Seven of us plus the son-in-law.'

I wanted to ask her what she'd thought of him, but I was having enough trouble getting her to the bit I really needed to hear without giving her an excuse to move sideways to another topic of conversation altogether.

'Olaf couldn't make it,' Therese continued. 'He's in design with Nico, and his wife was away that evening so he had to babysit. Patrick made a joke about that.' She stopped talking and looked down at her hands. 'Not a mean joke. Olaf thought it was funny too.'

I nodded. I was starting to get a much clearer idea of what Patrick had been like. It wasn't a particularly flattering picture. 'Was that normal for him?'

'He didn't make fun of people, if that's what you're asking.'

'I understand. I'm only trying to see if he was behaving differently that last evening.'

Therese paused. 'I don't think so,' she said eventually, maybe stuck between a desire to lie and make her boss a nicer person than he had been, and the realisation that it wasn't a good thing to lie to a detective in the middle of a murder inquiry.

'Did you talk to Patrick much that evening?'

'Only later. When I was getting ready to leave.'

'What happened?'

'It really wasn't a big deal. I don't know why you think it was.'

The more reluctant she was to tell me, the more I wanted to know. 'It could be important,' I said.

Therese sighed. 'Well, I'd been to the bathroom. It was down the corridor, a bit of a walk from where we were sitting. When I came out, he was waiting in the hallway. Do I really have to tell you this? I'd prefer not to.'

'Yes,' I said. I got a feeling that I knew where this story was going. 'You really have to. I understand you don't want to say anything bad about Patrick now that he's dead, but this might help solve his murder.'

'It really wasn't important,' she said again.

'If it has nothing to do with the murder, nobody else will need to know. Not his family, not your colleagues. We can keep it between ourselves.'

She tucked her hair behind her ear. Her hands were shaking. 'Some of them know already anyway,' she said.

That suggested to me that some people might have seen what happened. 'If someone else was a witness to this,' I said, because I could tell how hard it was for Therese to talk to me, 'would you like me to ask them what happened instead?' I had thought she wanted to paint Patrick in a better light, but now I suspected her reluctance meant that this was really difficult to relive. I hadn't appreciated that. It also made me think whatever had happened wasn't as unimportant as she kept insisting.

She shook her head. 'No, I should tell you myself. He . . . how shall I say it . . . he stopped me from going back into the restaurant. I told him I wanted to, but he wouldn't let me. He tried to kiss me. I think he was really drunk.'

I put my hand out and touched her arm. 'Take your time,' I said.

The perfect veneer of her face seemed to crack. Tears started to stream down her face. Ugly tears. Not the kind of tears that Karin had held in earlier; not tears of sadness at her boss's death, but tears because she was reliving something traumatic. 'He knew I wasn't interested. He knew I was seeing someone here. But he wouldn't let me go. He had me pinned up against the wall. His hands were all over me.

101

I couldn't get away.' She looked at the ceiling, clearly waiting for the tears to stop. She rubbed them away with a deliberate gesture, as if she wanted to get on with the story now that she had started it. 'I don't know what would have happened if Nico hadn't stepped in.'

I wanted to tell her that eventually someone would have stepped in and helped her, but experience had taught me that this wasn't true. I kept control of my anger, grateful on her behalf that someone had rescued her from that situation.

'When you say Nico, do you mean Nico Verhoef?' I wondered why he hadn't mentioned that.

'Yes. He saw what was happening, grabbed Patrick and pulled him away. I asked him not to tell anybody. Not any of our colleagues, especially not Fabrice. It wasn't a big deal, and I didn't want everybody to know.'

'He didn't tell me.' At least I now knew why.

'Good,' Therese said. 'That's good. I didn't go back into the restaurant. I waited for Fabrice and went straight home.'

'You didn't tell your boyfriend what had happened?'

She shook her head. 'I told him I'd had too much to drink and that was why Nico had called him to come and fetch me.' She looked at me. 'We both work there. We need our jobs. Fabrice would have been so pissed off. He wouldn't have let it go. Even if I wanted to leave, there was no reason for Fabrice to do the same. I kept quiet. That was the easiest thing to do, especially when Patrick wasn't there on Monday. That's why I didn't want to tell you either. Karin knew about the girl last year, and I thought she could tell you about that and leave me out of it. Please don't tell anybody.'

'I won't if I don't have to. I'll talk to Nico about it and ask him some questions. I need to know what he saw and what happened afterwards.'

'Of course. That's fine. Fabrice and I left immediately. I told him I didn't feel too good, and he gave me a hard time for drinking so much during company time.' She smiled. 'He's sweet. He held my hair when I was throwing up.' She paused for a few seconds. Her hands were shaking. 'I hadn't realised how shocked I was until I had to be sick. Isn't that weird?'

Chapter 13

I stayed behind in Patrick's office and wrote down my thoughts about the interview in my notebook. My anger was still simmering away just beneath my skin. So Patrick had been a boss with wandering hands if I believed Karin's statement, or a sexual harasser if I believed Therese. It didn't necessarily give me a lead in his murder case but it did give me an interesting insight into what this guy was like. Not the kind, nice husband and boss that I'd been told about so far, but a guy who liked touching up the pretty women who worked for him, who had called Therese to make sure she was going to be there and who had pinned her against the wall. She'd been so upset she'd thrown up.

The door opened and Nico came in.

I gestured towards the chair opposite me. He sat down without saying anything. I let the silence last.

'I'm sorry.' He finally filled the void. 'She asked me not to say anything.'

'I'm sure she meant that she didn't want you to gossip. She didn't know that we were going to be dealing with a murder inquiry. That changes things somewhat, don't you think?'

104

'I'm not sure what it would have to do with Patrick's murder,' Nico said with a defensive tone in his voice. 'I didn't think it was relevant. I didn't want everybody to know what had happened if Therese didn't want that herself.'

Perfect, so he thought the sexual assault would have looked bad for the victim not the perpetrator. 'Give me your version of events,' I said.

'Patrick was really drunk. I hadn't seen him drink that much in a while. He'd made sure that Therese was coming. He called her, asked what she wanted to eat, insisted really. I think she was avoiding him. She hadn't wanted to come. She'd been like that ever since she and Fabrice got together. I'd made sure she didn't have to sit next to him.'

'You knew what he was like then?'

'Before Fabrice, I didn't think she minded. She would smile at him.'

No doubt the kind of smile that women gave when they were uncomfortable about the situation but keeping their head down in order to hang on to their job. The kind of smile that was harder to maintain when your boyfriend was watching. 'I heard that someone complained last year as well.'

'That was nothing. He'd made a couple of remarks.'

I was surprised that he still thought that, after what he'd witnessed. Covering for his boss might have become second nature. It made me appreciate just how bad this grope in the hallway must have been for him to intervene. 'Therese said he was waiting for her when she got out of the bathroom,' I said.

'I didn't see that. I saw them in the hallway. She was trying to push him away. And he was . . .' Nico coughed. 'This is hard to talk about now that Patrick is dead.'

I knew it would be easier for him to talk about his own actions rather than Patrick's. I decided to help him. 'Therese was grateful that you stepped in. You pulled him away.'

'I grabbed his arm. He came to his senses when he saw me. He was embarrassed.'

Embarrassed at being spotted probably, not at what he'd done.

'He went back inside the restaurant. I stayed with Therese. She was really upset. She was shaking. I called Fabrice for her. She asked me not to tell him, so I said that she wasn't feeling well, had drunk too much, and could he come and get her. They live quite close by, so he was there in fifteen minutes.'

That matched with what Therese had told me. 'What happened then?'

'Patrick was in a foul mood. Everybody seemed to pick up on that and people started to leave.' He shrugged. 'Or maybe I'm reading too much into it and it was purely because Therese had gone home, so others could go too. It's often like that, isn't it? Once one person leaves, everybody starts to look at their watch. I went not long after. It was no longer a fun evening. I'd talked to the son-in-law, Arjen, I'd done my duty and I'd had enough.'

'What was Patrick's son-in-law going to do at the company?'

'I'm really not sure. Patrick was talking about trying new strategies, but I don't know why.'

'What does that mean: new strategies?'

Nico shrugged. 'Beats me. Patrick didn't tell me. Arjen never actually started, of course. I'm not even sure that Patrick told him much, but he was going to parachute the guy in. Maybe he needed a new job. Patrick was like that: he cared about his family. Now that's all fallen through.'

'Wouldn't he have kept you informed as the lead designer?' The only new strategy I could think of would be to try a new line of products, whatever that might be in the lighting business, and wouldn't they need to be designed? In the back of my mind I realised that I was probably thinking about it too simplistically, but what did I know about this business – or about business in general, if I was completely honest with myself.

'I don't think there were any new strategies,' Nico said. 'No new plans. It was a manufactured job for his son-in-law. There was no need for us to change anything. Things were fine as they were.'

I wished I had someone who could go through the books and tell me if there was a problem with this business. There was an obvious candidate for that in the financial fraud department, but I wasn't going to ask her.

I had to stay focused. There was clearly a problem with the way Patrick had behaved towards some of the women in his company. I shouldn't get sidetracked by thinking about what Arjen was being asked to do at the firm or what his prospective colleagues were thinking about him.

It wasn't that I thought Margreet was the kind of woman to have killed her husband because he had tried to shove his tongue down the throat of someone who worked for him, but it did mean that Patrick had a different personality from what we'd been told so far. He would not be the first person to behave inappropriately after he'd had too much to drink. The question was: was there anything else he had done whilst under the influence? Something that might have given someone a reason to murder him? Who knew what had happened after he'd left the Clipper drunk and in a bad mood.

He could have annoyed the wrong person, and someone could have taken a swing at him. I would have to read through the pathologist's report again, but what if he'd been punched and landed with the back of his head against a hard object, and that had killed him? There had been plenty of bruising on his face to substantiate that theory. It all depended on exactly which of those marks were post-mortem and which weren't. But I remembered what Thomas had told me about the shape of the wound and how someone had brought down a heavy object on the back of his head.

As I was still thinking about that, my mobile rang. It was my mother. She and Richard were having dinner at his daughter's house. If I wanted to come and meet them, I was very welcome.

She knew how to drive me mad. I was in the middle of a murder investigation. 'I'm a bit busy, Mum,' I said.

'Okay, well that's fine. If you're busy, I'll tell Richard you can't make it.'

After I'd disconnected the call, I thought that I could have told her who the victim was. She might care about this murder. She'd always liked Arjen, and I knew that she sometimes babysat for their daughter.

Now I wondered why Nadia hadn't asked her own mother to help out instead.

Chapter 14

When I got back to the office, Thomas and Charlie were deep in conversation. As soon as they saw me, they stopped. It was the kind of silence that fell when you walked into a room where everybody had been talking about you. But that didn't make sense, because I was pretty sure they'd been talking about Patrick van der Linde. What was it about the victim that I wasn't allowed to hear?

To fill the hiatus, I told them about what had happened at the company do: that Patrick had forcefully kissed one of the sales girls and Nico had stepped in.

'I hadn't heard about that,' Thomas said. 'I met with the son-in-law and he didn't mention it at all.'

Suddenly the silence made sense: they had been to interview Arjen again and didn't want me to know about that after yesterday's meltdown. 'I don't think they told anybody,' I said quickly, to show that I couldn't care less about them talking to my ex. 'Therese didn't want anybody at the company to know; her boyfriend works there as well and it would have made things very awkward. Nico said he hadn't told anybody either. The girl was upset and went straight home.'

'Is that possible?' Charlie asked. 'That nobody noticed something like that happening?'

'It depends on how much people had had to drink,' Thomas said. 'How late it was.'

'Plus how normal it was,' I added. 'There were rumours about Patrick. Apparently last year another woman made a complaint but it was brushed under the carpet and she left the company shortly afterwards.'

'Did she report it to the police?' Charlie said.

'I doubt it.'

'Even if she had, I don't think we would have done much with it,' Thomas said. 'Unless it was rape. Are we talking rape?'

'In Therese's case, no. He forcefully kissed her, had her up against a wall when Nico stepped in.' I thought about what Therese and Nico had told me. 'She said he had his hands all over her. But of course you never really know what happened.' Or what had happened on previous occasions. He could well have gone further. Therese throwing up afterwards indicated trauma, brought on either by the attack or by memories of a previous assault.

'It's really hard to prove any of this, and as the perpetrator was the owner of the firm, complaining would have been next to impossible,' Thomas said.

Just because that was factually correct didn't mean his comment didn't piss me off.

'It's not right, though, is it?' Charlie said. 'What a terrible place to work. My girlfriend told me about something that happened at her company too. A guy was touching one of her colleagues all the time, asked her to go out for drinks.'

'She could just have said no,' Thomas said.

'But he was her boss and he kept making the excuse that there were work issues they needed to talk about. It was very difficult. My girlfriend was annoyed with me when I told her it wasn't something for the police to get involved in.'

'You can just tell how that would play out,' I said. 'The boss would imply that he truly wanted to help the girl. That he didn't think he was touching her inappropriately, that he was only being friendly. That she had misunderstood his intentions. I've worked for people like that.'

'You have? When?'

'A long time ago. Luckily there aren't many of them. Most of my bosses and team leaders have been decent human beings.'

'You were too pretty for the guy to control themselves.'

I shook my head. 'It's never about that. It's not that they're head over heels in love. It's because they can. It's a power trip. Don't get me wrong,' I said as Charlie started to say something, 'I'm not talking about relationships at work. I'm talking about unwanted attention and people in authority who won't take no for an answer.'

'It can be an advantage for women too,' Thomas said, 'to have a boss who's like that. They get invited, promoted, involved in everything.'

It was on the tip of my tongue to jump at his comment, but I remembered Karin telling me that Therese had been quite flirtatious with Patrick until recently. Until she started dating Fabrice. 'Whatever the case may be, when it gets to the point where someone has you pinned against a wall when you don't want to be, I think we can agree there's a problem.'

'Do you think this has anything to do with the murder?'

'From what I've seen,' I said, 'men who don't behave like decent human beings around women often aren't decent human beings in other areas either.'

'What do you mean?'

'The boss who gave me difficulties was a shit to the guys in his team too. Anyone who thinks that having power means he can get away with touching up the women who work for him will think he can get away with other stuff too.'

'What you're saying is that Patrick probably isn't the squeaky-clean family man his wife portrayed him as,' Charlie said.

'Exactly.'

'I didn't get anything from the family,' Thomas said. 'Does the business sound dodgy? Anything that rang alarm bells?'

'Their products are manufactured in China,' Charlie replied, 'and then sometimes shipped directly to the clients.'

'That could be a front for something,' Thomas said. 'You should look into that, Lotte. Is it possible to get the list of the clients where that happened?'

'I can call Karin Lems. I'm sure she's got that information.'

'Perfect.'

It hadn't taken him long to slip into the role of boss. I reminded myself that this was what I wanted. This was what I'd suggested to Moerdijk.

It took me one phone call to Karin to request the information, and the list was in my inbox five minutes later. That made me think there was probably nothing suspicious about this working method, or that if there was, Karin wasn't aware of it.

If I was going to work on this case properly, I should start with the forensic documents. I would have looked at those first thing if I hadn't been trying to stay as far away from the case as possible. Now I checked through the photos. I always studied the photos, and it felt odd that I hadn't done so in this case. I hadn't felt the same need to get acquainted with the victim. I would normally have started with photos of his face, but now I was mainly interested in the ones that showed the back of his head. I read the forensic report at the same time: the shape of the wound implied that he had been struck with force with an object at least ten centimetres long. Forensics suggested that it could have been a brick, or something of a similar size and heft. Something with a straight, sharp edge.

Thomas and Charlie didn't return to the conversation they had been having when I walked in. Whatever angle they were working on, they obviously weren't going to include me. I started to feel uncomfortable at my own desk. I should probably just go home.

Instead of working late, as I had originally planned, I called Mark and asked if he could come with me to meet my mother's new family. I needed him to give me moral support. He said that of course he would. That made me feel a bit better.

I called my mother and told her we could join her and Richard for dinner after all. She sounded surprised, but gave me the address with only the slightest hesitation in her voice. Her tone had a hint of something else to it too. As if she had hoped I wouldn't come and was nervous now that I was going to make it after all.

She was probably worried that I would try to interrogate Richard about his life and check that he wasn't a criminal who was only after her money. That she had no money made this unlikely, so I wasn't particularly concerned about that. All I needed to do was meet Richard and his daughter and make pleasant chitchat. Have a relaxing evening. With Mark by my side, I might even be able to do that.

I checked my watch. I had an hour or so before I needed to leave. I was going to have a shower and get changed, and buy a bottle of wine and a bunch of flowers to take with me.

I went back to the pathologist's report and read through it again. Patrick could have died immediately after the company do, or up to five hours later.

'Have you found any sign of him after the dinner?' I asked Charlie.

'No,' he said. 'We checked CCTV from around the restaurant but didn't see him leave.'

Thomas shot him a glance.

'You think he was murdered there?' I was shocked. I'd assumed he'd drunkenly bumped into someone on his way home.

'Well, CCTV is sketchy in that area,' Thomas said. 'We just know he never went to the tram stop, or got on the ferry, or left through the front of the restaurant. But there's an open area at the back, so it doesn't rule anything out.'

I tried to picture where the Clipper was in relation to his house. What route would he have taken?

'Forensics checked out that area at the back but didn't find any traces of blood,' Thomas said. 'He could have walked anywhere. We might still catch him on CCTV somewhere else, but it will be hard. A needle in a haystack.'

'There's no CCTV at the Clipper itself?'

'Just inside and at the front,' Charlie said. 'Nothing at the back.'

I wondered if they'd contacted the restaurant while I was in there with Karin Lems. If forensics had been checking the area at the back, I hadn't seen them. It was possible of course that you couldn't see that space from inside the restaurant, plus I'd been concentrating on what Karin was telling me. Still, I thought that if officers had been walking around, I would have noticed them. They must have got there after I'd left.

If Patrick had walked along the water's edge at the back, he could have gone for miles before being caught on CCTV again. Finding the scene of the murder was going to be difficult, but it was crucial for the investigation.

Just as I was about to leave the office, I got a call from the duty officer. I had a visitor: Margreet van der Linde. She wanted to speak to me specifically. I shot a quick look at Thomas. I had told Margreet that I would be less involved in the investigation, that Thomas was leading it, and she had seemed to accept that, so if she was here asking for me, maybe there was something urgent. Karin had said she wanted to talk to me without Charlie there; what if Margreet also wanted to mention something she didn't feel comfortable talking to a man about? I should meet with her and hear it out.

I told the duty officer I would be straight down.

Chapter 15

Part of me was curious to find out what Margreet wanted to speak to me about, but a much larger part felt very awkward about this, especially in light of the things I now knew about Patrick.

'Can we go where we went last time?' she said. 'That little café? It's a bit strange talking here.'

Going outside meant that we would have to talk for at least the amount of time it took to finish our drinks, which could well be longer than I wanted to spend with her. Then I reminded myself that she'd recently become a widow and that none of what had happened had been her fault.

'Sure,' I said. 'I'm done for the day anyway.' I hoped she got the hint and would keep it short.

She was quiet as we walked across the bridge and I was happy enough with that. In Margreet's company, I was reminded that the man who had died had been loved; that whatever he had done, he'd been a victim of murder. We went inside the café and took a table at the window. It wasn't busy; at this time of day people were going home for dinner, not to a café for drinks. The crowds would come later.

'I talked to Nadia,' she said as soon as she sat down. 'I want to apologise. I'd never asked her about you before. I mean, I knew there was an ex-wife.'

She gestured to the man behind the bar and he came over. I had only ever ordered at the counter, but Margreet was the kind of person who would get them to come to her.

'I'm having a glass of wine,' she said, reminding me of Karin earlier today. 'What about you? The same?'

'Sure,' I said. I felt I was going to need the alcohol to get through this conversation. This wasn't about the murder victim but about my private life. 'Dry white, please.'

'Do you have Picpoul?' Margreet said. 'Or Chablis?'

'It's Sauvignon Blanc,' the barman replied.

'That would be great,' I said quickly. 'Thank you.'

'I'll have a large one,' Margreet added.

I pinched my thumb and index finger together to signal that I wanted a small one. The man nodded.

'Nadia told you who I was, then?' I said.

Margreet stayed quiet until the barman brought our drinks over. Then she continued exactly where she'd left off. 'As I said, I knew there had been an ex-wife, but I never gave her any thought.'

I wondered if she'd rehearsed what she was going to say before she met with me.

'Was that bad of me?'

'It wasn't your doing,' I said. 'It wasn't your problem.'

'I was mortified when Nadia told me how she knew you. I thought you were her friend. I have no idea what she was thinking of, going to you for help.'

As if that mattered. I was surprised that this was how she was feeling, seeing as her husband had died a week ago. 'She was very worried about her father,' I said kindly.

'I want to apologise,' Margreet said. 'I'm so sorry.'

'It's fine,' I said.

'Was it a shock? Did you know that your husband was having an affair?'

Did you know what yours had been up to? I could have asked. I took a sip of my wine. 'I don't understand why you want to know this,' I finally said.

'I want to know if my daughter is a bad person.'

I sat back on my chair and hooked one arm over the back. 'I found out when my husband told me he'd got your daughter pregnant.' I kept my voice steady, but Margreet flinched as if I'd hit her.

'I'm so sorry,' she said. 'I never believed those stories; I always thought that surely the wife would know. Would have an inkling.'

I had been too engrossed in the pain of my daughter's death to appreciate that my husband had been finding solace elsewhere. 'Often the wife has no idea whatsoever,' I said. I looked at her steadily.

'If my husband had done something bad, do you think I would know?' she asked. 'You're a police officer. What do you think?' There were tears in her eyes.

I couldn't tell if she was crying because she was thinking about her husband or if she was actually considering the possibility that he had cheated on her. Seeing as we now had a much better idea of what kind of person he really had been, it wouldn't surprise me if she had had her suspicions about his behaviour. Maybe she had even seen him do something. 'What kind of bad things are you talking about?'

'Something that would get him killed.'

I narrowed my eyes. 'Was there anything like that? Is there something you're worried about, or have you found something out?'

She was still crying. 'I don't know. It's all the things together: meeting you, hearing what Nadia had done to you, Patrick being murdered; it makes me wonder if there was anything else I didn't know. I feel as if I've been living in this bubble, accepting everybody's words, everything they told me, without questioning anything. Believing them. Now I'm doubting everything.'

'Did Patrick tell you something that you're now doubting?' I wanted to stay with the investigation. I wanted to talk about the murder, not analyse Nadia's affair and my divorce.

'He would often come home late. He'd been drinking, I could smell it on him. I could even smell that he'd been smoking, though he was supposed to have stopped years before. He used to say that it was only smoke on his clothes from other people's cigarettes, but now that there's a smoking ban everywhere, that doesn't make sense, does it?'

I kept quiet. I wasn't going to give her any hints as to what else Patrick had been getting up to, but if her own mind was heading in that direction, I wasn't going to direct her thoughts either.

'So if he smoked and lied about that, I keep wondering what else he was lying about.' She buried her face in her hands.

I fished a packet of tissues out of my handbag and gave them to her.

'Was he lying about the drinking? What was going on at the company?' Margreet took a tissue out and dabbed her eyes. 'I thought I knew what he was like.'

I didn't tell her. I didn't confirm her worst fears. I didn't want to tarnish her husband's reputation in her eyes. If he'd been a power-abusing git who inappropriately touched the women who worked for him, that wasn't her fault, in the same way that Arjen's cheating hadn't been my fault either. If Arjen had suddenly died, in a car crash, for example, I would have much preferred to think that he'd been great and had loved me forever. I could do Margreet the courtesy of allowing her to have good memories of her husband. If it became the core of the investigation, or the motive for murder, I would ask her about it, of course, but I didn't feel it was necessary at the moment.

'This is a murder case,' I said instead. 'If there's anything that you think we need to know, anything at all, you should tell us. We're trying to find out who killed your husband. If there were problems at work, problems at his company, you must tell me.'

'I don't know anything,' she said. 'And I feel stupid for that. I let Patrick do everything. I have no idea what our finances are like, Nadia is helping me with that. Everything is in his name. I can't even pay my bills.' She put her head in her hands and sobbed.

I gave her time. I threw a quick glance at my watch without her noticing. I had to leave in the next half an hour to get to the dinner in time. I sent Mark a quick text to ask him to pick up some wine and flowers.

Margreet rummaged around in her handbag, got a handkerchief out and blew her nose. 'I'm sorry,' she said. 'I hate crying.'

'It's normal. Don't worry about it.'

'You must see a lot of miserable people. I thought I was coping just fine.'

'How can you be?' I said.

'I hate it that I cry about not paying the bills, not about my husband.'

'You're crying about all those things at the same time. Don't be hard on yourself.'

'I don't even know why I wanted to talk to you. What I wanted from you.' She put her handkerchief back into her bag. 'It seemed important an hour ago. I wasn't thinking straight. Asking you about your divorce, about Nadia. I shouldn't do that, should I?'

'It's best if we keep the two things separate,' I said. That was an understatement, of course, and the thing I was battling with myself.

'But there was probably something wrong with your marriage already for your husband to have cheated.'

'Let's not talk about that any more.' The bitterness I felt inside, that I'd managed to hold back so far, spilled out. 'I want to see this as a normal murder case, not the death of the father of the woman my husband had an affair with.'

Margreet paled and I instantly felt guilty. I wished I could take my words back.

'I'm sorry,' I said. 'I didn't mean it like that.'

'A normal murder case,' she repeated. 'That's terrible. That Patrick is a normal murder case.'

I was surprised that this was what she'd got upset about. But to be fair, I shouldn't have said that part either.

'My husband is dead, and for you this is a normal case.' She pushed her chair back. 'I won't bother you any more,' she said. 'As you mentioned, I should really talk to your colleagues. That's what you asked.' She put her coat on and left.

I swore under my breath, but I didn't stop her. I felt awful. That she was finally going to do what I'd asked her to do made no difference. That she'd asked about something that was painful to me was no reason to lash out. That her husband had been a cheat, like mine had been, didn't make what I'd said right. The mistake was all mine. Whatever my opinion of Patrick and his daughter might be, Margreet had done nothing wrong. I had no reason to make her feel worse than she was already feeling.

The rest of the bar was empty. I was now the only person sitting there, two half-drunk glasses of wine on my table. It was tempting to finish mine at least, and maybe even empty Margreet's into my glass too, but I shouldn't drink too much before going to my mother's dinner party. However much I would like to sit here in silence and enjoy a nice glass of wine, arriving half-cut would really set me up perfectly for disaster. It was going to be tricky anyway, and the less I drank, the better it would be.

Margreet had walked off without paying. I went up to the bar and settled the bill for both our drinks, then popped back into the office to pick up my stuff. Thomas and Charlie looked at me in surprise.

'We thought you'd left for the day,' Thomas said. He shuffled a heap of papers together. I wanted to ask what they were looking at, why they would clear things away as soon as I came in, but then I realised that this was what happened when you said you didn't want to be a main part of the investigation: you were on the outside. You didn't get included. I told myself firmly that it was fine. This was the price I had to pay.

'Someone's coming in,' Thomas looked at his watch, 'in about five minutes.'

'Who?'

'Arjen Boogaard.'

I flinched at the sound of the surname that had once been mine. I tried not to read too much into the fact that they had him coming in after they'd thought I'd left for the day. 'What for?' I asked.

'We want him to talk us through the timeline of that company do. Who was there, what did they say, did he see anything. Things like that.'

'You want to ask if he noticed anything going on between Patrick and Therese?'

'Amongst other things. But really to get the timings straight.'

Now I understood what they had been talking about when I came in earlier; they must have been preparing for the interview.

'You guys get on with it without me. Just check if he

knew what exactly Patrick wanted him to do. Work-wise, I mean.'

'Are you sure?'

'Getting the timeline straight doesn't need three of us, and I need to have dinner with my mother.'

'Well, okay, we'll go downstairs now.'

Charlie took the pile of papers with him. It made me smile. He'd learn quickly enough that there was no point in having all your notes with you when you were interviewing a witness, but I liked his eagerness and attempt at detail. It was not his strong point – I knew that, he knew that – but it seemed that he was working hard to rectify it.

He looked like a student with all that paper under his arm.

Bless.

I responded to a couple of emails that had come in, then logged off from my computer, grabbed my handbag and put my coat on. I was nervous about the meeting with my mother's fiancé and his daughter, but hanging around here wasting time wasn't going to help.

As I came down the stairs, I saw Thomas and Charlie ushering Arjen into an interview room. That surprised me. I had thought they would have used one of the more informal areas, rather than the one with all the recording equipment.

It made me intrigued as to why they really had him coming in. If it was just about the timeline, surely they wouldn't need an interrogation room. The only reason I could think of was that they were going to ask him about

Therese, or maybe the money situation at the company. These were all areas that were crucially important to the part of the investigation I was involved in.

I was making up reasons why I was going to do what I was going to do anyway.

Chapter 16

It would be embarrassing if Thomas and Charlie knew that I was looking at them interview my ex-husband, so I ducked into the observation area behind the one-way mirror after they'd gone in. I had always liked sitting there in the dark, watching my colleagues as they interviewed someone. I flipped the switch on the sound and the men's voices came through clearly, but with that slightly tinny quality that the electronics added.

Now that Arjen couldn't see me, I could study him. It was the first time I'd seen him without Nadia present since our divorce. Did he look good? It was so hard to tell. There was more flesh on his face – he'd definitely put on weight – but he'd kept his hair. What did I expect? We'd only been split up for four years. It wasn't enough time for him to have altered much. Apart from putting on ten kilos.

Nadia must be feeding him well.

'Can you talk us through what happened that evening?' Charlie asked.

'Nothing unusual,' Arjen said. He had his arms folded across his chest, and a frown line that I remembered well was showing between his eyebrows. A couple of days ago, I would have interpreted his posture as being annoyed at having to come to the police station. Since then, we'd found out what his father-in-law was really like, and I could now see a second interpretation for that frown.

He's defensive, I wrote down in my notebook, but it was the 'I forgot to put the bin bags out' look, not the 'I screwed my secretary and got her pregnant' one. I could still read him like a book, especially if my concentration wasn't pulled away by his wife and child.

'I was with my father-in-law for most of the evening. He was drunk but still compos mentis, if that's what you're getting at.'

It really pissed me off that he classified a drunken Patrick forcefully kissing Therese as a bin-bag-level misdemeanour.

'We're not really *getting at* anything.' Thomas stressed the repetition of Arjen's words. 'We want you to tell us what happened that evening. Walk us through it. What time did you arrive? Let's start there.'

'I went to Linde Lights first. That was just after five p.m. Patrick had asked me to be there at five, but I was a bit late. Traffic was bad.'

'You drove?' Charlie said.

'Yes. I wanted an excuse not to have more than a couple of drinks.' He shrugged. 'Patrick would always drink a lot, but if I was going to work there, I wanted to keep my wits about me in front of my new colleagues.'

I could see Charlie taking a note of Arjen's answer. He seemed even more like an eager student than when he'd walked to the interview room with all those papers under his arm.

'So yes, that was just after five. Patrick introduced me to the staff. I'd met Nico Verhoef before but none of the others.'

'Where had you met Nico?'

'He came to my wedding.'

I didn't even choke. I was getting much better at this.

'Your wedding to Nadia, Patrick's daughter.'

'Yes. He knew Nadia well and he came to the reception. It was nice to see a familiar face when I did the rounds of the company.'

'So you met all those new people, then went straight to the restaurant?' Thomas's voice was harsh. I wondered if he was pissed off with Arjen on my behalf, that he so lightly talked about his second wedding in front of his ex-wife's colleagues. I should buy Thomas a drink at some point, I thought. It was nice to have someone on your side.

'The table was booked for six p.m.'

'Not everybody came,' Charlie said.

'No, Patrick said sales and design only. I'm not sure why, but that was his choice.'

'Did everybody come straight away?'

Arjen shook his head. 'One girl, Therese, I think, was really late. Patrick had to call her. I'm not sure what time exactly she got there. It was after seven, I know that, because I thought Patrick needed to have some food or otherwise he'd be quite drunk. I wanted to order some nibbles, olives and bread, but he said we'd spoil our appetites. I think that was a joke.'

'What time did people start to leave?'

'The girl who was late to arrive was also the first to go.

130

She said goodbye to everybody around nine-ish, nine thirty maybe. Again, I'm not sure exactly. If I knew I was going to be examined on it, I would have paid more attention.' He smiled.

Thomas didn't smile back. 'Did you notice anything around the time she left?'

Arjen raised his eyebrows. 'With her?'

'With her, with someone else.'

'No, not really. Should I have done?'

'I don't know.'

'I was talking to Gerry and Patrick. Therese was at the other end of the table. I didn't talk to her at all.'

'Did Patrick stay at the table all evening?'

'He got up to go to the bathroom a couple of times. I didn't really notice when that was. Sorry.'

'Did the mood change at all during dinner?'

'I noticed that everybody left all of a sudden. I don't know why.'

I knew why. I wondered if anybody else at that table had known why.

'Gerry, Nico, Patrick and I were the last ones there. Patrick insisted we finished the bottle of red that had been opened. I didn't want any more, I counted myself lucky that I was driving. When we were done, it was after eleven. I know that because I texted Nadia to say that we were finally finished and I was coming home.'

'Everybody left at the same time?'

'Patrick told us to go first. He said he wanted to pay the bill,' he smiled, 'but we knew why he wanted us to leave. We knew what he'd get up to.'

Thomas narrowed his eyes. 'What *did* he get up to?' Like me, he was probably thinking about Therese.

'He probably wanted to order another glass of wine, then sit outside and smoke a cigarette. He always did that. He thought his wife didn't know, but you could smell the smoke on him.'

'You knew that he did that?'

Arjen smiled. 'Everybody knew. Everybody apart from my mother-in-law, who was convinced that he had given up smoking.'

Was he really that obtuse that he had no idea what other things his father-in-law got up to?

'You didn't go to have a chat with him?'

'Why would I?'

'And that was the last you saw of him?'

'Yes. I said goodbye to him, then to Gerry and Nico. We all went in different directions. I offered Nico a lift, but he was walking to the Azartplein stop to take the tram home. He wanted to clear his head, he said. Gerry got on his bike. That was it.'

'You didn't speak to Patrick afterwards?'

'What do you mean?'

'It seems a clear enough question: did you talk to your father-in-law after the dinner?' There was an edge to Thomas's voice. It was something I recognised. He'd asked the same thing twice now. That was also something I recognised.

'Why would I have?' Arjen folded his arms. 'What about?' There was that defensive look again.

He was lying, I thought. Or at least he clearly hated being asked about this. Had he known about what Patrick had done that evening?

'To talk about his behaviour?' Thomas asked.

'He just got drunk. There wasn't anything to talk about.'

'You, Gerry and Nico all left together and that was the last time you had contact with Patrick?'

'I sent him a text to thank him and say that I'd talk to him the next day.' Arjen took his phone out. 'Here. That's what I sent when I got home. "Thanks for a nice evening."'

A nice evening. It had been anything but. Could Arjen really have been oblivious to what had happened? I found that very hard to believe. It was much more likely that he was covering for Patrick. He must have thought that Therese and Nico had kept their mouths shut out of respect for the dead and therefore this would never come to light.

Was Nadia's father more important than the girl he'd sexually assaulted? Was that the kind of behaviour that Arjen had expected from him anyway? The kind of behaviour that he thought was fine for a company director? If he didn't get angry about things like this, what did that say about him?

Thomas asked him if he was going anywhere over the next weeks and said that they would call him if they had any further questions.

I left the observation area quickly and went down the stairs to the side exit. Arjen would come this way if he'd cycled, and because the weather was nice, there was no way he would have driven.

I saw him come around the corner before I'd even left the little courtyard garden.

'Arjen,' I shouted after him. 'Can we talk for a second?'

'Hi, Lotte.' He stopped, looking surprised. 'I was just in the police station, talking to your colleagues.'

I could of course let him know that I'd been watching the interview. But it was best not to tell him that. Not only would it seem weird, but he might tell Thomas, who would definitely be annoyed with me. He would accuse me of checking his work, or make fun of me for wanting to snoop on my ex.

'There's something I want to ask you,' I said.

'What about?'

'About Patrick's murder, of course. What did you think? The weather?'

'I don't know, Lotte. There are quite a few things that you might want to talk to me about.'

'Nope. Just one. Just the murder.' And Patrick's behaviour and your reaction to that.

'What specifically do you want to know?'

I had to go to my mother's dinner, so this street corner would have to do. The statues on the outside of the station served to remind me what the duty of the police was, and that I was performing that duty right now. This wasn't a chat with my ex; this was me talking to a witness.

'Did you notice anything odd about Patrick that last evening?'

'No, he seemed his normal self. He didn't kill himself, if that's what you're thinking.'

'That was not what I was thinking. Did he tell you why he wanted you to join the company?'

'He wanted me to see if another strategy, another way of working, would be more profitable.'

'Was the company not profitable enough?'

'It doesn't work like that, Lotte. You have no head for these things, I know, but surely even you understand that companies always look for ways of making more money. That doesn't mean they have a problem.'

'You're saying Linde Lights had no problems?'

'Not that I'm aware of.'

'I think they had a huge problem. I think Patrick was their problem.'

Arjen narrowed his eyes. 'What do you mean?'

'His behaviour, Arjen. His behaviour towards the women in his company. Did you know about that?'

'What the hell are you talking about? Patrick wasn't like that.'

'No? You're saying that he was a good father and husband?'

'Yes. From what I've seen, he was a decent man.'

'That's not what I heard. I heard what happened at the company dinner.'

'Nothing happened!' He rubbed a hand through his hair. 'Your colleagues were asking me something very similar. I have no idea what you guys heard, but you heard wrong. He was a good boss.'

'The kind of *good boss* that you used to be as well?' My words were bitter in my mouth. 'Do you think that's acceptable behaviour? It isn't!'

'Are we back to that? Is everything about me? Just let it go, Lotte. Let it go.'

'Patrick sexually assaulted one of the women reporting to him. In the corridor of the restaurant.'

'That isn't true.'

'It's true, Arjen. Believe me. Your *decent* father-in-law, the *good boss*, had to be dragged away from a woman. A woman who hadn't wanted to come to the dinner because he'd probably done that kind of thing before.'

'Don't tell Nadia. Or Margreet.'

I laughed. 'Why not? The precious daughter shouldn't know that her father was up to that sort of thing at work? Oh wait – it's what *she* did at work as well, with her boss. It all makes sense now.'

'Don't you dare, Lotte.'

I read anger from his face. It wouldn't take that much needling to push him over the line.

I stepped away from it. 'Let me remind you that I'm a police detective. I'm investigating a murder. I have to explore every avenue that might have had something to do with Patrick's death. That includes his unwanted sexual advances.'

'How do you know it was unwanted?'

'He had her against the wall, Arjen. Someone had to pull him away. She was crying and throwing up afterwards. Does that sound consensual to you?'

Chapter 17

My mother greeted me at the door half an hour after I'd left Arjen standing outside the police station. I'd gone home, calmed down and got changed. Not the ideal preparation for meeting your future stepfather, but it would have to do.

'Be nice,' my mother hissed before she introduced the elderly man by her side. He was short and portly and looked at me with obvious concern. I had no idea what Mum had told him about me. Had he expected that I was going to come in with a gun and sit him down for a serious conversation?

I smiled at him, put my hand out and introduced myself. I even added, 'So nice to meet you.'

His hand shook in mine. Whether it was Parkinson's or nerves, I couldn't tell. He was a bit older than my mother, I thought, but not much.

'This is my partner, Mark,' I added.

'I've heard a lot about you two,' Richard said, 'and I'm so pleased you could finally make it.'

I shot a look at my mother. Finally? This was the first time we'd actually been invited. I got the sudden suspicion that my mother had refused a bunch of invites on my behalf.

If I hadn't told myself to be good, I might have got annoyed and even said something I'd later regret. Instead I felt for Mark's hand, close to my side. He gave mine a little squeeze.

This was going to be fine. But only because he was there to support me.

We went inside and met Elise and her husband Michael. It was easy to spot the family resemblance between Elise and her father.

Michael held out a glass of wine to me. I liked him already. 'Dinner is pretty much ready whenever you are,' he said.

I looked at my watch. It had all been a bit of a rush. I'd had to cycle to Mark's place first so that we could arrive here together, but I thought we'd arrived at the time my mother had stipulated. Had she made us intentionally late? 'Have you been waiting for us?'

'No, no, not at all,' Michael said, as if he was answering the question in my head. 'I like cooking things that sit on the hob for hours and don't spoil. It's less stressful that way, don't you think?'

I handed Elise the flowers that Mark had bought after my panic call.

'Great,' she said. 'I have a couple of vases out already, but you can never have too many flowers. These are wonderful, I love them. It will make the house feel like spring is here already.'

Richard, who I was certain would never ask me to call him Dad, pulled out a seat for me next to him. Mark was directed towards the head of the table on my other side.

Michael was opposite me, Elise next to him and my mother at the other end of the table. Couples got to sit next to each other.

'You look very familiar,' Elise said to Mark. 'Didn't you do some work on our offices in the Zuidas?'

She made it sound as if Mark had personally painted the walls.

'I pitched for it,' Mark said. 'We didn't win the business.'

'Oh, didn't you? I thought it was your lot that made the changes.'

'No, we came in for a few meetings, I remember you from those, but you went with another project development firm.'

'Oh yes, of course, you came in for the redevelopment of our old building, not the completion of the new one. I mixed the two up.'

'That's right. We talked about how many people you'd be able to put in there.'

Elise nodded. 'In the end, we sold it and moved to new premises altogether.'

'That always seemed on the cards,' Mark said. 'We couldn't fit the number of people in that you wanted.'

'How long ago was that? Two years?'

'A little longer, I think. Four, probably.'

I exchanged a smile with Michael opposite me but didn't interrupt the conversation.

'God, doesn't time fly? That's right, though, we moved into our new buildings three years ago. We're already out of space again.'

'Your firm is growing quickly.'

'We took on a lot of people last year. We're working on a few new strategies; it's quite exciting.'

'How do you do that?' I asked. Arjen had been hired to come up with a better strategy for the lighting firm.

'Do what?' Elise stared at me as if she'd forgotten for a second that I was there.

'Decide on a new strategy.'

She didn't immediately answer.

My mother shot me an angry look from the other end of the table. She probably knew better than anybody else there that I was asking for professional reasons. She hated it when I brought up work at a social event.

'Sorry, was that a stupid question?' I said.

'It's not a stupid question at all,' Elise replied with only the tiniest hint of condescension. 'You have to figure out what the new market directions are going to be and decide how best to take advantage of them. We have a strategy committee that meets every month to discuss this. It's really interesting . . .' She stopped herself mid sentence and smiled at her husband. 'Or really boring if you've heard it all a million times already.'

She was nice, I decided. They were all nice.

'Can I top you up?' Michael held out the bottle.

'Yes please. We cycled here so we could both drink.'

The people were nice, the wine was very nice too. The food was nice. It was probably the most relaxed dinner I'd had in a while with my mother also at the table. So much better than the time we'd argued about how long you had to boil pasta for. Michael was clearly a much better cook than either my mother or me.

'Now there's only my son left to meet,' Richard said. 'He's in Norway at the moment but will come back for the wedding. It will only be a small affair, all of us in the town hall.'

'I asked my mother if she was going to wear white,' I said with a grin.

'No, no! Shh!' Michael interrupted me. 'You can't tell us what she's going to wear. That's bad luck.'

'Is it?' I turned to Mark.

He shrugged. 'Not my area of expertise.'

'But I don't know what she's going to wear anyway,' I said, 'so I can't tell you.'

'I bet you could find out,' Michael said, and tapped his nose. 'That should be a small job for a super-detective.'

'Super? Hardly.'

'I saw you on TV,' he said. 'When you interrupted that interview.'

'Ah yes, that. Not my finest hour.'

'Don't get her to talk about her work,' my mother said. 'Otherwise she'll be discussing dead bodies and nasty crimes within minutes.'

'Like Elise, I'll just say that I think it's very interesting, or really boring for people who've heard it all a million times already.'

Elise laughed. 'I see we're going to have to be careful,' she said, 'otherwise we'll have our words used against us.'

'Lotte normally gives people a warning about things like that,' Mark said. 'That everything you say can and will be used against you.'

'I'm not as bad as all that,' I said with a smile. For the first time since my mother had told me she was going to get married again, I really believed that this was all going to be fine. I leaned back in my chair and picked up my wine. I might even have gone as far as to say that it seemed like a good idea. Underneath the table, Mark put his hand on my knee.

My mother stared at me. I winked at her.

When we'd all finished eating and had had dainty chocolates and coffee, Michael started to clear up. Mark and Elise were in deep conversation about the financial repercussions of new government guidelines for environmentally friendly building. I followed Michael to the kitchen. He started to rinse the plates and handed them to me. I stacked them in the dishwasher.

'It was so great to finally meet you both,' he said. 'We really like your mother and are so happy that Richard has found someone again.'

'Likewise,' I said. We might not have had a lot in common, but they were very friendly and this evening had gone better than I'd expected. 'Mum has been by herself for a long time. They're sweet together, aren't they?'

Michael smiled. 'They are,' he said. 'And she loves our daughter too. She really likes children, doesn't she?'

I took the plate that he held out to me and put it in the bottom shelf of the dishwasher. I gave the spraying arm a spin to make sure it wasn't obstructed. Michael was looking at me. I realised he'd expected an answer. 'Yes,' I said. 'She's really fond of children.' I sounded pretty normal and was pleased with that. I knew my mother wouldn't have divulged to Michael what had happened to me: that I'd had a couple of miscarriages and then lost my daughter. She would have thought it was private. She probably hadn't even told Richard.

'It was so funny,' Michael said. 'I have to tell you this story. When Elise and I first met your mother, we got totally the wrong idea.'

Maybe they had known who I was – he'd seen me on TV, after all – and thought that my mother would be like me.

'We went to her flat and this couple were there, with their little girl. I thought they were you and your husband at first. I mean,' he rinsed a glass under the tap, 'the woman was a little younger than I thought you were, but he was the right age. The kid was very cute; she had this toy, a little pony.' He held the glass out to me and I took it. 'With your mum, they were a perfect little family.'

He'd met Arjen. My mouth was dry. I grabbed a clean glass from the cupboard to get myself a drink of water. I'd had too much wine and felt a bit light-headed.

'I said: "Lotte, how nice to finally meet you," and your mother gave this uncomfortable smile and said that she wasn't her daughter; that her name was Nadia and she was only babysitting for them. Wasn't that funny? I got completely the wrong end of the stick. I guess I was expecting to see you.'

It was that last sentence – about seeing what you expected to see – that made me think about Thomas's behaviour during the interview. He'd asked Arjen at least twice whether he had talked to Patrick after the dinner. I'd recognised Arjen's defensive body language, and Thomas was experienced enough to have noticed the same thing.

I remembered that fleeting moment during the interview when I'd thought Arjen was lying. Then I'd convinced myself that he didn't want to admit that his father-in-law had been a creep.

Thomas wouldn't have felt the need to think the best of him. He would also have caught the lying. He might well have thought that Arjen had lied because . . .

Realisation hit me.

Thomas thought that Arjen had murdered his father-in-law.

I only realised that my grip on the glass had loosened when the sound of it smashing on the tiled floor jolted me.

'Oh no, I'm so sorry,' I said, and bent down to pick up the shards.

The thoughts kept going around and around in my head. They had called Arjen in for an interview after they'd thought I'd gone home. I only found out about it because I'd come back to the office after meeting with Margreet. Thomas and Charlie had stopped talking whenever I was within earshot.

Surely not.

'Don't worry about it,' Michael said. 'I do that all the time. They're not expensive.' His voice was distant.

That couldn't be the direction in which Thomas's thoughts were going. Could he have interpreted the defensive posture over knowledge of the sexual assault as being defensive over having killed someone? Misinterpreted Arjen's guilt?

'Leave it,' Michael said. 'Leave it, I'll get a broom and sweep it up. Careful.'

I was embarrassed about having smashed their glass and looked around for a container to put the pieces in. It was important not to put broken glass straight in the bin bag, otherwise the bin men could cut their hands on it. A milk carton was good for that.

'You're bleeding,' Michael said.

I looked down at my hand and saw blood dripping down onto the floor. I hadn't even felt the glass cutting into me.

'Oh my God. Elise! Elise!' His voice ended in a shout.

'It's fine,' I said. 'It's just a small cut.'

Michael rushed out of the kitchen. I stared at the shard in my hand and didn't know what to do for a second. Then I snapped out of my trance and rushed over to the sink, careful not to step on the rest of the glass. I turned on the tap and washed away the blood. It came streaming out of a cut along the length of my index finger. I used my other hand to close the wound. I needed to apply pressure to stop the bleeding. My hand was now dripping a mixture of water and blood into the sink. There was blood on the floor. I didn't think the cut was all that deep; it was purely because I'd been drinking that I was bleeding so much.

My mother came into the kitchen and paused on the threshold. I could only imagine what she thought of the mess I'd made.

'You're always like this,' she said softly, so that nobody else could hear. 'Couldn't you be normal just for once? Why did you have to ruin this evening?'

Mark came in behind her and wrapped his arm around my shoulders. 'Let me look at that,' he said. 'Do you need stitches?'

I still held the wound closed with my other hand. 'It looks a lot worse than it is.' My voice didn't waver or falter. 'I'm sorry about the mess. If you can find some kitchen roll, or plasters, then I'll stop dripping blood all over the floor.'

'Yes, here.' Mark grabbed some kitchen roll and passed me a couple of sheets. I wrapped them around my hand. They were soaked through quickly.

'You shouldn't have drunk so much,' my mother said. 'Then this wouldn't have happened.'

Elise came in with a brush and dustpan. She was very pale.

'Give me that,' my mother said to her. 'You're not good with blood. I'll do it.' She knelt down at my feet and swept up the glass. The blood left long smears behind. She looked up at me. 'You should go home,' she said. 'I'll clear up here.'

'I can help,' I said.

Mark's arm around my shoulder steered me out of the way. 'You need to have that looked at,' he said. 'I'll take you to A and E.'

'That's really not necessary,' I said. 'I'm fine.'

Michael arrived with a roll of bandage and held it out to me, counting on me to know what to do with it.

'Get me some cotton wool,' I said. 'Something to soak up the blood.' I sounded like a police officer ordering people around.

Mark ignored me. He took the bandage from Michael, pushed more kitchen roll into my hand and guided me out of the kitchen. He picked up my handbag from the floor and got our coats. 'Let's go,' he said.

'I think I said something wrong.' I heard Michael's voice behind me. 'She looked really upset.'

'She just had too much to drink,' my mother said. 'I'm sorry about all this. Your lovely floor, I hope it won't stain.'

Because we'd come on our bikes, I had to leave mine behind and sit on Mark's luggage carrier, pressing my cut hand tightly against my chest, the roll of bandage in between to soak up the blood, holding on to Mark's coat with my other hand.

'If I'd known you were going to be this dramatic, I would have brought the car,' he joked.

I smiled. My hand didn't even hurt that much. I rested my face against his back. 'It was just an accident. Everybody made such a big deal out of it.'

'You were standing in a puddle of blood and broken glass. It might not be a big deal for you, but it looked really dramatic. I'm sure everybody will remember it for a long time. It's one way of making a lasting impression.'

I was sure he'd heard what Michael had said about upsetting me, but he didn't ask what had happened, and accepted what I said about it being an accident.

We were lucky that it was the quiet time at A&E. The normal household mishaps – the fallen kids, the broken arms – had been dealt with, and the drunken accidents would come later. Even if my mum thought I had done this because I'd been drinking too much, I didn't think that two or three glasses of wine at dinner and half a small glass with Margreet would have made me drunk in any way.

Four stitches later, I was sent home with my hand swaddled up and with clear instructions that I had to keep moving my fingers to stop them from getting stiff.

Mark insisted on calling us a cab. When I protested, he said that he wasn't going to cycle back with me in this state. I looked down at my clothes and saw what he meant. My coat was probably ruined, as was my nice top. I wanted to call my mother to tell her I was okay, but she was annoyed with me and I knew it was better to call her tomorrow. I felt like lying down and getting some sleep. My hand had started to throb.

I remembered falling as a child and my mum would always be more worried about my clothes than about any injuries. A grazed knee would heal, she'd say; ruined clothes had to be thrown away. Even tonight she'd been more concerned about the floor in Michael and Elise's house than about my hand.

She was right, of course: if the blood had stained the tiles, they would never get that out. My hand would be fine in a few days when the stitches had dissolved.

Mark helped me undress. I'd better buy a big bunch of flowers for Elise and Michael, for when I went to collect my bike from their front doorstep tomorrow. 'I ruined everything, didn't I? And it was such a nice evening.'

Mark gave me a hug. 'You dropped a glass. It could have happened to anybody.'

'It really was just a stupid accident,' I muttered.

'Of course it was,' he said.

Chapter 18

I called Thomas the next morning and told him that I'd been in a small accident and would come in later. I was in two minds as to whether I should ask him about the investigation, but before I'd made my decision, he'd disconnected the call. Mark had gone to work. He'd said I should take it easy today, but my concerns swirled around my brain. My hand wasn't in too bad a state, swaddled up in bandages and a little bit sore, but nothing that a couple of ibuprofen wouldn't solve.

What was going on in my head was harder to deal with.

I made myself breakfast in his kitchen, using his amazing coffee machine to get my first cappuccino of the morning and devouring a slice of bread with cheese. I couldn't sit around too long, because I wasn't the only one who wanted food, so I took the tram back to my flat to feed my cat.

Pippi meowed loudly as soon as she heard the key in the door. It was nice to be welcomed but it also made me feel guilty that I wasn't spending enough time with her. I'd play with her for a few minutes before going to the office.

I held up my hand. 'Look at this,' I said. 'Hope you feel sorry for me.'

She rubbed her head against my legs and meowed again. I knew what she was telling me: a bandaged hand shouldn't be a major impediment to feeding her. She was right, of course.

I opened a sachet of cat food and put it in her bowl in the kitchen, cleaned out her litter tray and refreshed her water. Then I sat down on the sofa and listened to her eat. I felt bad about leaving her alone so much of the time, but I hadn't been able to come up with a better solution. She jumped onto my lap after she'd inhaled half the contents of her food bowl and purred loudly when I scratched the little soft spot behind her ear.

'Your owner was very clumsy, Pippi,' I said. 'I dropped a glass and cut myself. Got four stitches to show for it and a huge bandage.' I reached for my bag – without disturbing the cat, of course – and got my phone out. I thought about calling my mother, but she would only make a fuss, and I wasn't in the mood for fuss. I wasn't in the mood for anything. I sat on the sofa and stared out over the canal. Had I ever felt this paralysed, this unable to act, in the middle of an inquiry?

The more I thought back to Thomas interviewing Arjen, the more I knew my realisation of last night had been correct: he saw him as a suspect. How long had that been going on? What had triggered it? There was nothing I had come across that would point the finger at my ex-husband: no motive, no evidence. Quite apart from the fact that I couldn't see him as a murderer because I knew him, I couldn't understand why anybody else would either.

There was something Thomas had discovered that he hadn't told me about. That was the only plausible explanation. Something about Arjen. Something about that evening, maybe. I rubbed Pippi's head. It was absolutely inconceivable that Arjen had killed his father-in-law. Whatever Thomas thought he'd found, he was wrong. That meant that he and Charlie were concentrating on the wrong angle. I knew what it was like to go off in the wrong direction early on in an investigation: other motives, other evidence, could get ignored if it didn't fit in with the hunch of the lead detective, especially if the team was under-resourced, which we clearly were. It was like taking a left turn where you should have taken a right, and then keeping going, certain that you'd made the correct decision but getting further and further away from where you wanted to go. What you needed was someone to open a map and show you where you'd gone wrong. The tricky thing was that they wouldn't take my word for it. Not with my ex-husband involved.

In an investigation, finding irrefutable evidence for the right direction was the equivalent of opening that map. I needed to focus on what was going on at the company, because nobody else would.

Urgh, I hated anything to do with numbers. Even Arjen had said I didn't know anything about business. It popped into my head that maybe he'd said that to annoy me. To keep me away? Or to prod me into taking action? He'd known me for long enough to understand what I was like.

I had to do this because otherwise they would keep honing in on Arjen and we would never get back on track.

I comforted myself by thinking that the financial side wasn't the only obvious angle of investigation. Why had Patrick brought Arjen in as a strategist? That couldn't be Thomas's motive for Patrick's murder, because if it was, he would have kept me well away from the company. Second-guessing what Thomas was thinking was doing my head in. All I was certain of was that what he wanted me to look into wasn't relevant, but a way of keeping me out of the way. I'd bet that by now he regretted telling the CI that I should be part of this investigation. Actually, in view of his suspicions, I was surprised that he hadn't gone to Moerdijk and had me taken off the case. I guessed that I wasn't getting in the way, I wasn't interfering. I should continue to do that. Not talk about my ex-husband at all, and investigate other angles.

Having made that decision, I pushed Pippi from my lap and went into my study. I always used my big architect's table to make drawings of the cases I worked on. It helped me to think. The empty white sheet mocked me. I picked up a blue marker pen and wrote Patrick van der Linde's name in the centre.

What did we know? He'd been bashed on the back of the head, then thrown into – or had fallen into – the IJ and drowned. He'd floated all the way out towards the Orange Locks. It was bothersome that we had such a wide window for his time of death, but I knew it was difficult to be more precise, with the temperature fluctuating from the edges to the centre of the water and not knowing exactly how long he had been floating for. So yes, sometime after the do.

Had his murder had something to do with the company? There was of course his sexual harassment of Therese and the fact that Therese's boyfriend Fabrice worked there. I wrote their names down on the left-hand side of the page. Then there was the family. Margreet, Nadia and Arjen. I wrote their names on the right. Looking at these names, I thought it still quite possible that Patrick had been murdered by a stranger. He could so easily have got into an argument with someone on the way home. There was no concrete evidence about the actual place where he had been murdered.

Or maybe something else was going on at the company. I had the list of the Chinese suppliers they were working with. Goods were being sent straight from China to companies in the Netherlands. Was that suspicious? It wouldn't be that hard to add something to a shipment of small lights. To take a cut. How did the company make money anyway?

There was nothing to be gained from staring at the page, I decided. I left my flat to go to the office and then realised I should pick my bike up first. I got on the tram to Amsterdam Zuid, where Elise lived. It was ten stops away from my canal. A young girl wearing headphones looked at my bandaged hand and gave me her seat. This was a result! Being injured wasn't all bad.

I got off the tram and walked down the street to Elise's house. Last night I'd thought I'd better bring them a big bunch of flowers to apologise, but I'd forgotten all about that. I could unchain my bike from their railings and send them a note later.

But as I was unlocking it, the front door of the house opened and Elise came out.

'Lotte,' she said. 'Come in. Are you okay? We were really

worried and phoned your mother this morning. She said she didn't know how you were.'

I waved my bandaged hand. 'It's just a few stitches, that's all.'

'Come in. I've got tea ready anyway.'

It would be rude to refuse. I locked my bike up again and followed her into the house. It was odd to think that these people were going to be family. That officially this woman was going to be my stepsister. When those things happen when you're both in your forties, it's strange. At this age, you expect your family to shrink, not grow.

'Is your floor okay?' I asked. 'I hope I didn't ruin it.' See, I was slowly turning into my mother: caring more about damage to objects than to people.

'No, not at all. It came up clean no problem. See for yourself.'

I followed her to the kitchen, which was once again spotless and tidy. There was no sign of the mess from the night before. 'If the blood hadn't come out, I could have given you the number of a firm who are really good at . . .' I saw the look on her face and stopped talking. People didn't like to think about who cleaned up the crime scenes we were involved in. People didn't like to hear about blood, especially not people who worked in normal office jobs.

'Luckily we didn't need that.'

No. Luckily not.

'Would you like a cup of tea? I've made a pot of green, if you like that.'

'Sure,' I said. I suddenly remembered what we had talked about last night, before my dramatic exit. I restrained myself from asking Elise about this until she had at least poured me a cup.

'Michael isn't in right now,' she said. 'But he wanted to apologise. He felt really bad about what happened.'

'Why? It wasn't his fault. I was clumsy. It was just an accident.'

'He didn't know.' She leant forward to give extra emphasis to her words. 'He had no idea that the guy he'd met at your mother's place was your ex-husband. He was absolutely mortified when your mother told him.'

'He couldn't have known.'

'He realised it couldn't have been nice for Nadia either, that he called her by your name.' Elise tried not to laugh. 'He was so embarrassed.'

'Really, tell him not to worry about it. It's not his fault that my mum didn't bother to explain the situation to him.'

'I guess she couldn't have done that with them still in the room,' Elise said. 'Can you imagine? She'd have had to say: no, no, that's not my daughter, that's my ex-son-in-law's wife.' The smile that she'd been trying to suppress danced around her mouth. Like Mark, she seemed to have the knack of seeing the amusing side of everything.

It made me see the funny side too. 'I didn't cut myself because of that. I should drink less when around sharp objects. That's the lesson I learned.'

'It's nice that everybody is still friends,' Elise said. 'That your mother babysits for them. So often you hear about really acrimonious divorces. My parents' divorce was unpleasant.'

'Your parents are divorced too? I thought your father was

155

a widower.' Had my mother told me that, or was it just the impression I'd got?

'My mum died last year, but they'd got divorced in the nineties. My mum fell in love with our neighbour. It got very messy, huge rows about us, what was the best thing for teenagers, nobody asking us what we wanted.'

'My parents got divorced when I was five. I was too young to be asked anyway. My own divorce was acrimonious, but at least it wasn't messy. The courts decided what I was owed and I left it like that. No children, no pets; just money to argue over and that was sorted out quickly enough.'

'Oh, I thought it had been amicable, given that your mother was still meeting him.'

'Amicable. No, I wouldn't call it that. But my mother didn't see the need to cut ties just because he and I had fallen out.'

Elise nodded. 'I see. And you? Are you still in touch with his parents?'

'Nope.' I said it shortly. 'They hate my guts.'

'I'm sorry. I shouldn't ask all these questions.'

'It's all in the past. It's been a while now. I'm sorry I didn't get to meet your daughter last night,' I said to change the topic.

'She's a teenager. She's got better things to do on a Friday night than hang out with her parents, her grandfather and her grandmother-to-be. Fifteen going on twenty.'

'Wow, fifteen. You and Michael don't look old enough.'

'I can get used to having a sister if she keeps giving me compliments,' Elise said.

'That can be my job description: official provider of compliments.' I picked up my cup with my non-bandaged hand. Doing things with my left hand was awkward and I had to concentrate on not spilling my tea. All the talk about families and divorce had made me think about the problem I was trying to solve. 'Can I ask you something about your work?' I said. 'I hope you don't mind. It's to do with a case I'm working on.' I thought full disclosure was probably the best way to go.

'Is this where you tell me what my rights are?' She smiled to indicate that this was a joke.

'You said something last night about strategy, and I wondered why companies would go for a new one.'

She frowned. 'What do you mean?'

'Well, if a company is looking for a new strategy, does that mean they're in financial trouble?'

Elise burst out laughing. My question must have been even funnier than the embarrassment around Nadia's misidentification.

'I'm guessing not,' I said.

'Sorry. No, it doesn't mean that at all. It's a natural thing for a company to do, to find new areas to sell to, new products, all of those things.'

'Even if it's a small firm?'

'It's a bit different if they're trying to completely change everything they're doing. That would be strange and a potential sign of trouble, but if they're purely looking to add a new strategy, that would be good business sense.'

'It's a company that specialises in lighting. They're not that big. Fewer than twenty employees.'

'Are they profitable and expanding?'

'I think so, but I'm not sure.' I took a note of that question.

'Are they keeping their old product lines and just trying out something new?'

'I don't really know.' I wrote that down too.

'Do they have trouble paying their bills?' With every question, she was using easier language until she asked something that I could actually answer.

'I talked to the woman who pays their invoices and she said not.' I would double-check that with Karin.

'To be honest,' Elise said, 'it sounds as if they're fine. I would suggest talking to the person in charge of this new strategy. That's the best way to find out.'

That might be the best way to find out, but it was the one thing I really shouldn't do.

Instead, there was the perfect candidate to help me out. We didn't get on and I had turned down the CI's offer of her assistance, but I knew that it was time to eat humble pie.

After I had left Elise's house, I went directly to Stefanie Dekker's office without even taking my coat off or dropping my handbag on my desk. Part of me wanted to avoid talking to Thomas for a bit longer, but also, if I had time to think, I might change my mind.

Chapter 19

'I need help,' I said to Stefanie without preamble.

'Really?' she said. 'I was told you were all set.'

'Yeah, well, things have become complicated.'

'Don't they always?'

'Even more than normal,' I said.

I could see that she had cut out and framed the article about her and hung it on the wall. It reminded me of the articles in Patrick's office: whenever there was something to brag about, he seemed to have displayed it, and only the fact that the cut-outs weren't recent indicated that currently there was nothing to celebrate.

'Are you stuck with the financial side of a case? Is that why you've come running to me?'

I already regretted coming here, but I didn't say anything, because she was right.

'There must be other people who can help you out, seeing as you were so adamant about turning down my offer of help in the first place.'

'Don't be like this.'

She looked very smug. She was obviously enjoying

herself. 'Are all your friends busy doing something else? I thought you had that young kid traipsing around with you.'

'Charlie? He's not that young; I certainly wouldn't call him a kid.'

'He's a kid compared to us.' Stefanie tapped her pen on her notebook to get me to hurry up. 'But you didn't answer my question: isn't he working with you?'

'It's a bit tricky,' I said. 'He and Thomas are working on one angle and they wanted me to work on the financial side.'

Stefanie frowned. 'You? But you're terrible at that.'

'I know,' I said through gritted teeth.

'You're bad at it and it bores you to tears.'

'I know.' That was the issue, otherwise obviously I wouldn't have been there.

'Okay, well if it's such a problem for you, I can make some time. Give me what you've got and I'll look into it.' She gave a theatrical sigh. 'See, that's the nice person I am. Plus, I think it would put me in your CI's good books.'

'That's not quite what I had in mind,' I said.

'Why not? Didn't you want me to check this for you so you can join Thomas and Charlie on whatever angle they're pursuing?'

I looked behind me. The door to the office was open and everybody in the corridor could hear what we were talking about. I got up and shut it. 'They don't want me involved in their part of the investigation.'

'Oh, poor Lotte, have the boys excluded you?' She couldn't have been more sarcastic if she'd tried.

'Yes, but that's not it.'

'Do they think you're not good enough?'

'It's got nothing to do with that. It's because I think they've got a suspect and I know the guy.'

'Friend of yours?'

'Hardly.'

'Someone you slept with?'

That made me laugh. 'Yes, someone I slept with. My ex-husband, in fact.'

Stefanie gave me an open-mouthed stare. 'Your ex-husband? Didn't he cheat on you?'

'Yup. And the father of the girl he cheated on me with is the man who's been murdered.'

Stefanie grinned. 'Why didn't you say this at the beginning? It sounds too good to miss. Count me in. I guess you want me to help prove that he's guilty?'

'Guilty? No, I honestly can't see him killing someone.'

'Do you still like the guy?'

'I hate his guts, but I can't think of a single motive for the murder. Plus, I can't see him bashing someone's head in and then throwing his body in the canal while he's still alive.'

'Is that what happened?'

'I think it's Thomas's working hypothesis right now, but we don't even know yet where the victim was murdered.'

Stefanie stared at me. 'I understand why they're keeping you away. You're trying to pick holes in their investigation already.'

'I don't mean to. I just want to do my part of it properly.'

'Because that could throw up a different suspect.'

I shrugged. 'Either way, it needs to be done.'

'Sure, but now you suddenly care. You didn't before, and

you told the CI that you didn't need my help. Now your ex is in the picture for it and you want to do it right.'

'It's also because Charlie is working with Thomas, leaving me by myself and—'

'You protest too much,' Stefanie interrupted me. 'If what you're actually asking me is to investigate this with you, I'll happily help you out. Especially if it means seeing you squirm. Are we going to meet the new wife?'

'God, I sincerely hope not. My part is to focus on what happened in the victim's company. There's the financial side that I need your help with, but I think we should also follow up with a case of sexual harassment.'

'Sexual harassment?'

'He had one of the women working for him pinned up against the wall during a company do. Had to be pulled off her.'

'Who? Your ex-husband?'

'No, the guy who was murdered.'

'Jesus. Well, that's definitely an angle to look into.'

'Yes. She has a boyfriend and he works for the same company.'

'Was he there that evening?'

'No, but he came to pick her up.'

Stefanie nodded. 'Okay, and then you want me to check if everything is all right with their financial situation?'

'Yeah,' I said. 'I have a feeling there were issues – they'd brought in a strategist to explore other avenues, but I have no idea what they were. I don't even know how the company makes its money.'

'You know none of that means there are financial problems, right?'

'Yes, people keep telling me that. It's just a niggle. You can set me straight immediately. Rule it out and that's fine.'

'Okay,' Stefanie said. 'Okay, I'll help. I just want to ask one thing: what are you going to do if your ex actually did it?'

Chapter 20

'What the hell did you do to yourself?' Thomas said as soon as I walked into our office. Without breaking eye contact, he closed a folder on his desk and pushed it to the corner.

He had found out something he didn't want to share. I might try to have a peek when he went for lunch. I knew better than to ask him about it.

'Oh, this?' I said instead. I waved the hand with the bandage that the A&E nurse had so carefully put on. 'I cut myself on some glass yesterday. It was a stupid accident. Four stitches.'

It was of course possible that there was nothing in the folder about Arjen, but that Thomas wanted to exclude me in general.

'That's a big bandage for four stitches,' Charlie said.

'I'm sure it would be fine by now with just a plaster, but I got a seat on the tram this morning, so I might just keep it for a bit longer.'

'I once had a cut on my hand,' Charlie said. 'They stitched it and put one of those kiddie plasters on. You know the ones I mean: with teddy bears. I looked like an idiot. I think it was the doctor's idea of a joke.'

'Had you been in a fight?' Thomas said.

'Nah, I came off my bike on a patch of ice and cut my hand on the brake levers. It was really nothing.'

'Falling off your bike is a kiddie accident,' Thomas said. 'That's why you got a kiddie plaster.'

'I got my foot on the ground but my shoes were slippery too and there was no grip.'

There was something unnatural about their conversation and the tone they were using.

'I did some work this morning,' I said brightly. 'I talked to someone who works in product strategy to see if that would point towards financial issues. She said that the best person to ask is the one in charge of the new strategy, so that we can see what the purpose of the change was. Did you talk to Arjen about it when you interviewed him?'

'You know what we talked about.' Thomas's voice was sharp. 'You were watching every second of it.'

There was no point denying it. 'They established the exact time of death, then? You were focusing so much on that company dinner.' At least I could pretend that I didn't know he saw Arjen as a suspect.

'We haven't managed to locate the victim after the Clipper,' Charlie said. 'He didn't use his card anywhere, made no calls. We tracked his phone. Unless he left it behind or switched it off, he didn't go anywhere.'

'But he was found on the opposite bank. That's a three-hundred-metre drift. Isn't it more likely that he crossed the river and was killed on the far side?'

'He didn't get on the ferry. It was the first thing we

checked. There were only three crossings he could have taken before the ferry stopped running.'

'He could have driven,' I said.

'His car was parked outside his apartment. It had been there all day.'

'So he was murdered as he walked home.'

'I think it happened behind the restaurant,' Thomas said.

'By a stranger? Someone he met?' I obviously knew that this wasn't his theory. 'All the people from the company had left already.'

'Someone could have come back,' Thomas said.

'What, on the off-chance that Patrick was still there?'

'It was well known that he'd have a smoke before going home.'

I could piece Thomas's hypothesis together: Arjen had come back to the restaurant and killed Patrick as he was having a cigarette outside. 'I think I should have a chat with the people at the Clipper. Look into their CCTV footage.'

'I told you before that they don't have CCTV at the back,' Thomas said.

If Thomas thought that Arjen had come back, had someone actually seen him? Or maybe he'd made a call from there and their suspicions were based on his mobile records. No, that didn't make sense, because they would only have pulled his phone location records after they'd got suspicious about him.

'I'd like to hear what the staff at the restaurant noticed about the group that night,' I said. 'Have you checked all of that already? Requested the CCTV footage from the restaurant area itself?'

He shook his head.

'Okay, let me look into it. We shouldn't rule out the sexual harassment angle. Maybe I can see what happened during the dinner itself.'

Thomas threw me a look that meant that he was considering stopping me, but he didn't say anything.

I went into the ladies' and undid the bandage on my hand. The cut and the area around the stitches were deep red, but the rest of my finger felt fine. I did the exercises they'd given me at the hospital, then replaced the bandage with a sticky plaster. It was a huge improvement, even if it would no longer get me a seat on the tram. It looked far less dramatic now.

I got on my bike and cycled over to the KNSM Island. It was a nice ride along the water on a sunny day. Even though it was still chilly, the air had a hint of warmth in it, a promise that spring was close. A band of thick dark cloud was looming on the horizon. On days like today, it was almost compulsory to be outside, because you never knew how long this weather would last. In a couple of hours, the rain might be back. I kept my hand safe in my pocket and let the afternoon sunshine caress my face. One of the advantages of being a police detective was that you weren't stuck at your desk all day. I didn't think I could do that. Cycling through the city was one of the perks of my job, and it gave me a sense of freedom.

I locked my bike to the railings of the Clipper. I noticed the waiter who had served Karin and me the day we'd met there. He still had his hair tied back in a man bun. He smiled at me and came over. It was hard to tell if he recognised me or if that was his professional greeting for anybody who entered the place. It was a large space, too big for the number of people who were here this afternoon. Apart from me, there were only two other customers. That didn't warrant the Clipper's two floors. If a place like this wasn't filled on a regular basis, it would go bust quickly.

The waiter noticed that I was looking around but interpreted it in the wrong way and said I could sit anywhere I liked. I showed him my badge and told him I had some questions for the manager. His demeanour hardly changed. He'd call her over, he said. In the meantime, would I take a seat? I asked if he could bring me a cappuccino.

It arrived with the message that the manager would be with me in a few minutes. I didn't mind waiting. It gave me the chance to check out the place in more detail. When I'd been here with Karin, I hadn't realised that this restaurant was going to be of importance. There was an open staircase in the centre. The upstairs area was half the size of downstairs and all the tables were at the back, by the window. It would be the best place to sit, giving a view over the water. If I hadn't been here for work, that was where I would have wanted to sit. Staring at ships was endlessly fascinating. I'd probably caught the bug as a child, when my mother would take me to watch the boats clear the Orange Locks; or maybe she took me because I already loved watching the boats so much. Maybe I'd been unfair when I thought that we only went there because it was free of charge.

It dawned on me how little I actually knew about what had happened the night of the company dinner. I didn't know where the group had sat; I didn't know at precisely what time everybody had arrived and left. I understood why Thomas had asked Arjen all those questions, but there was a much better way of doing this part of the investigation. In the corners I could see the round eyes of the restaurant's CCTV system.

I had just taken a note of where all of them were when the manager came over. She was a dark-skinned young woman, dressed in the black trousers and black shirt that seemed to be the uniform for this place.

I introduced myself. 'Can I ask you a couple of questions?' I said. 'Please have a seat. I'll keep it short.'

She reluctantly pulled out the chair opposite me. I got my notebook out. 'Were you working on the night that Patrick van der Linde and his group came here?'

'I was.'

'Did you know him? Did he come here a lot?'

'Yeah, this place is really close to his office, so they were here often.'

'They were good clients.'

She frowned. 'He brought big groups here; they would have dinner and drink quite a bit, so yes. Good clients in that way.'

I caught the edge of what she was saying. Her facial expression belied her words. 'But not in other ways?'

'Last time he was here, his credit card bounced and he got very angry.'

'His card bounced? On the night of the company do?'

'Yeah. And all the others had already left. He said he'd come back the next day to pay and that it was purely an issue with the bank. I said that wasn't possible; that I was very sorry but it was such a large bill. If it had only been a bottle of wine, I would have let him off. But dinner for eight and drinks – it was too much.'

'Then what happened?'

'I asked him if he had any other credit cards. I could tell that the one he gave me was a company card, and thought maybe he could put it on a personal one. He started shouting that I was unreasonable, that this wasn't the way to treat a loyal customer. That people like me were the reason companies went bust.' She sighed. 'I wanted to say that it was non-paying customers like him who were the reason that restaurants went bust. But instead I said: "I can't afford it. If I could afford to give you credit, I would, but I can't." Look at this place.' She gestured at the empty tables. 'I've got to keep ticking over until summer, when the city is heaving with tourists and we'll get the overspill. Until then, I need every cent I can get.'

'But he paid up in the end?'

'Yes. I think he put it on a personal card. Would you like me to check?'

'Please. That's what I came here for: the time stamp on the bill. If you have a copy of what they consumed, that would be useful too.'

'Sure. Give me a minute.'

'And can I get the CCTV footage of that night?' I said.

'I talked to your colleagues the other day,' she said as she got up. 'There's no CCTV at the back.'

'Not of the back; from the cameras here.' I pointed at the ones on the ceiling. 'You still have that, don't you?'

'Yes, I can get it for you.'

'One more thing: who was the waiter at their table that night?'

'Oh, it was Gregor. I'll get him for you too.'

Shortly after the manageress left, Gregor ambled over and took a seat without being asked. It was the guy who'd brought me my cappuccino earlier. 'I didn't know you were the police when you were here last time.'

He did remember me, then. People with good memories for faces were really useful.

'You were working the night Patrick van der Linde and his colleagues were here?' I asked.

'Yeah.' He pulled a face as if he was drinking a particularly bitter cup of espresso. 'I know you shouldn't speak ill of the dead, but still . . .'

'Still?'

'I didn't like him. He went too far. He once touched my colleague's bottom, and when she said something about it, he complained that he was getting bad service. Nasty man.'

'Did you see what happened that night?' It was quite possible that this waiter was the witness that Thomas had found.

'With the woman? Yeah, I saw that. I saw him get up after she'd gone to the bathroom. I knew what he was like, so I checked to see if she needed help, but the other guy had already stepped in.'

'You mean Nico?'

'I don't know his name. He was here a lot with Patrick. He was sitting across from him that evening. Tall guy.'

I nodded. 'Yes, that's Nico.'

'He stayed with the woman, made sure she was fine, so I went back to work.'

'I'm curious about something,' I said. 'Do you think anybody else noticed?'

Gregor shrugged. 'I'm not sure. It was away from the eating area. Just around the corner there.' He pointed it out. The corridor leading to the bathrooms was at the other side of the room. 'You can't see it from here.'

'And where were they sitting?'

'They had the table by the window, over there.'

I got up and walked over to the table he'd indicated. It was tucked away. They must have wanted a bit of privacy for their party, or maybe management knew it was going to be a noisy dinner and wanted to make sure they didn't disturb anybody else. I sat down. Gregor joined me at the table. I scanned the room. There was no way you could see the hallway from here either, and I didn't think you would be able to hear anything, especially if you were talking to someone.

'I'm surprised Nico noticed,' I said.

Gregor didn't ask me what I was talking about. 'Maybe he had to use the bathroom. At the same time as his boss. To have a private chat.' He winked.

'You think they were doing drugs?' I found it hard to believe. Nico didn't seem the type.

'No, I really did mean just to chat. I've seen that guy do it before; he'd follow his boss out and talk to him in the corridor. Only this time he saw something he wasn't supposed to see.'

At least Nico had done something. He could have gone back to the table and ignored the scene in the corridor.

'Did you notice when everybody left?'

172

'Not really. I was tidying up. I remember Patrick shouting at my boss at the till. Then he went for a smoke.'

'Where?'

'Out the back; there's a patio overlooking the water. We have ashtrays there.'

'Was there anybody else out there?'

'I don't think so. It's quiet this time of year. Most people had left even though it was a Friday night.'

'Would you have seen if there was someone else there?'

'You can't see the patio from here. I saw Patrick go out, but I didn't look too closely. We were clearing up, getting ready to close.'

Thomas didn't have a witness then. There must be something else. I thanked Gregor and finished my coffee while I waited for the manager to dig out the CCTV footage. She also had a copy of the receipt and the bill ready for me. Turned out the party had spent more on wine than on food. They'd drunk a lot. I remembered that Arjen had said he'd hardly drunk anything because he'd come by car. The others must have made up for that.

I paid for my coffee, though I had to insist, because initially Gregor refused to take my money, then decided to check on the smoking area. I went across to the window, but all I could see was the water. Gregor had been right: from inside the restaurant, the patio was out of sight. I opened the door. There were steps going down. That explained it.

To call it a patio was a stretch; it was a small patch of ground, completely concealed from view, perfect for someone who wanted to hide the fact that he smoked. From one corner a path ran along the water, probably leading out to the street. Thomas had said that Patrick hadn't been spotted on the CCTV at the front of the restaurant, so either he had been murdered here or he had followed this path. I gave the area a quick scan. No sign of a struggle, or any blood, but then a week had passed.

I went down to the water. The restaurant had installed a single railing to stop people falling in after they'd drunk too much, or maybe to discourage them from going for an afternoon swim with enough alcohol in their system to make them feel it was a good idea to cool down fully clothed. There were no sharp edges anywhere, nothing that could have caused the type of wound that Patrick had on the back of his head. There were large buckets for cigarette butts on either side, but they were round, with no straight edges. It would also have been tricky to lift an unconscious body over the railing. I didn't think this area was the murder site, but there was nothing factual to base my opinion on; purely experience talking.

An oil tanker came past. Only a few months ago, one of them had rammed into the gates of the Orange Locks and damaged them so that they'd had to be closed for days. It was odd to think that the only visible border between Amsterdam and the villages surrounding it could be closed due to a ship's captain messing up.

An enormous cruise ship followed the oil tanker, as tall as the buildings on the other side of the water. It was a floating block of flats. I shuddered as I thought about the number of tourists it would drop into Amsterdam's town centre. I remembered the morning we'd found Patrick's body, and how I'd thought it was a good thing he hadn't fallen from a cruise ship, because that would have been a nightmare.

It had turned out to be a nightmare anyway.

I couldn't help but think that the list of people who had reason to kill Patrick was getting longer the more I found out about him. The fact that his credit card had bounced suggested to me that the company bank balance was not as solid as I'd been told. This could be another area where people had been hesitant to speak ill of the dead. Another area where it was just easier to keep their mouths shut.

It was time to renew my acquaintance with Karin, the woman in charge of invoices at Linde Lights.

Chapter 21

Just as I arrived at Linde Lights' front door, Karin came out. Stefanie wasn't here yet to join me. I had only had to walk five minutes from the restaurant on the corner; she had to drive all the way from the police station. Most likely she was stuck in traffic somewhere, but she said she'd be right over when I called her.

I stopped Karin. 'Can we talk for a minute? I have a few questions for you.' We could always start and leave the more in-depth financial questions for when Stefanie arrived.

'I have to go to a meeting,' Karin said. 'Can we do this later?'

'Patrick's company credit card bounced.'

'Yes, I'm off to speak to the bank manager right now.' She looked at her watch. 'In fifteen minutes actually.' She started walking in the direction of the little car park behind the office.

I followed her. 'There are money problems then?'

Karin didn't break her stride. 'I don't know what's going on. People have clearly heard that he died and now they're here like vultures, trying to claw their money back.'

'There are a lot of debts?'

She bleeped her car unlocked. 'It's a cash-flow problem,' she said. 'Anybody who was owed money wants it now, instead of in ninety days as per usual, and anybody who owes us cash is delaying.'

'But Patrick's card bounced before his death.'

She opened her car door. 'I really have to go. I'm going to talk to the bank and clear it all up. I'll call you afterwards.'

'Please do. You have my number.' I gave her my card again to be sure. 'If I haven't heard from you by the end of the day—'

'I'll call you as soon as we're finished.'

I had no reason to detain her longer. I wanted her to get answers from the bank and then she could report back.

She pulled the door closed and started the engine.

The voice in the back of my mind said that in other cases I had been more determined. I had also been more suspicious and would not have relied on one of the company employees to get this information for me. But then Karin had been extremely cooperative so far.

I had just got my phone out to call Stefanie and tell her to turn back when she pulled into the car park right next to me. She opened her door.

'Sorry,' I said with one hand on the car roof, to stop her getting out. 'The person we needed to talk to has just left. Let's go back.'

'You've got to be kidding me,' she said. 'I've come all the way here and now you're telling me to leave again?'

All the way? It had only been a fifteen-minute drive. 'The woman who's in charge of the finances had to go meet with the bank. Until she's got the information, there wasn't much point in keeping her here.'

'There's never just one person at a company who knows that things aren't going well.' She got out of the car, slammed the door behind her and beeped the lock. 'Let's talk to someone else.' She stomped off towards the main entrance. She was wearing very high heels but was still shorter than me. Clearly it wasn't a competition, but winning without having to make any effort was quite satisfying and I could wear shoes that were easier to walk in than Stefanie's. I strode past her effortlessly and arrived at the front door of Linde Lights first.

If we wanted to talk to other employees who knew what was going on, our best bet was probably the company's lead designer, Nico. I could see him through the glass wall of the tiny reception area. He looked up from his desk, as if he'd felt someone looking at him, then waved and got up to open the door.

I introduced Stefanie to him. They shook hands.

'Shall we use Patrick's office again?' Nico asked.

'Yes please.' I was thinking of this as my interview room now. It didn't seem to be used for anything else anyway.

Before we got there, a young man approached Nico. 'I fixed your printing problem,' he said. He was good-looking, with short-cropped blond hair.

'Thanks, Fabrice.'

Fabrice. So this was Therese's boyfriend. He hadn't been here when I came to the company first time round.

'I just needed to update the drivers. It didn't take me long at all. I'm sorry—' He checked himself when he noticed that I was listening carefully. 'Sorry I didn't do it sooner.'

It was obvious that this wasn't what he was going to say originally. I got the impression that maybe Fabrice and Nico hadn't got on that well before, but that now Fabrice had a reason to be nice to the other man. Perhaps Therese had told him what had happened at the restaurant.

'This is Detective Lotte Meerman.' Nico introduced me. 'She's investigating Patrick's murder. And Detective Stefanie Dekkers. Did I get that right?'

'Detective Inspector,' Stefanie corrected him.

Nobody cared about using the proper titles.

'Shall we go?' I said to Nico, to end the awkward conversation.

Once we were in Patrick's office, Nico closed the door behind us.

'I'm guessing Fabrice knows what happened?' I said.

'I think everybody does,' Nico said. 'It wasn't me. I didn't say a word.'

'Did Karin tell you what was going on with the finances?'

Stefanie shot me a look. She obviously thought I wasn't asking the questions subtly enough.

'She asked me for advice this morning. It seems we're running out of cash. But it's only a cash-flow problem.'

'Patrick's company credit card was refused on the night of the dinner,' I said. 'When he tried to pay at the Clipper, it bounced.'

'I didn't know that.'

'You'd already left,' I said.

'Yeah, things got a bit uncomfortable.'

'I can imagine.' I smiled. It had taken guts to interfere. It was always hard to go against your boss, especially if you were close enough that you'd been invited to his daughter's wedding. 'Did Patrick tell you beforehand that he was bringing his son-in-law in?'

'He told me that morning. He said we should try something new. Instead of doing more of the same, we should look into different markets and new ways of monetising our products.'

'How did you feel about that?'

'It made no difference to me. I designed stuff, he sold it. That was how we worked. If there was a way to get more money from my designs, of course I was all in favour of that.'

That made sense to me. Nico was the artistic one, Patrick the businessman. I could see how that would have worked well.

'Did he say what kind of different markets?' Stefanie cut in, bored with my ineptitude.

'I don't think even he knew exactly what the plan was. It sounded very explorative and in the early stages. Doing things differently doesn't mean that we were doing it wrong before.'

The fact that the company seemed to be running out of money implied to me that that wasn't the case. Stefanie could confirm that for me later. 'But there must have been a reason for Patrick to want to do something else?'

'He was only looking into other possibilities. That's all. It might be that nothing would have come from it.'

Arjen wouldn't have thought of it in that way, I was sure. Unless he was just doing his father-in-law a huge favour.

What had Nadia said when I'd met them at their house? That he was getting bored of being a house husband. But I just couldn't see him doing something pointless, even as a favour to someone.

'When did you move into these offices?' Stefanie asked.

'When? About ten years ago now, I'd say.'

'What about office supplies? Who orders those?' She'd decided to take control of the questioning.

'Karin does all of that.'

'What does the company pay for?'

'What do you mean?'

'Do you have a work phone?'

'It's my own.'

She pointed at the notebook he was holding. 'Did you buy that, or did the company?'

'That's mine too.'

'Laptop?'

'It's mine, because I need specialised software.'

'Did the company reimburse you for that?' She was taking notes, working through a checklist in her head.

'I didn't ask for my money back. I'm a director in the company; it's okay for me to buy my own things.'

'What about the others? Do they have to bring in their own pens and notebooks?'

'There's nothing wrong with that, is there? Everybody already has a pen.'

Stefanie nodded. 'I get it.' She closed her notebook; obviously she'd got to the bottom of whatever it was she wanted to know. 'That's all from me.' She looked in my direction. 'We'll know more when we talk to Karin later.'

I nodded. 'Thanks for your time,' I said to Nico.

As we walked out, a woman came through the door. 'Nico,' she said. 'I got you a coffee – mocha, no cream.'

'Thanks, Isabel.' From the look on his face, I got the impression that he wasn't used to people fetching him coffee.

One intervention had turned him into the company hero.

Fabrice was smoking outside the office building. He noticed me and I went over to talk to him.

'Therese told me what happened,' he said.

'It's good that she did.'

'Yeah, I guess so. I thought it was weird when I went to pick her up and she was outside with Nico.'

'Why?'

'The two of them didn't really get on. There'd been some argument about a client who wasn't happy with the designs. Nico blamed Therese; she blamed him.'

He was very forthcoming with information and I wasn't going to stop him. 'When you saw them together . . .'

'I thought it was weird. It was also weird that Nico went back inside as soon as I got there. I asked Therese what had happened and she said she'd drunk too much and didn't feel well. That was all.' It was possible that he just wanted to talk to someone about it. Sometimes a stranger can be a good sounding board.

'And then what happened?' I asked the question as if we were having a casual chat.

'Then I drove her home. That was it. That was all.'

'She didn't talk about what had happened then?'

'No. She told me yesterday, right after she told you, I think. She said that since she'd told the police, word would get around. She wanted me to hear it from her, not through the office gossip. She should have told me sooner, of course. It's hard to be angry and pissed off with a dead guy. I wish I'd been the person to help her rather than Nico.' He stubbed his cigarette out on the wall. 'But it's nice for him that he got to be the hero. Every dog has its day.'

Chapter 22

The grey clouds that had been a threatening presence earlier had by now drifted overhead, and inevitably it started to rain. Fabrice rushed into the office. The rain wasn't too heavy but I would probably be soaked before I got to the police station. Normally I would cycle, holding an umbrella in one hand, but with the stitches, that would be difficult. When Stefanie offered me a lift, I didn't refuse. I could pick my bike up again later.

We got in the car.

'What were your questions about?' I asked.

'I was doing what you wanted me to do – looking for signs of financial distress. That they've been in the same offices for ten years and aren't particularly overcrowded means they haven't grown. Getting people to provide their own stationery, their own laptops, their own phones, it's not a good sign. I think you were right about the financial problems. The next step would probably have been not paying the staff, or hiring people on a commission-only basis.'

'So that's what you do? Go around and check out the pencils and stationery cupboards?'

'Yup. Stationery cupboard police. That should be my new job title.' Sometimes it surprised me that she had a sense of humour.

'That guy I was talking to is the boyfriend of the girl that Patrick van der Linde sexually harassed the evening of his death.'

'You think that's a motive for his murder?'

'Could be, couldn't it? He had her pinned up against the wall and Nico intervened.'

'Interesting that the boyfriend didn't seem too pleased about that.'

'I get the impression that Nico wasn't all that well liked before this incident.'

'At least the girl had a witness. These things are so hard to prove.'

'I didn't think that was your department's responsibility.'

'I've come to find it quite a useful warning signal for fraud.'

'What? Office sexual harassment?'

Stefanie nodded. 'The kind of guys who do that are often the ones who don't feel bad about committing other offences. It's never just about the girl. Or hardly ever, I should say.'

'You're branching out from checking stationery,' I said, but I'd had similar thoughts as well.

'It's how we got the guy in our previous case.'

We had just reached the main shipping port. A flow of tourists disembarked from one of the cruise ships; a better class of tourist than the ones that hung out to get drunk in

185

the centre. Maybe it was the boat I'd seen come in as I was at the Clipper.

'What, stationery?'

'No, sexual harassment. Just as we were about to give up, I heard that none of the secretaries would go into the kitchen when the main guy was there. It gave me a reason to have another look at his stuff.'

'Because you felt bad for them?'

'No, because I thought he was probably the kind of piece of shit who would have siphoned money off. I had another dig around and found his Cayman Island accounts. Very satisfying indeed.' She shrugged. 'It's not always the case, of course, but it's a very definite red flag for me these days. The immoral ones are always immoral in a number of ways.'

I nodded. 'I see your point.'

The stream of people coming off the boat were heading towards the station, where they would intermingle with the other tourists. These ones were well dressed, probably American and most likely retired.

'I hope you do see my point,' Stefanie said. Her voice had a meaningful tone that I didn't like.

'What do you mean?' I asked.

'Didn't your ex-husband cheat on you?'

Back at the police station, I checked out the CCTV footage I'd got from the Clipper. Not that I wanted to prove Stefanie wrong – there was no way that Arjen would have killed Patrick – but because I wanted to know exactly what had happened that evening. I wanted to know what had led up to Therese being harassed, what the party at that table would have seen and whether Arjen had been aware of any of the goings-on. The camera had a view along the main room in the restaurant; Patrick and his group were on one side of the picture. I kept wanting to angle what I saw on the screen to get them in the centre, but of course I couldn't. The image was a bit grainy, but the group were clear to see.

The first to arrive were Patrick, Arjen, Nico and a man I didn't recognise. I fast-forwarded the footage to where Therese turned up. At that point, there were seven people at the table. She waved at everybody when she entered and took the seat furthest away from Patrick. As far as I could tell, Arjen didn't even look up from the conversation he was having with the guy opposite him, but it wasn't easy to see.

I found the moment when Therese got up to go to the bathroom: 9.14 p.m. according to the CCTV. A couple of minutes later, Patrick followed her out. Nico turned around when his boss left the table. He kept looking over his shoulder. Then he got up too. It all lined up with what he and Therese had told us. I had no specific reason to doubt them, but I liked to check everything. What I was interested in was what Arjen did next. He looked up from his conversation a couple of times, but it was hard to tell if he was paying attention to what was happening or just waiting for Patrick to come back to the table.

I forwarded it to the moment when they all left to go home. It was the same four people at the end who had been there at the beginning. They got up, and the footage never showed them again. This camera didn't show the door. I should check the CCTV recording from the front of the restaurant. Arjen had said that Patrick had stayed behind after the other three left.

When Thomas and Charlie returned from wherever they'd been – they didn't bother filling me in – I told them what I'd been doing: that I'd spoken to Fabrice and that it seemed there had been a problem with Patrick's credit card.

When I finished, nobody said a word. The silence felt oppressive. I sat staring at my screen for a few more minutes, rewinding the footage a bit, but didn't see anything that didn't line up with Therese and Nico's version of events, or that implied anybody had seen what had happened to Therese.

I stopped watching the screen, decided that sometimes you had to make the first move to make amends. It was nearly time to go home anyway. I called my mother. I didn't actually apologise, but I asked her if she wanted to go shopping for a dress.

We met outside the Bijenkorf, Amsterdam's smartest department store. My mother looked at my finger, now only covered by a plaster.

'That was a whole lot of drama for nothing,' she said. 'Mark was acting as if it was a major wound.'

'Four stitches,' I said.

'You ruined their kitchen.'

'I did not.' I took her by the arm and guided her through the doors. 'I went to see Elise this morning and I can report that their kitchen is fine and not in need of any repairs.'

'That's good to hear. What was that all about anyway?'

'I dropped a glass. It was a stupid accident, that's all.'

'Michael thought he'd upset you. He's such a nice guy, I don't think he'd ever upset anybody. Not on purpose anyway.' She shot me a look that told me clearly it was entirely my own fault for taking things out of context.

'He didn't say anything to upset me,' I said. It was best not to mention that it had been the moment that I'd realised Arjen was being seen as a suspect.

'So you met with Elise this morning.'

'I had to pick up my bike and we had a chat.'

'A chat?' She stopped in front of the perfume counter. 'It was about work, wasn't it? You do that: talk to people only when it has something to do with a case you're working on.'

I didn't answer her. She was right, after all. I just pulled her arm and dragged her along before the woman by the counter could spray us with the latest scent.

We took the escalator up to the first floor, where the women's fashion was situated, but a quick look round made it clear it was all a bit too young for my mother. About five decades too young. The trick was always to find the brand that was fashionable but not too youthful. And also affordable.

'Let's ask someone for help,' I said.

'I can pick a dress by myself.'

'Fine. Pick something.' I grabbed a dress from the nearest rail. It was a black affair, slashed to mid thigh. 'Something like this?'

'No,' she scoffed. 'Clearly not that.'

I put it back. You'd have to be under thirty and extremely

skinny to carry off a dress like that. 'Do you have something in mind?'

'Something tidy,' my mother said.

'Tidy,' I said. 'What does that even mean? Who wears something tidy to their wedding? What you're wearing now is tidy. You can save money by wearing this.'

'Richard says he'll pay for it, but I don't want that.'

'I'll buy you an outfit,' I said. 'As long as it's not tidy.'

My mother walked towards the escalator to go up to the next floor. 'I've got money,' she said.

'I'm not saying you haven't. I'd just like to buy it for you.'

'I know you always had some strange ideas about Arjen and Nadia coming to see me.'

'Mum, let's not talk about that now.'

'But they pay me. Babysitting their daughter – it's a job.'

'It doesn't matter.'

'It does matter. They were looking for someone right around the time you were in the news a lot. Arjen came to see me because he wanted to check that you were okay, without actually having to talk to you. But then he ended up telling me that Nadia was going back to work and they wanted someone to babysit and were having difficulty finding someone they could trust. I offered. It was an easy job; they paid well. It allowed me to afford little extras.'

'Why didn't you tell me?'

'You'd have said I should stop doing it and that you would give me money instead. Which was very much what I didn't want.'

There was no denying she was right. 'Why didn't they ask Nadia's mother?'

'How do I know? Maybe she was busy, maybe they didn't want to bother her, maybe she hates kids. Sometimes it's easier to pay someone for help. Not to be beholden to anybody. The same way that it's easier to work for money than to ask for it.'

'I'd rather have paid you than have Arjen and his wife employ you.'

'I know. That's why I didn't tell you. I knew you'd be like that. You don't want anything to do with them any more and have gone out of your way to avoid them. You should talk to him.'

'I talked to him the other day.'

'Okay. Well, that's good,' my mother said. 'It's good that you're talking again.'

It was best not to tell her that we talked as part of a murder investigation. 'Why is it good?' I asked instead. 'What difference does it make?'

'Because now you won't get too angry if I use the money I saved up from babysitting to pay for my dress.'

That made me smile.

I wondered what it said about Arjen that he'd employed his ex-mother-in-law as a babysitter. He must have known she could do with some extra money. I knew I was trying to refute the thought that Stefanie had put in my head earlier, but surely he'd been helping my mother out? That must make him a decent person, mustn't it? Not the kind of man she would investigate and find embezzling company funds. He couldn't have done it to create problems between my mother and me because why would he have wanted to do that?

I pushed the thought out of my head. I didn't want to think about Arjen any more. 'You're honestly not going to let me buy you a dress?' I said to pull my mother back to the matter in hand.

'No.'

'Can I get you anything else? Shoes? A hat?'

'All you need to do is come to the wedding.'

'Of course I'm going to come to the wedding,' I said and hooked my arm through hers. 'I wouldn't miss it for the world.'

'Richard is a good man.'

'I didn't say otherwise.'

A sales assistant came up to us. 'Can I help you at all?'

'Yes,' I said. 'We're looking for a dress for my mother. For a wedding.'

'You're going to a wedding? That's nice.' There was a hint of condescension in her voice that rubbed me up the wrong way.

'She's not *going* to a wedding, she's getting married.' I hooked my arm tighter around my mother's. 'And we're planning on spending all the money she's earned over the past years on something really nice.'

'Sure,' the woman said, not missing a beat. 'Let me help you find something special.' She rummaged through the rails of dresses for something she deemed appropriate and came up with a full-length dress in pearl grey. 'How about this?'

'It's too long,' my mother said. 'I don't want a long dress. And I don't want grey either. A wedding is festive. I want to wear a happy colour.'

I didn't think I'd ever seen my mother wear a happy colour.

'I want a red dress,' she continued. Being condescended to seemed to have driven her towards making extravagant choices. I liked the attitude – so much better than 'tidy' – though I wasn't sure red would be a good colour for her.

'How about pink instead?' I suggested.

'Pink is for old ladies,' she said. 'Or little girls.'

There were some arguments you just couldn't win, so I let her get on with buying a red dress.

As the saleswoman checked various dresses for size, my mother studied the price tag on the one closest to her. I expected her to walk away quickly, because this section was expensive, but she nodded to herself as if that was exactly how much she'd been planning to spend on a dress for her wedding. If she wanted to blow all the money she'd made from years of babysitting on this one dress, then who was I to stop her?

The woman came back with a dress in a soft red that bordered on pink but stayed on the right side for my mother to be okay with it. It definitely was not an old woman's dress. It was a little longer than knee-length, but not too long.

She held it up in front of my mum. 'What do you think? Would you like to try it on?'

I thought she'd made a good choice. I accompanied my mother to the changing area. She went into the changing room by herself and came out five minutes later wearing her not-pink dress.

She looked great. She looked happy.

Had I ever seen her glow like this? Whatever I might think about her getting remarried, however much I might think it was unnecessary, if this was how it made her feel, I should support her. I should be grateful to Richard for making her happy. I definitely had never managed that. I had seen my parents' wedding photos. She'd looked happy then too, snuggled up against my father. That happiness hadn't lasted.

Maybe this wouldn't last either.

But did that actually matter? Should you write something off from the start because it might all end in tears? Should I be upset with her for babysitting for Arjen and Nadia all these years if it allowed her to buy her this ridiculously expensive dress? That was her choice.

I decided that she could do whatever job she wanted. She'd kept quiet about babysitting for a long time because she knew it would hurt me. She'd probably thought that doing it in secret would get her the best of both worlds. I shouldn't be upset; I should be happy that it allowed her her little extras.

I should be happy because my mother was happy.

It felt right to think that way.

'What's up with you?' she said.

'Nothing,' I said. 'You look nice.'

Chapter 23

I was playing with my cat, getting her to chase a length of string over and over again, when my phone rang with a number I didn't recognise. It was probably Stefanie trying to annoy me by telling me again how my ex-husband was suspicious because he'd cheated on me. I should store her number so that next time I could avoid her calls.

But instead of Stefanie, it was a man's voice. A voice I knew extremely well.

'Lotte? It's me. Can we talk?' he said.

My initial response was to say no. Even before I had known that Arjen was a suspect I would have been reluctant, and now I should tell him that it was totally out of the question. 'Why?' I said instead. I dangled the string in front of Pippi and smiled as she leapt at it.

'I'm at the bar on the corner of your canal. I can wait here for you if you're not home yet.'

'What's it about?'

'There's something I need to tell you.'

I pulled the string back. 'Whatever you want to tell me, let's do it at the police station tomorrow' would have been the sensible answer. 'Wait,' I said. 'I'll come down.' I grabbed my coat and handbag and went down the stairs.

The bar on the corner had a circular beer advertisement hanging outside. I didn't come here that often because it was always busy with tourists. Arjen had only chosen it because it was the nearest place to my flat, though I didn't remember ever having told him where I lived.

I pushed the door open and quickly scanned the bar. A group of well-dressed elderly tourists, the type who would have come from one of the cruise ships, were ordering drinks in English. A Spanish couple were arguing loudly in a corner. Arjen was sitting at the table at the back, an almost-empty wine glass in front of him. He must have started drinking before he'd even called me, as it hadn't taken me much more than a few minutes to get there.

'I'm so sorry,' he said as soon as I arrived at his table. 'I know I messed up.' He drained the wine in his glass.

I sat down heavily. My legs refused to support me any longer. I didn't want to believe that he could have killed someone. I forced myself to think about practicalities. If he was going to confess, I should caution him. I should record our conversation. I should probably stop him from talking and get Thomas or Charlie over here. Or even Stefanie.

Instead I stayed motionless, my body so heavy it was impossible to move.

'Hold on one second,' he said. 'I think I need another drink for this.' He got up.

It crossed my mind how happy Stefanie was going to be at being proved right. This, of course, was the very least of my problems. What if Arjen was going to tell me but refused to repeat it to the others? If it came down to my word against his, would anybody believe me – regardless of whether I was a police officer or not?

With Arjen at the bar, this was the perfect opportunity to phone Stefanie to come over, but I didn't make the call. I did press the record button on my phone, though, so that I had evidence of what he was going to tell me.

He came back with two glasses of wine. 'White okay?'

I nodded. I still drank the same thing; I still had the same telephone number.

He took a large gulp from his glass and looked down at the table. 'I might as well get this over with. I know I shouldn't have done it, but everything was so messed up.'

My hands started shaking.

'I'm so sorry, Lotte. It just happened. I never stopped to think about what I was doing, and before I knew it, there was no way back.'

There was no way back? Why? Because at that point he'd rolled Patrick unconscious into the canal?

'And then we found out that Nadia was pregnant . . .' He fell silent. 'I know how much it must all have hurt, and I want to apologise to you.'

Nadia was pregnant. He wanted to apologise. To me. Realisation dawned. This wasn't about murdering Patrick. He was talking about his affair.

I sat back and burst out laughing.

The shock at my reaction showed on his face, then he smiled cautiously in return. 'What's so funny?'

It wasn't necessarily funny. Part of my laughter was purely the reaction to the breaking of the tension, I knew that.

'You call me in the middle of a murder investigation because you need to tell me something, and then you apologise for cheating on me four years ago. I wasn't expecting it, that's all.'

'You don't think I have anything to do with Patrick's death, do you?'

I didn't respond to that, though Stefanie's reasoning had seemed so sound, right up to the point where she applied it to my ex. 'Whatever,' I said. 'It's the first time I've laughed about you sleeping with Nadia and getting her pregnant, so that's a major win.' I laughed again and lifted my glass of wine. 'Cheers,' I said. 'To small mercies.'

He shook his head. 'You've changed.'

'I hope so. About time.'

'I thought you were going to kill me that night.'

'I could have done,' I said honestly. 'But that was four years ago.'

'Are you happy?'

'Yes,' I said. 'Yes, I'm happy.'

'That's good.' He drank some of his wine. 'I felt I had to do this, because you're working on Patrick's case. I had to clear the air. Now it all seems unnecessary.'

I frowned. 'If I hadn't been investigating your father-in-law's murder, you wouldn't have apologised?'

'I would have waited a few more years. Just to be on the safe side.'

Part of my sense of amusement died away as suspicion came flooding back. I wasn't too keen on people wanting to get on my good side during a murder investigation. I realised that this all seemed rather conveniently planned.

I looked at him, this man I knew so well, and tried to decide if he was playing me. I didn't like that I felt so wary. His body posture was open, his arms rested on the table and his upper body leaned slightly forward. I didn't think he was lying. I think he wanted me to believe what he was saying. Even if his apology was genuine, it had come at an extremely opportune moment, and that made it feel like a form of manipulation.

'Waiting a bit would have made for better timing,' I said.

'I wanted to say something when you came to our house,' he said, 'but I didn't know how to bring it up – not with your colleague there.'

'Nadia was there too.'

'Yes. Yes, I guess so. But she doesn't really understand. That's why she insisted we talk to you when her father went missing.'

'I had wondered whose smart idea that was.'

'Also, Lotte, I get what you were saying about Patrick. But the man has died. Do we have to talk about all the things he's done wrong? Do we have to drag his name into the gutter?'

I narrowed my eyes. 'He was murdered. What he has or hasn't done could be crucially important. I suggest you cooperate fully with the investigation.'

He smiled. 'It's weird to see you go into work mode.'

I didn't return his smile. 'Arjen, I'm serious. If there's anything you haven't told us, you need to fix that. As soon as possible.'

'Please don't tell Margreet,' he said. 'Don't tell her about that girl. That's why I wanted to see you tonight, to ask you that.'

'Wow, was that the deal? You apologise and then ask me to keep my mouth shut?' I wondered if he saw me as anything other than his ex-wife. As if for him it was all personal and he didn't realise that I also had a job to do.

'That's not what I meant,' he said. 'I don't want her memories of her husband ruined if at all possible.'

I also wondered if I saw him as anything other than my ex-husband. I did not see him as a suspect, for example. If I had, I wouldn't be having a drink with him.

'She's going to find out anyway,' I said. The least I could do was remember that he was my cheating ex-husband, regardless of the apology. 'Too many people know what Patrick got up to.' I finished my wine and pushed my chair back. 'There's no point hiding the truth from her.'

Chapter 24

The next morning, I was in the office before Charlie and Thomas. It had been my plan to steal a quick glance at the files on Thomas's desk, but he arrived before I had a chance. He was early today even though it was Sunday. The stitches on my finger were itching and I tried to rub it as gently as I could. Scratch without disturbing the wound. I should mention meeting with Arjen last night, but then it came to me that I really had nothing to tell. We hadn't talked about Patrick. Plus, Thomas would give me a ticking-off for seeing him by myself. He would be right to do so, but that didn't mean I wanted to hear it.

'How are you?' he asked.

'Fine. You?'

'Busy.'

'I asked Stefanie Dekkers to help me out with the financial side,' I said.

'Yeah, I heard. Well, that's good, I guess. I didn't think you two got on.'

'She's good at what she does,' I said. And her suspicion of Arjen might end up helping me understand the case against him. 'What have you guys been working on?'

'Still piecing together what happened that night.'

'I checked the CCTV footage from the Clipper.'

'There isn't any.'

'There aren't any cameras at the back, but this is inside.'

'Anything interesting?'

I shrugged. 'It all lines up with what we've been told. It's hard to make out, but it seems that Patrick did follow Therese out. That's what the waiter at the Clipper confirmed as well. It's what I've been concentrating on. It still strikes me as a motive for murder.'

'Good,' Thomas said. 'You do that and the finances.'

My mobile rang. It was Karin Lems at Linde Lights. That she was supposed to have called me as soon as her meeting with the bank manager finished had completely slipped my mind. 'Hi, Karin,' I said. 'Do you have all the information from the bank now?'

'Yes. I'm sorry I didn't call you last night, but there was something I needed to double-check at the office.'

'Okay. We'll come right over.'

'I can just tell you on the phone.'

'No,' I said, 'I'll come with my colleague. She's a financial expert. We'll be there in twenty minutes or so.' I was keen to get out of the office, and there was no point in talking to Karin without Stefanie anyway.

She asked me to come to their workplace because then she would have all the paperwork to hand and there wouldn't be anybody else there today.

When we got to Linde Lights, Karin was waiting in Patrick's old office. I introduced her to Stefanie. Today Karin wore square orange earrings. There were dark circles under her eyes.

'What did they say at the bank?' I asked.

'We're overdrawn to the limit and they won't extend our line of credit.' She gripped a couple of sheets of paper as firmly as if they were a life buoy. 'Apparently it had happened before, but Patrick had shored up our financial situation each time.'

'Did you know about those problems?' Stefanie asked.

'I had no idea.'

Stefanie shot me a look. 'I thought you were in charge of the finances,' she said to Karin.

'Not really. I'm in charge of invoices,' Karin said. 'I'm more an admin assistant.' She was already distancing herself from the mess the company found itself in.

'Did you know that Patrick shored up the finances?'

'The bank told me he'd injected large sums of money, but I didn't know about that.'

'If you do the invoicing, surely you see all the money that comes into the account? Including the inflow of capital.'

'The bank said it came into the second business account.'

'Ah, I see.' Stefanie got a notebook out. 'And there was money flow between the two accounts?'

'That's right. Whenever the balance in our regular account went over a certain amount, I would move the money to the other account. Not that this had happened recently.'

'And Patrick's credit card was linked to this second account?'

'He called it the capital reserve account. I didn't know he had a card linked to it.'

'So he used the second account for personal expenses?' I asked.

Karin shook her head. 'It was the company's saving account.'

'It's not that unusual,' Stefanie said. 'And you didn't have access to this account?'

'I could have checked the balance, I guess, but I never did. I'm busy and I don't have time to look at random things.'

'But you are a signatory to that account.'

'Yes.'

'Did the bank tell you how often Patrick shored up the financial situation?'

'Only twice. He made two lump-sum payments. Once in 2016 and once two years ago.'

'Could you give me the exact dates?'

'Hold on a second.' Karin leafed through a pile of paper. 'The fourteenth of April 2016 and the twenty-fifth of September 2018,' Karin said. She turned the page around and gave it to Stefanie.

'Thank you, that's fine.' Stefanie wrote it all down. 'Where does this leave you guys?' Her tone had changed. Instead of being a sharp interrogator, she sounded sympathetic. The questioning part of the interview was apparently over.

'I don't really know what we're going to do now. We can't pay any of our invoices.' Karin started to tear up, moved by the death of the company as much as the death of her boss. 'I didn't know about any of this.'

'Will the bank extend you a line of credit?'

She shook her head and the orange earrings flashed like warning signs. 'They said it wasn't possible any more. That they had told Patrick the same thing a month ago.'

'He didn't mention it to you?' I asked.

'He didn't say a thing.'

'Would anybody else have known?'

'I don't think so. Because I had to process all the invoices, Patrick would have told me before anybody else.'

I wasn't sure if that was true. For example, he could have told people when he'd drunk too much at the company do. He could have let it slip to Nico over coffee. In my opinion, it was absolutely possible that he would have wanted to keep this quiet from the person in charge of the invoices.

If it hadn't been for the shape of the wound on the back of Patrick's head, suicide would have seemed a possibility: a businessman who knows his company is about to go bankrupt is refused credit by the bank and kills himself after having bought his employees drinks one last time. Only people don't commit suicide by bashing their heads backwards against a sharp-edged object.

Karin and Stefanie were talking about money: invoices, debt repayment schemes and ways of filing for bankruptcy that would not involve firing all employees immediately. Stefanie asked about selling the company: what assets there were, what the position was with the creditors. It was all rather boring, but the two of them seemed to find it riveting. I guessed that if your livelihood was about to disappear, all these numbers became hugely important. With no one officially running the company, the woman in charge of invoices had suddenly had this huge weight dumped on her shoulders. Talking to Stefanie was probably helpful.

When they'd finished, after what seemed ages, I asked Karin what Fabrice's surname was.

'Timmer,' she said. 'Fabrice Timmer.'

Stefanie and I walked from the Linde Lights offices to the Clipper. She'd asked if she could have a look at the scene of the company dinner. Despite her high-heeled shoes, it didn't take us longer than ten minutes to get there. We crossed the ground floor of the restaurant and went down to the patio at the back.

'Do you still smoke?' I asked.

'I've almost given up.'

'Almost?'

'I'm doing my best. I thought I had a lot of self-control, but it's been hard. Places like this help.' She gestured at the dismal little patch of ground with the bins for cigarette butts. 'It's purely functional and a bit depressing: the outdoor equivalent of a smoking room. Do you remember when we used to have those?'

It was surprising that the restaurant hadn't made more of this area; the wide expanse of water was rather amazing. I guessed it was too small a space to do anything much with. 'I remember we used to have a smoking room in school, where all the cool kids hung out.'

'I didn't know you used to smoke,' Stefanie said.

'I didn't. I was as far from being a cool kid as possible.'

'That figures. So is this where it happened?'

'I don't think so.' I pointed at the railing. 'It would have taken a lot of effort to get a man over this balustrade.'

'You're saying that because you don't want Arjen to have killed him here.'

'That's not the point. Forensics went over the area. Sure, it was a week since he'd been killed, and it had rained, but they didn't find any evidence of blood. No signs of a struggle. Nothing to show that someone had bashed a man's head in with a brick.'

'Nobody saw him leave the restaurant, though. He's not on CCTV.'

The area was largely enclosed by the railing; clearly the restaurant wanted to ensure that people didn't just do a runner from this space that wasn't covered by CCTV. I pointed to the path that I'd seen the previous time I'd checked the patio. 'Here's my guess. It would have been a short cut for him, instead of going through the restaurant and out again.'

We both squeezed through the gap in the railings and followed the little path along the water, past the back of the restaurant and the neighbouring shops. The path was made from red gravel, a colourful strip in the otherwise barren soil. 'You see my point,' I said. 'If you can do it in your shoes, there's no reason Patrick couldn't have done the same. And this path leads straight to the Barcelonaplein.'

'It's a bit grim, isn't it?' Stefanie said. 'Imagine this as your route home.'

'It isn't too bad. At least there are no cars. It's a quiet walk. It would be deadly quiet at night.'

'He could have met anybody here.'

'My point precisely. I'm betting the murder took place somewhere along this path, where there's nothing to stop you from pushing an unconscious man into the water.'

'He was still alive when he went in?'

'Yes, there was water in his lungs. He drowned. It's only knee-deep at the edges here.'

'You think someone hit him on the back of his head and then pushed him in?'

'That's exactly what I think, and it would be really hard to do at the Clipper.'

Stefanie nodded. 'But really easy here.'

'Exactly. We could test it out if you like. I could give you a push and see how far you'd go. It's a nice downhill roll.'

'Very funny,' Stefanie said, but she took a step back from the edge. 'A push and momentum would have taken him directly into the water. I don't want to see your point, but I definitely do.'

'See, I can teach you something.'

The path opened out a little. We'd come to a building site. There was no activity there; nobody was working. Even the building materials themselves looked derelict. Maybe the company developing the site had gone bust. A blue tarpaulin rattled in the wind. As it billowed back, it revealed a pile of bricks.

'We need to get forensics out here,' Stefanie said.

I nodded and made the call.

In the car on the way back, Stefanie did her best to explain the financial issues at Linde Lights to me. We'd pointed out the path at the rear of the Clipper to the forensic team and then headed out. They'd made it clear we'd only be in the way as they checked for residue of blood splatter.

'I would love to go through all the company's sales figures,' Stefanie said. 'That would make for very interesting reading.'

I laughed. 'Whatever floats your boat. Go ahead and do it if you like.'

'Not that it's got anything to do with this murder,' she said, 'but it would make a great case study on how not to run a company.'

'With the second account and all that, you mean?'

'We should check where the lump sums came from.'

'From Patrick's personal account, wasn't it?'

'Yes, both payments were made by him, but where did he get the cash from in the first place?'

'He was a company director. He was probably rich.'

'This is a tiny firm, Lotte. An unsuccessful tiny firm at that. What I saw from the paperwork was that he paid in around half a million euros each time. That's a lot of money.'

'But he used the company account to pay his bill at the Clipper. If he did that all the time, he probably didn't have many outgoings.'

Stefanie shook her head. 'All we know is that he used the company account to pay for a company dinner. There's nothing wrong with that.' She pointed at the large file she'd put on the back seat. 'Karin gave me the statements for that account. I'll check what else he did with it.'

'Go nuts,' I said. 'Have fun.'

'You don't seem to care much about this.'

'It's not my thing,' I said. It would have been fairer to say that I found it really boring.

'I'll write a summary in language you'll understand. I'll even draw you a picture.'

'I'm not an eight-year-old.'

'You just have the financial understanding of one. No, sorry, come to think of it, my daughter understood much more at eight than you do today. You're more like a finan-cial five-year-old.'

It reminded me of the conversation I'd had with my stepsister-to-be, where her language became clearer and clearer the more she understood that I wasn't getting what she was trying to say. 'At least I was right in thinking there were financial difficulties,' I said in my own defence. 'That they were looking at new strategies because they were in trouble.'

'It was far too late for them to think about new strategies,' Stefanie said. 'They had to think about how to pay the latest invoice. I've seen it in small firms before, where the owner keeps putting in his own money to keep the place afloat. I wonder if they were successful at one point and then the business climate changed. Companies are spending less money on billboards and advertising, and that hits firms like these who provide the hoardings.'

'Was that what they did? I thought it was lights.'

'Did you even look at their website? Their main business was outdoor advertising and small merchandise. I think my daughter has a T-shirt made by them; she got it at some gig of this boy band she's crazy about. It's pretty neat. The lights respond to the bass notes or something, and the logo on the shirt flashes to the beat – as long as it's loud enough.'

'How do they make it do that?'

'I don't know, Lotte, you could ask their lead designer.' Her exasperation with me was only too clear in her voice. 'I'll go through their records, but it seems the downturn just hit them hard. If the margins are small to begin with, then a company can get into trouble really quickly.' She parked the car. 'I'll get back to you. That's what you wanted me for, wasn't it?'

Back at my desk, I checked the police database to see if any of the people working at Linde Lights showed up. Nico and Therese were pretty clean. Nico had had a speeding ticket three months ago, Therese a parking ticket. I was tempted to run my mother's husband-to-be's name through the database too. It would only take seconds. I really shouldn't.

'Have you guys made any progress?' I asked Charlie, just to keep my mind, and fingers, away from temptation.

'Just this and that.' He kept looking at his computer screen.

Next I checked Karin. She had a completely clean record. Thomas came in.

'I took your advice,' Charlie said, as if he felt he needed to cheer me up. 'I tried to weigh up what was worse: cleaning up or being cleaned up.'

'What the hell are you talking about?' Thomas said. 'Why would you listen to her advice?'

'What did you decide?' I asked, ignoring him. 'Are you cleaning up?'

Charlie nodded. 'I've thrown away so much stuff,' he said. 'But my place looks as if a bomb hit it. It's a total mess.'

That was what my life felt like: as if a bomb had hit it.

'It's weird, isn't it?' he said. 'You try to tidy things away, and it makes it so much worse.'

'It's rubbish that you've accumulated over the years,' I said. 'It'll take a while to sort through all of it.'

'I'm enjoying it in a way. Throwing everything out makes it feel that we're making a fresh start. Together.' He blushed. 'Does that sound weird?'

'Yes,' Thomas said. 'And I have no idea what you're on about.'

'Not weird,' I said. 'I think it's rather sweet. And I'm pleased you decided to do that.'

'We need to go,' Thomas said to Charlie.

I didn't ask why. He wouldn't tell me anyway. Instead I searched for Fabrice Timmer in our database and found that he had prior.

Three years ago, he'd been arrested for GBH. He'd punched a guy in a drunken fight. In the end, nothing had come of it and the case had been dropped, but this was very interesting.

I felt a sense of relief. Compared to looking into the company's finances, I was suddenly on much firmer ground. Even though I was being shut out by Thomas and Charlie and lectured by Stefanie, I didn't feel like a huge idiot any more.

Amazing what one little bit of information could do.

Stefanie might think this was all about money, but on the other hand there was a girl who had been harassed and her boyfriend was the kind of person who punched people. As grounds for murder, I liked this one much more than money or whatever reason Thomas might have to think that Arjen was involved.

'Look at this,' I said. 'Therese's boyfriend. We should talk to him.'

'Ready?' Thomas said to Charlie. He didn't even look at me.

'Thomas, it's the boyfriend of the girl that Patrick touched up.'

Charlie hesitated. I got the feeling he wanted to stay behind and look at what I'd found.

'This seems very similar to what happened to Patrick,' I said. 'Three years ago, he—'

'Later, Lotte.' Thomas cut me short. 'If you want to do something useful, could you go and talk to Margreet? She's been calling me continuously.'

Charlie got up and put his coat on, and they both disappeared. I was left sitting at my desk, not sure what had just happened. Thomas and I had had our run-ins in the past, but I'd thought we'd sorted things out over the last year or so after working closely together on a number of cases.

I'd never thought I was going to be ostracised in my own office.

Other people might reach for the chocolate when they felt like crap. I typed my mother's fiancé's name into the database and hit enter. Nothing. Wow. Not even a ticket. It would have been remiss of me not to check that my mother wasn't marrying a criminal, I told myself. Not that he looked like a criminal, but it was better to be safe than sorry. Now at least she couldn't blame me if it all went horribly wrong.

Not that it would, of course.

Then forensics called me. They'd found nothing. There were no signs of blood on that particular spot by the pile of bricks. Did I want them to look further along the water?

It was clear from the tone of the question that the correct answer would be no. There was a shortage of resources and we couldn't have a team looking for a needle in a haystack along kilometres of waterfront. I told them not to bother and thanked them for their work.

Chapter 25

'I was surprised when you called,' Margreet said when she opened the door. 'I thought I was supposed to talk to that Thomas Jansen guy. I called him quite a few times, but he never seemed to have time.' She seemed more together today. The circles under her eyes were deep and dark and she looked as if she'd aged a decade in the last few days, but at least her socks matched and her cardigan wasn't inside out. 'I think he's avoiding me.'

'It's not that he doesn't want to talk to you,' I said, covering for Thomas. 'He just has a lot going on.'

'And you don't?'

'Something like that.' I hoped my smile didn't look as fake as it felt. 'This is my colleague Stefanie Dekkers.'

Stefanie had of course complained when I'd asked her to come with me to the Barcelonaplein. She'd suggested that I was using her as my personal taxi driver. There might have been some truth in her comment, but she was ultimately interested enough in meeting other people related to Patrick's murder that she drove me here without giving me too long a lecture.

'Well, come on in,' Margreet said.

We followed her into the flat. I hadn't had a good look around when I came here the first time. At that point, we hadn't been sure that it had been murder, and I hadn't known she was Nadia's mother.

'When did you move here?' I asked.

'Twenty sixteen,' she said. 'I wasn't sure at first. I loved our old house, but Patrick said we didn't need six bedrooms. He was sensible like that.'

A long hallway ran through to the kitchen. There was a large lounge and, I guessed, two bedrooms. It was a decent-size flat, roughly the size of mine on the canal, but it must have been a definite step down for her, and I could guess the reason for that. Now that Stefanie had pointed out that managing directors of small companies didn't necessarily have half a million euros lying around to invest in their own companies, I could see the signs.

We were standing in an awkward triangle in the middle of the room. Stefanie was looking around her, probably estimating the value of the property. 'Did you own your other house?' she asked.

'Yes. We got a good price for it. Patrick had such an amazing head for business. It was just before the housing market turned. We sold it at precisely the right time.'

'What did you do with the money? Buy this flat?'

'No, we're renting this one. Patrick said it was more tax efficient because we'd no longer have a mortgage.'

'Was this in April?' Stefanie said. 'April 2016.'

'Yes, it must have been. Why?'

'That's when Patrick personally invested more money into

his company. I wondered if the cash came from the sale of the house,' she said.

'Oh, I wouldn't have thought so. Would you like a cup of tea?'

'I'm fine, thanks,' I said.

'You said that Patrick put more money into the company? That sounds unlikely.'

'You didn't hear anything about financial problems at Linde Lights?' Stefanie asked.

'There can't have been. He always worked so hard,' Margreet said. 'Actually, before you sit down, let me show you his office. Then you can see for yourselves how success-ful he was. He worked a lot from here in the evenings.'

We followed her to a room off the main hallway. She opened the door carefully, as if she was displaying a sacred area. 'I haven't gone through his things yet. This is exactly as he left it. I'm sure the people working for him will want to collect it all at some point. It will be very useful for them, don't you think?'

I nodded, though I wasn't sure what exactly I was look-ing at. It was a poky room, with a desk at one end, dominated by the computer screen, and filing cabinets along the sides.

'See this.' She pointed at a square glass trophy. 'They kept getting awards for their innovative designs.'

I bent close to examine it. It was very ugly; something you would only keep because it had your name engraved on it. *Linde Lights. Innovation Prize 2004.*

'This is well over a decade old,' Stefanie said. She'd clearly noticed the same thing I had, only she had no qualms about mentioning it to the grieving widow. 'How have things been going recently? Did Patrick talk about the company?'

'A decade? It only seems like yesterday we went to collect that.' She picked up the award. 'Yes, you're right. I never would have guessed it was that long ago. It was a great evening. Nadia came with us too. Such a special occasion.'

How nice that he'd brought his entire family.

'Patrick was beside himself with pride,' she continued, 'and Nico was so happy I thought he'd explode.'

I scanned the room. As with the press clippings in Patrick's office at Linde Lights, there was nothing here that was recent. How long could a company survive on past glory? Past innovation?

'Did Patrick say anything about how work was going recently?' Stefanie asked again. 'Did he talk about new deals they'd won?'

'We didn't really talk about his work much,' Margreet said. She picked up another award. That one was from 2003. 'He was always busy. It was different when Nadia worked there; she still lived at home back then, and the two of them would talk about it over dinner, so I would hear about it as well.'

That surprised me. I hadn't known that Nadia had worked at Linde Lights.

'Why did she stop working for her father?' I asked.

'The two of them were always arguing,' Margreet said with a smile. 'She thought they should diversify, he thought they should concentrate on what they were good at. They would have the same discussion every evening, until she got fed up with it. It was Patrick's firm in the end. He would never budge. He wanted to run things the way he thought best. You can understand that.'

I could understand it, only it seemed that he'd run it into the ground in the last years and had used his own money to shore things up. He must have kept Margreet completely in the dark about that. He had sold their house from under her without telling her what he was going to use the proceeds for. I wondered if that had been legal. I wondered if he'd asked her to sign something.

There was nothing else to look at in the small office, and we went back to the sitting room. Margreet indicated one of the two sofas, and Stefanie and I sat down side by side. She offered us tea again, and once more we refused. She took the other sofa but seemed unfocused now that she had nothing to do.

'Was the house in your name as well as his?' I asked.

'Oh no, everything was in Patrick's name.'

Stefanie's face told me quite clearly what she thought about that.

'I didn't get involved in the finances much,' Margreet continued. 'It's a real headache now. I don't even have access to my bank account. Luckily Nadia and Arjen are helping me out.'

I was concerned that the problems with paying the bills at Patrick's company would spill over into Margreet's life. I took some comfort from the fact that their personal credit card hadn't been maxed out, because that was what Patrick had used to pay the bill at the Clipper. Part of me wanted to sit Margreet down and tell her that she should really check her finances. More precisely, I wanted to tell her to let Stefanie help her check her finances. I hoped for her sake that there was money left. I hoped that Patrick had had life insurance. I sincerely hoped that she was going to be fine, though I had a nasty suspicion that she was not going to be. I worried that all the cash had gone, sunk into a company that now needed another heap of money. The sale of a six-bedroom house could easily explain the 2016 payment. I wondered where the later money had come from.

'Did you have any other properties?' Stefanie asked. 'Something you sold in 2018?' She was clearly thinking along the same lines as me.

'Another house? I think you've got the wrong idea,' Margreet said. 'We're not the kind of people to have a second home in the south of France or Tuscany.'

The doorbell rang.

'That must be Arjen,' she said. 'I hope you don't mind. He insisted on coming when I told him you were going to be here.' She smiled sheepishly. 'It's weird. It's really weird.'

You tell me, I wanted to say.

She went to open the door. Stefanie mouthed something at me. I ignored her.

'Hey,' she whispered. She prodded me in the arm.

'What?'

'That your ex?'

I waved her words away as if they were nothing more than annoying flies.

She nodded and grinned as if that had answered her question perfectly.

Having Stefanie here made me feel that Arjen's appearance was also a judgement on me. Would she think that my ex was attractive, or would she consider the slightly overweight man who had stepped into the room an embarrassment? Was my desire to defend him really a desire to defend myself? He didn't always wear jeans that were a bit tight around his waistline. He didn't always wear boring polo shirts. He scrubbed up quite well, I wanted to tell her.

Margreet sat back down on the sofa and looked at her hands. 'How's Nadia? She was so angry with me when I said I'd had a drink with Lotte.'

'You had a drink together?' Stefanie said in a casual tone that wasn't fooling anybody. If she was concerned about that, she definitely shouldn't know that I'd had a drink with Arjen last night.

'Sorry,' Margreet said. 'I shouldn't have mentioned it.' She seemed confused, uncertain how to behave in this situation. 'I shouldn't have mentioned Nadia's name, should I?' How to behave in front of your son-in-law's ex-wife wasn't covered in any social handbook, I was sure.

'It's fine,' I said. When Stefanie and I had turned up, Margreet had been relaxed, but Arjen's presence seemed to have reminded her what the relationship between us all was. 'Why was she angry?'

'It's been really tough for her,' Arjen answered when Margreet stayed silent. 'Her father's death hit her hard.'

'It's been hard for me too,' Margreet said. 'But she felt the need to come around here and have a go at me.'

I could understand Nadia's anger. That time we'd met, Margreet had asked me about my relationship with Arjen;

221

she'd asked me if I'd been aware that he'd been cheating on me with her daughter. Even without knowing what we'd discussed, it would have felt like a betrayal to Nadia.

'She seems to think that she can come here and say terrible things about her father. Sure, he wasn't a saint, but who was? Let's face it, her own husband isn't a saint either.' Margreet looked first at me and then at Arjen.

He didn't respond, and an uncomfortable silence fell.

I had to bite my lip to stop myself from grinning. Even if I would have preferred that Margreet hadn't done this in front of Stefanie, I liked seeing her assertive spark. It made me think she wasn't as vulnerable as I'd assumed.

'Patrick had an affair, seven years ago,' she said, 'and Nadia never forgave him.'

'But you did?' I asked.

'We went to couple therapy,' Margreet said. 'It really helped us. It made a huge difference to Patrick especially. It made him understand his drinking. He told the therapist that if he drank, he felt young and attractive again. He felt like everybody loved him. Every woman in the room, but every man as well. In reality, of course, he was just a drunken middle-aged man.' She reached for her cup of tea. 'I ended up feeling sorry for him. And jealous maybe, because alcohol never had that effect on me. It would be great, wouldn't it, to think you were suddenly young again.'

'Did he stop drinking?'

'Yes, he did. The therapist made him understand that he was only using it as a crutch. Patrick also accepted that the way he behaved when he was drunk wasn't acceptable. I'd seen that myself; he'd get all chatty and flirty with young women.'

'He did that in front of you?'

'That just showed that it didn't mean a thing,' she said. 'He didn't think anything of it. But having a daughter the same age as those women made all the difference. He understood that really it was embarrassing. That he embarrassed Nadia. That he upset me. It was tough to kick the booze, but he decided it was worth it.'

But he had definitely been drinking at the night of the company do.

'Do you remember,' she said to Arjen, 'he didn't touch a drop at your wedding. Sorry,' she added, 'I probably shouldn't have mentioned that. Anyway, Nadia has never wanted to give her father any credit for changing his behaviour. Changing it for a while, at least.'

'It didn't last?'

'He had to drink for work. He told me that he needed to build his contacts, that it was impossible otherwise.'

'When was this?'

'I think it all started again a year ago. Maybe a little longer.'

'When things weren't going so well with the company,' Stefanie said.

'I guess so. I guess that's what it was.'

'You mentioned you'd been trying to get in touch with Thomas,' I said. 'What did you want to talk to us about?' Maybe she'd waited for Arjen to get here before bringing up certain topics.

'It's only practical things.' Margreet bit her lip. 'We'd like to organise the funeral and need to know when we can do that.'

'I'm sorry,' I said. 'It will be a little longer.'

'Do you know how long?'

'It depends on how long the investigation takes.'

'Surely we can bury him?' Her voice rose. 'I hate to think of him there. All alone.' She reached out and took Arjen's hand. He squeezed it. Whatever momentary coldness there had been between them, it seemed healed by the sadness of thinking about Patrick.

I thought about what to say. I could explain to her that we would still need his body for any forensic investigation. We could not release it until the investigation had been closed. There had been a few cases where forensic evidence at the last minute had made all the difference.

But I wasn't explaining this to a colleague, I was talking to a woman whose husband had been murdered, and whatever my opinion of this husband might be, he was someone she'd loved.

'I'm really sorry,' I said instead. 'We will contact you as soon as you can bury him. I understand how important this is to you.'

'Okay,' she said. 'Okay. I shouldn't have asked you to come here. I should let you get on with the investigation.'

'It's okay,' I said. 'You can call us.' Staying in touch with victims' families was an important part of what we did.

'And I'll do my best to answer all your questions too,' Margreet said, as if we'd come to an arrangement. 'You were asking about money, weren't you? Now that Arjen is here, he might be able to help with that.'

'What money?' Arjen asked.

'Patrick made two large payments into his company's account,' Stefanie said. 'One in April 2016, which might have come from the sale of the family home, and another one roughly two years later.'

Arjen looked over at Margreet. 'Did you know about this?'

'I'm sure that's not right,' she said. 'We did sell the house, but he never mentioned needing it for the company.'

Arjen scratched the back of his head. 'To be honest, he did ask us for an investment two years after that.'

So Patrick had tapped up his son-in-law for cash.

'Oh my God!' Margreet said. 'You didn't tell me about that. Nadia never said anything.'

'I didn't give him any money at that point, so there was nothing to tell.' Arjen looked at me. 'He asked me again last month, and I said I'd consider it if he gave me full access to the firm's books. I wanted to see if it was viable before I stepped in.'

'Was that why you became a strategist there?' I asked.

Arjen shrugged. 'It was a vague enough job title that I could ask everybody plenty of questions.'

I was reminded of Stefanie saying how it was too late to change strategy when you needed to find ways to pay the invoices.

'What did you find out?' she asked.

'I never got started. He went missing that evening.'

'Why didn't you tell me any of this?' Margreet said.

'Nadia and I wanted to keep it between us until we'd made a decision. How are you coping money-wise?' he added.

Why was he changing the subject so quickly? What was it that he didn't want Margreet to ask about? Or was it that he didn't want *me* to ask about something? That niggle of doubt came back again.

'I still can't get into any of the bank accounts,' she said. 'They've all been frozen. I can't even pay the phone bill, as it's all in his name. At the bank, they asked me for proof of address and I've got none of the things they wanted: no credit card statement, no utility bill, no driving licence. Nothing's in my name. I don't know what to do.'

'What about the rent? When is that due?'

'I don't know. I feel so stupid that I don't know any of this.'

'If they call you about the rent, give them my number and I'll pay it for you.'

'Thanks, Arjen. Have you guys sorted out your childcare problems? You said your childminder was getting married.'

He shot a quick glance in my direction. 'Yes, we're looking for someone new.'

'I can always do it,' she said. 'I'd like to help you too.'

'Wouldn't you be too busy?'

'No, not at all. The flat gets really quiet. I'm not used to it. I'd like to think about something else. Have something to do. Having the little one here would be great.'

'Okay,' Arjen said. 'I'll talk to Nadia.'

That surprised me. I'd have thought he would have jumped at the chance. I realised that it was Nadia who didn't want their daughter being looked after here. I couldn't think why; it wasn't as if my mother's place was better than this. Far from it, in fact.

'Thanks for coming,' Margreet said. 'I should let you get on with your work. If I find anything to do with the financial situation, I'll give you a call.'

Stefanie handed her a card. 'You can call me too. Either one of us. We'll be happy to help.'

'I'll head out as well,' Arjen said. He kissed Margreet goodbye and walked out with us towards the lift.

'Congratulations, by the way,' he said as we waited for it to arrive. 'I heard. I meant to say that last night but completely forgot.'

I was careful not to look at Stefanie. 'You heard about my mother's big decision?'

'Yes, she told me.'

The lift doors opened.

'I'm coming round to the idea,' I said. 'I thought it was weird at first, her getting married again, but now I see it's making her happy, so it's all fine. I heard that you met his daughter and son-in-law.'

'Ah, yes. They thought Nadia was you.'

We stepped in, side by side, Stefanie behind us.

'That didn't go down well,' Arjen said.

'I can imagine,' I said. 'When you left the Clipper that night, did you see anybody?'

'Do I need an alibi?' There was a jovial tone to Arjen's voice.

Yes, you do, I wanted to say. 'Was there anybody waiting for Patrick, I mean? Anybody you'd seen at the company.'

'I don't think so. I probably wouldn't have recognised them anyway.'

'And this second payment, the one Patrick asked you for, you don't know anything about that either?'

'I can't think of anything they sold at that time. I'm worried about Margreet: she could be in a tough spot financially.'

'Are you going to look after the company?'

'No, I have no real interest in it. I wanted to help Patrick, but that was it. Lighting isn't my thing.'

'They've got problems paying their bills,' Stefanie said.

'It might have to be closed down. I could help wind it up, but that's it.'

'I think Karin Lems would appreciate some guidance,' she said. 'She was in a real state today. I gave her some tips, but it's a big responsibility for her alone.'

'I could help, or Nadia. We'll talk about it.' Arjen pulled his hand through his hair. 'Anyway, thanks, Lotte.'

'For what?'

'I thought you were going to tell her about the girl. That's why I came over. Thanks for keeping quiet.'

'I'm not keeping quiet. I would tell her if it was important for the investigation that she knew. At the moment, it isn't. I won't shatter her illusions unless I have to. But I think you should tell her that her husband wasn't quite what she thought he was.'

We left the small box of the lift and exited onto the shared garden in the middle.

'He wasn't as bad as you think,' Arjen said.

'Arjen, he sexually harassed one of the women working for him.'

'He kissed her. Sure, that isn't great, and I don't want Margreet or Nadia to know, but he was having an affair with her.'

'An affair?' I couldn't keep the incredulity out of my voice.

'That's what he told me, at least.'

I stopped walking and swallowed down the saliva that had suddenly rushed into my mouth. 'He told you? When did he tell you that?'

'Never mind when.'

I realised he wasn't seeing me as a police detective at all. He still thought these conversations were private chats, and that he could choose what to tell me and what to keep silent about. 'When did he say that?' I asked again. I needed to know when he'd had a chance to discuss Therese with Patrick.

Stefanie stared at me. I remembered her asking me what I'd do if I realised my ex was guilty. I still didn't believe that, but I was starting to understand why Thomas saw him as a suspect.

I would have continued the conversation; I probably would have made it clear to him that when you were talking to a police officer, it really was the best policy to be honest if you had nothing to hide.

If I'd had more time.

But I didn't.

Because at that very moment, Thomas's car came speeding

around the corner. He stopped beside us and he and Charlie jumped out.

I could only watch as Thomas read Arjen his rights and arrested my ex-husband on suspicion of the murder of Patrick van der Linde.

Chapter 26

I walked back to the office. I didn't want to sit in a car with Stefanie and listen to her gloat about how she'd been right. I had to consider what to do, and walking back to the police station would give me at least forty minutes of thinking time.

As I strode along the canal, I realised that forty minutes wouldn't be enough to come up with a way to fix this mess. I stopped at the side of the water, spotted an empty bench and sat down. A father and his little son played along the edge. The kid tottered and teetered on his tiny feet in their tiny shoes. The dad waited, clearly in no rush on this sunny afternoon, and let the kid explore and point to his heart's content. He knelt down to take a photo at child height.

The first thought that popped into my head was that I needed to get Arjen out. The next was that I shouldn't think like that, even though I couldn't believe Arjen had murdered Patrick. But I also had to accept that Thomas and Charlie wouldn't have arrested him if there'd been no evidence. It was just that I didn't know what that evidence was. They'd barred me from anything involving my ex-husband, stopping me from taking part in a crucial section of the investigation just like the red-and-white-striped traffic barrier was supposed to stop cars driving along the canal's edge.

The little kid was fascinated by the barrier, as if it was placed there especially for his entertainment. He didn't look at the water at all. It was possible that the red of the barrier was more interesting than the grey-green of the canal. But he was also paying more attention to what was there to stop him than to what gave him freedom. Watching him run his chubby little hands across the traffic barrier made me think that I should also study my obstacle carefully and consider how to approach it.

I couldn't go in screaming or accusing. I couldn't go in all defensive either, but neither could I tell them that they were doing a good job and praise them for arresting the obvious murderer. I needed to find out what they had on Arjen and then weigh up that evidence against what I knew about Arjen as a person.

If I couldn't lift my barrier, I had to sneak along the side of it. I nodded to a seagull floating on the water. I had a strategy. I had figured out what I was going to do.

'I'm really disappointed in you guys,' I said before I'd even taken my coat off.

Thomas and Charlie sprang apart as if they were a cheating couple and I was the wife who had come home. I was surprised that they were here instead of in the interview room. They must be waiting for Arjen's lawyer to turn up. It gave me the chance to ask them some questions.

'I couldn't tell you,' Thomas said. 'You must understand that.'

'I thought we were working on this investigation together,' I said. 'That means you should tell me when you're about to arrest a suspect, not spring it on me. That's not how this works.'

'I couldn't take the risk.' On his face I saw guilt. It was mirrored on Charlie's, and he was worse at hiding it than Thomas. He felt guilty for having excluded the person who had got him this job.

That look on Charlie's face made me think of how Arjen had looked when they'd arrested him. What I'd seen wasn't guilt, but confusion. He hadn't expected to be arrested; he was utterly surprised. Not because he hadn't thought he'd be caught, but because he'd had nothing to do with Patrick's murder. He'd been defensive a few days earlier when he'd been trying to conceal Patrick's philandering. Wouldn't he have been even more so during the arrest if he'd had something to hide?

'The risk of what?' I said. 'Of me telling you that this was a mistake? That he's not the type of person to have murdered someone?' I was more adamant than I'd intended.

'This.' Thomas pointed a finger at me. 'The risk of you behaving like this. I knew you were going to say something like that.'

'Like what?' I could feel my blood pressure rising and struggled to keep my voice under control. Do not shout, I told myself. To show anger would be counterproductive.

'You're pissed off.'

'Only because you arrested a suspect without telling me. I was wondering what the two of you were talking about, why you were excluding me. Now I know. You wanted to make this arrest without the voice of reason stopping you.'

'The voice of reason?' Thomas laughed.

I could have hit him. Instead I offered a placating smile, as if his reaction wasn't hurtful. 'I know him well; I can be useful,' I said.

'I know you can never be objective where your ex-husband is concerned,' he said. 'I wasn't sure if you would want to think him guilty or innocent, but either way, I was certain that your personal view of him would get in the way. I didn't want to put you in a difficult position. Wasn't that why you said from the beginning that you didn't want to be involved in this investigation? I know you're pissed off, and you're not going to believe me, but I was trying to be considerate.'

I took a deep breath and counted to ten before I spoke. 'How certain are you?'

'We wouldn't have got an arrest warrant based on nothing,' Thomas said. 'A witness saw them arguing behind the restaurant after everybody else had left. We found two wine glasses: one with Patrick van der Linde's fingerprints and one with Arjen's.'

So that was when Patrick had told him that he'd had an affair with Therese. I sat down heavily on my chair. I didn't want it to be possible. I'd thought he had nothing left to hide. 'He told me he went straight home.'

'That's what he said to us too, when we brought him in for questioning,' Charlie said. 'That he lied about it, on top of the forensic evidence, really doesn't look good.'

I remembered that. I'd watched that interview from the observation area. It was the moment I'd first started to get an inkling of the fact that Thomas saw him as a suspect.

'Who's the witness?' I wanted it to be someone with an ulterior motive. Someone who could be a suspect himself.

'The manager of the restaurant. She told us there had been problems with the bill, and she'd wished the other guy had come back sooner so he could have paid, instead of her having an argument with Patrick about it.'

She'd told me about the problems with the bill too. She hadn't told me about Arjen coming back to the restaurant. Probably because I hadn't asked her about that, I told myself. This wasn't suspicious or odd. I'd focused on Patrick failing to pay the bill because I'd been looking for money issues.

'They finished their bottle of wine, but ended up shouting at each other,' Charlie said. He was more forthcoming with information than Thomas.

'About what?' I asked, though I had a pretty shrewd idea.

'She couldn't hear. We'll find out when we speak to Arjen.'

'You didn't ask him that last time? About this argument, I mean.'

'We had the witness, but we were waiting for the fingerprints and DNA test to come back,' Charlie said. Thomas shot him a look but didn't tell him to stay quiet. 'We took his DNA when he was here last time.'

Arjen hadn't told me that either.

'There is another suspect,' I said. 'Someone else we should look into.'

'We're looking into Arjen Boogaard,' Thomas said. 'He's our main suspect at the moment.'

'But—'

'I don't think you should be involved in this, Lotte.'

'He isn't a family member,' I said. 'I know him. I can be useful,' I offered again.

Thomas looked at me with what could only be described as pity. He felt really sorry for me.

There wasn't much that I hated more.

'We're going to interview him as soon as his lawyer gets here,' Charlie volunteered.

'Listen to me. There's another suspect we need to invest-igate,' I said. 'Someone who actually has a motive. We should cover all possibilities.'

'Of course. That's a good thing for you to work on.' Thomas did a lousy job of hiding the condescension in his voice.

'Therese's boyfriend, Fabrice, has prior. That's what I was trying to tell you yesterday, but you weren't interested. He beat up a guy in a drunken argument four years ago. Combine that with the fact that Patrick sexually harassed Therese and there's definitely a motive there.'

'You check that out,' Thomas said. 'You're right, we shouldn't focus purely on this one suspect. Why don't you go and do that now?'

I was trying to hide it, but inside I was seething. Normally, there was no way I would have taken this tone of voice from Thomas lying down. I would have pulled him up on it. Now, though, I had to pretend that I was taking it all in my stride. That I was fine with not being listened to, with having my status as the most experienced officer in the team effortlessly eroded by his assumption that my judgement was clouded.

He wanted me nowhere near Arjen when they were questioning him, that much was obvious, though I didn't know what he thought I'd do. I wouldn't give information to his wife, or even to his defence lawyer if that was what he was concerned about. If he was certain of his evidence, he shouldn't mind me trying to poke a hole in it. Surely that would only push him to build a better case.

Unless he wasn't really all that certain, of course.

I couldn't help but be concerned about the fact that Arjen had lied to me. It wasn't as if he hadn't done that before, but I thought he'd known better than to lie about police matters. Surely he knew me well enough to understand that I took my job seriously, that we were in the middle of a murder investigation and that his lies would come out eventually.

I forced myself to visualise that night. I had to try to understand Thomas's mindset. If I thought about everything that had happened at the restaurant, I could easily imagine that Patrick and Arjen had argued. I could picture the two of them outside, drinking and talking. That was easy. I could even imagine that it got physical. I'd never seen Arjen in a fight. I'd never seen him hit anybody. But I could imagine him throwing a punch, sure.

If he had hit Patrick, causing him to fall and hit his head on the edge of the pavement or a piece of metal, and then had walked away, not knowing how bad the injuries were, for example, I could almost imagine that.

But that wasn't how Patrick van der Linde's death had happened. Forensic evidence had shown it was probable that the impact had been from above, someone hitting the back of Patrick's head with a heavy straight-edged object – in other words, a brick.

And it was this next step, the escalation of the fight, that I had problems with. I couldn't imagine Arjen picking up a brick and bashing Patrick's head in. I couldn't imagine him dumping him in the canal, still alive.

Thomas's phone rang and cut through my thoughts. 'We'll be right down,' he said, and disconnected the call. 'The lawyer's here,' he said to Charlie. 'Ready?' He didn't look in my direction as together they left the office.

Rolling an unconscious man into the water, still alive: I had a really hard time squaring that behaviour with the type of person I knew my ex-husband to be.

I hid my face in my hands. If it had been anybody else, I would probably have agreed with Thomas, and would have been excited about the arrest. It was the fact that I knew Arjen so well that skewed my thoughts. It was what made me certain that someone else had killed Patrick. It was why I kept focusing on Fabrice; why I was keen to find proof that it had been him, regardless of whatever forensic evidence Thomas had found.

But as I pulled up Fabrice's records again, a second conclusion offered itself. What if Thomas's evidence stood up and he had the right perpetrator, only Patrick's death had happened differently to how we'd assumed?

238

Chapter 27

Arjen and his lawyer sat side by side in the interrogation room. This was the point when the clock started to tick and we would have twenty-four hours to get enough to officially charge him.

The smart thing to do would be to go and interview Fabrice. After all, he was the number one suspect in my eyes. But my idea that Arjen might be guilty, just not of murder, made me invested in hearing what he was going to say. What he was going to admit to. I wanted to hear something from him that ruled that possibility out.

I'd sneaked into the observation area again. Even though I'd waited for a few minutes after Thomas and Charlie had left, just to make sure they didn't see me, I didn't think I'd fooled anybody. After last time, Thomas probably expected me to be there.

'You went back,' Thomas said. 'You met with Patrick outside the restaurant, had another glass of wine and ended up arguing.'

'Yes,' Arjen said. 'That's right.' He didn't look at his lawyer. He didn't pause and think. His answer was immediate. It meant that he was trying to come across as open and cooperative.

It was the smart choice.

'That's not what you said last time.'

'My father-in-law had died. I didn't want to drag his name through the mud. Everybody wanted to keep quiet about what happened that night, and I'll admit I was no different.'

'You understand that this is a police inquiry? That you have a duty to tell the truth?'

'My client was not brought in as a suspect,' the lawyer interrupted. 'I think I'm right in saying you hadn't cautioned him at that stage.'

Thomas ignored the comment. 'What did you argue about?'

'The woman. His behaviour.'

'You mean Therese?'

'Yes.'

'So you were aware of what Patrick had done.'

'I'm still not sure what he did,' Arjen said. 'I know what you think he did, but those things are hard to verify.'

'It seemed rather clear-cut in my eyes,' Charlie said.

'You might think so.' Arjen exchanged a glance with his lawyer. 'But all I can say for certain is that I saw him get up and follow her.' He was trying to balance agreeing with the detectives and defending his father-in-law. He still didn't see police officers in the way people being interviewed normally did. He saw them as people to discuss matters with. I realised it was an extension of having once been married to a detective. These were my colleagues, the type of people he'd socialised with when we'd been together. Not the type of people who could arrest him for murder. He needed to change this. He needed to take the situation seriously. His lawyer needed to make him, if nothing else.

'When he came back a bit later,' Arjen continued, 'he looked pissed off. I wanted to know what had happened, so I got up from the table. Then I saw Nico and Therese sitting on the steps outside, and she was crying. I heard her ask him not to talk about it to anybody, and I went back inside.'

'Explain it to me,' Thomas said in a sarcastic tone of voice, 'because I don't understand. You didn't ask Patrick what had happened? Or did you already have a pretty good idea?'

'I know what you're getting at,' Arjen said.

Thomas raised his eyebrows at Arjen using those words again. This time he didn't pull him up on them.

'I did ask him about it, but afterwards. Outside the Clipper, as you said. I knew he'd stay behind for a smoke; he always did that behind Margreet's back. I asked him why Therese had been upset, and he told me it was because Nico had walked in on the two of them. She had wanted to keep the affair a secret from her boyfriend and thought that Nico wouldn't keep his mouth shut. You can understand that, can't you?' He waited for an affirmative nod from Thomas that didn't come. 'Patrick asked me not to tell Margreet.' He ruffled his hair in a gesture I recognised; he always did that when he was embarrassed.

I used to find it cute. Now I was disturbed by it. Was it because of what he had been forced to reveal about his father-in-law, or did it indicate he still wasn't telling the whole truth? Was there one more layer hidden underneath what he had admitted to?

'Patrick swore that whatever had been going on between him and Therese had finished, and they'd only had a kiss for old times' sake.'

'Did you believe him?' Charlie sounded genuinely curious.

Arjen shrugged. 'He said they'd been having an affair, that she called an end to it when she started dating that guy in IT. But that she'd been looking at him all evening. They'd had a bit of a snog – his words, not mine – and then Nico turned up and got totally the wrong idea.'

It hadn't been like that, I was sure of it. Therese had been looking at him because she was keeping an eye on him. She wanted to stay out of his way. She and Nico had both told me that Nico had pulled Patrick away. I was pretty sure he wouldn't have done that if he'd thought the kiss was consensual.

'Why the argument, then?' Thomas said. 'If that's all that happened, why the heated discussion? You make it sound amicable, but that's not what the manager described to me.'

'You have to understand, Patrick was drunk and not pleased that I asked him about it. He was embarrassed, and whenever he was in the wrong, he'd become belligerent. I believe it was a consensual kiss, but that still meant he was cheating on his wife, my mother-in-law.'

'Then what happened? You punched him?'

'No. God, no. Of course not. He asked me to keep quiet and I said I would.'

This wasn't enough to hold Arjen. He had a believable story. Unless Thomas and Charlie had something else on him, they'd have to let him go. But it was very possible I didn't know the half of it.

I was looking for reasons why he hadn't done it. I was willing to believe him. They would look at it from entirely the opposite angle. They would think that of course he would say that – what else was he going to say: that he'd killed him? Of course he wouldn't. Denying it with a plausible story didn't make him innocent.

I was drawing circles on my notebook when I felt a hand on my arm. It made me jump. I'd been concentrating so hard on what was going on on the other side of the window that I must have missed the click of the door opening.

It was Chief Inspector Moerdijk. 'You need to get out of here right now,' he said.

I grabbed my notebook and got up to follow him out. He dropped his hand from my arm as soon as we were outside the observation area. He wouldn't want anybody in the corridors to see him dragging me along.

'My office,' he said.

I followed him without a word. He didn't start to talk until he'd shut the door behind me.

'When you told me you didn't want to be involved in this case, I should have accepted that,' he said. 'What's happened is partly my fault. I should have listened to you.'

'I hear that a lot.' I tried to lighten the mood. It was a mistake. He wasn't interested in being amicable.

'You can't be involved in this case any more.' He was deadly serious.

'Of course I can.' I had to be. I needed to stay involved now. Whatever I'd told him before, when I'd wanted out, I now felt completely different. 'I won't mess it up. I promise.'

'Do you think your ex is capable of murder?'

It was a good thing I had my notebook with me, because doodling circles helped me to think. It wasn't a question of whether Arjen was capable of murder, but what the right answer was to what the CI had asked. 'Everybody is capable of killing someone,' I said carefully, 'if the situation calls for it, or if they're unlucky. If they cause an accident.'

'What about Patrick van der Linde. Do you think Arjen could have murdered him?'

There was no right way to respond to any of this. I had to come across as if I had an open mind, but I didn't want to sound as if I thought Arjen was guilty. 'I think that if Boogaard killed him, it didn't happen the way we currently imagine.' I used his surname because that was what I would have done with any other suspect at this point.

'You're not ruling it out.'

'I trust that Thomas and Charlie have done a good job so far.' Even if they had deliberately kept me away from it. 'They wouldn't have cautioned him if they weren't certain of their case. However, I think there are some other suspects too, and it would be a mistake to rule them out at this stage and solely focus on Boogaard. If you take me off the case, it won't be easy to follow up on the other avenues, and we need to do that.'

'What have you got?'

'The boyfriend of the girl that Patrick van der Linde

sexually harassed has got prior for assault. We know he went to the Clipper to pick her up, and he could easily have come back later. He'd have had pretty good grounds to have a go at van der Linde.'

'The same grounds that Boogaard had for arguing with him.'

'Correct. Only it would be a bit more personal. You'd get angrier with the guy who assaulted your girlfriend than with a man who cheated on your mother-in-law.'

'Yes,' the CI said. 'I can see that.'

'He came to collect his girlfriend from the venue. She thought he didn't know what was going on, but this was a small firm. Even without her telling him anything, I'm sure he had a pretty shrewd idea what Patrick van der Linde was like.'

'But Boogaard was the last person to be seen with van der Linde.'

'As far as we know. Look, it would have been hard to get him into the water from the back of the Clipper, but if someone saw him walking home along the waterfront path, it would have been much easier to shove him in. There's a sheer drop at the back of the Clipper; you'd need to get an unconscious man over the railings. Further down, it would take far less effort.'

'You think that after Boogaard argued with him, someone else had a go?'

'It's been difficult to establish the exact time of death. We don't know precisely where he entered the water. It's all been guesswork so far. But we haven't found any traces of blood at the Clipper, and I would have expected there to be some if Boogaard hit him there.'

'You don't think he did it.'

'As I said earlier: if he did it, it didn't happen the way we imagine. I can see van der Linde and Boogaard arguing.' I kept the exasperation out of my voice. 'I can imagine Boogaard punching him, and van der Linde falling and hitting his head. What I have a hard time with is imagining Boogaard tipping him over those railings at the back at the Clipper.'

'Did you tell Thomas that?'

'Things have happened so quickly, I haven't had a chance to talk to him about it yet,' I said.

'Seriously? There wasn't one moment when you could have told him he probably had the location of the murder wrong? That forensics should check somewhere different?'

'I had forensics check one of the possible locations, but they didn't find anything.'

'But you didn't tell Thomas. That's not how teams should work. There's no excuse for whatever has been going on. Get your act together.'

Why hadn't I told him? It might have ruled Arjen out. I'd been annoyed with Thomas for excluding me. I'd thought I knew better than him. It hadn't been a decision as such to keep it to myself, but I realised I'd wanted to treat him in the same way he'd been treating me. It had been petty behaviour that had only come back to bite me.

'So you think the murder took place somewhere en route from the Clipper to Patrick's flat?'

'Yes. And everybody knew where he lived.'

'That doesn't rule Boogaard out,' the CI said.

'You're right. He could have decided to walk home with Patrick and got into a fight with him on the way. Who knows what Patrick said to him? Or someone else could have returned to have words. Or just to beat him up.'

'Does the boyfriend know where van der Linde lived?'

'He worked at Patrick's company. He must have known that Patrick liked going to the Clipper because it was close to his home.'

'That doesn't mean anything. You know I run to work, but do you know where I live?'

'I don't know your exact address, but I know roughly which area it's in. That's all you need.'

'Fine,' the boss said. 'Investigate the boyfriend by all means. I won't stop you doing that. But don't interfere in Thomas's handling of the case or meet with your ex's lawyer. Be careful, basically. Stay away from your ex, too. Remember that we've got CCTV near the holding cells. I don't want you anywhere near him.'

'I can do that,' I said. 'I can definitely do that.'

'And go home for the day. I don't want you in your office when Thomas and Charlie get back from their interview. Give them space to discuss what they need to, without you there. Stay out as much as possible.'

I'd wanted to prepare for the Fabrice interrogation, but I could do that from home, so I nodded to indicate that I understood and would do what the boss wanted.

'And fix things with Thomas!'

I didn't ask how I was supposed to do that if I had to stay away from him.

I walked out of the CI's office intending to go to my flat to do some work. But my plans were interrupted by a call from my mother.

Chapter 28

I got on my bike and cycled to my mother's flat. It was odd to think that she wouldn't be living there in a couple of weeks. It wasn't our normal evening for eating together, but she had asked me to come over. She'd sounded upset.

She opened the door without saying hello, or asking me if I'd had a good day, and came straight to the point. 'They fired me.'

'Who did?'

'Nadia called me to say that she didn't want me to babysit for her any more.'

'It's because you're getting married,' I said. 'Her mother's going to do it.'

'It's not that, is it, Lotte?' She gave me a sharp glance. 'How long have you been planning for this moment?' Her voice rose.

'What are you talking about?'

'You've always wanted to get back at him for leaving you. I know that. I know what you're like. You waited four years and now you have your chance.'

'Hold on. Are you talking about—'

'Nadia told me you've arrested Arjen.'

'Mum, I did no such thing. I wasn't involved in that.'

'You've been working on the case.'

'Yes, but I had nothing to do with Arjen's arrest.'

'I don't believe you.'

'Fine. Don't. If you think I'm capable of arresting an innocent man just because he divorced me four years ago, then you don't know me at all.'

'Michael told me why you cut yourself; that it happened after he'd told you the story about Nadia and Arjen being here. You got upset about that.'

'I dropped a glass. Have you never dropped a glass? For goodness' sake, what do I have to say to convince you?'

'You don't. Go through your stuff and sort it out. I don't want it in the house any more.'

'What do you mean?'

'I'm not taking your old stuff with me to Richard's. Decide what you want to keep and get rid of the rest. I'll be next door.'

'Wow. I can't believe you,' I said.

'And I can't believe you. Nadia told me exactly what happened: that you were meeting with Arjen and had set up for the other guys to come and arrest him.'

Well, I had been talking to him at the time, but I'd had no idea they were coming. I didn't bother telling my mother that, as I knew that she wouldn't believe me anyway. As she wouldn't believe that dropping that glass had been a stupid accident. As she wouldn't believe that I was trying my best to clear Arjen's name. 'I don't believe Arjen is a murderer,' I said instead.

'So what is this? You just lock him up overnight to scare him or something?'

'He's been lying to the police. It made him look very suspicious.'

'He was lying to you because it's you.'

'You're saying it's okay for him to lie to the police?'

'You're not a police detective in his eyes; you're his ex-wife. I'm sure there are things you wouldn't want your ex to know.'

'That would be perfectly reasonable,' I said, 'if he had lied only to me. But he didn't. He lied in an interrogation by my colleagues, when I wasn't in the room, and that was what got him into trouble.' But I knew what my mother meant, because I'd thought something very similar myself as I'd listened to the interview before the CI dragged me away.

'Get him out,' my mother said. 'You know he's not a murderer, so get him out.'

If only it was as easy as that. 'What do you suggest I do? Open the cell door and let him escape? There are procedures.'

She shook her head. 'You're more interested in your job than in doing the right thing. You're not objective.'

Nice to know that my mother and my colleagues agreed on that. 'I'm keeping away from it because I can't think about it objectively, don't you see? It's the same reason we don't investigate family members. I have too much history with him. Who knows what he's been up to for the last four years? I don't think he's capable of murder, but there's no telling what happened between him and his father-in-law.' I shut up abruptly. I shouldn't talk to her about any of this, as it was very possible that she would call Nadia and repeat it as soon as I left the flat.

'What do you want me to clear out?' I said, to change the topic back to what I was here for.

My mother gestured around the room. 'All of this. Go through it and take what you want to keep. Anything that's still here tomorrow morning, I'll take to the dump.'

'You don't want any of it?'

'Like what?'

'I don't know. Mothers sometimes like to keep things their children have made.'

She sighed. 'I've already gone through it. Anything I wanted, I've taken.'

'What are you doing with all your furniture?'

'Why? Do you want any of it?'

'No thanks.' I laughed. 'I have a flat full of stuff. I was just curious.'

'I'm not taking anything. Richard's house is lovely and I don't need any of my old things. I want to make a fresh start.'

'You're going to move in with just a suitcase?'

'Yes, I'm planning on taking only my clothes. There's nothing else from here that I want. This hasn't been a particularly happy place for me.'

'You've lived here so long.'

'I don't know why I didn't move ages ago. It's convenient, but it's a bit small and not very nice.'

'Because this was what you could afford,' I said.

'You're right. I was stuck here.'

I thought about Margreet, now living in a flat on the Barcelonaplein after her husband sold their house to pay the bills at his company. I wondered if she felt stuck there, as my mother seemed to have felt stuck in this flat.

I went into my old bedroom and opened the drawers of the chest nearest to me. What did I want to keep? Here were my university books. Any information in them would be dated by now. My papers were useless.

Even when Arjen and I had got divorced and I had moved out of his house in a rush, I hadn't gone back to my mother's flat to collect any belongings. I hadn't asked her if I could borrow pots or pans. To be honest, I hadn't asked her for anything. She probably would have loved to help me, but I hadn't even considered coming here.

Was that for the same reason that my mother had given for wanting to move out: that this place felt like failure? This was the place I had left behind. The place I had outgrown as I'd become an adult. But my mother had been stuck here for decades. It was great that she was leaving it now. Some of the furniture here was stuff she had taken with her after her own divorce, pieces that were too big for the space. Items that would have reminded her every day for over thirty years of what had gone wrong in her marriage.

It was a good thing she didn't want to keep any of them; not the table nor the chairs. Not the ancient sofa.

I closed the door to my old room behind me. 'You're doing the right thing,' I said to her. 'Getting rid of everything. Feel free to get rid of all my stuff too.'

'You don't want anything?'

'Nope,' I said. 'You can recycle the lot.'

'That's typical, making me deal with it.'

'I can organise movers to clear the place out,' I said. 'If that's helpful.'

'No,' my mother said. 'It's fine. I've got people coming in at the end of the week. But your things will end up in a skip. I'm warning you, don't come crying to me later when there's something you desperately wanted.'

The skip could well be the best place for the majority of the past. 'If there was anything I desperately wanted, I would have come for it years ago. I would have taken it with me when I moved out.'

'Final warning,' she said.

I gave her a hug. She struggled against my embrace and I let go. 'Be happy,' I said to her. 'I want you to be happy.'

'Off with you.' She gave me a push against my upper arm. 'Go home.'

I waved and started walking down the stairs.

'Be happy yourself,' she shouted after me.

'I'm doing my best.'

And I thought that maybe I was doing just fine.

Chapter 29

I called Stefanie the next morning, and asked her to meet me at my flat, so that we could interview Fabrice together. She said she'd be there in half an hour. That was perfect. I could use the intervening time to feed my cat and prepare for the interview. Pippi was pleased to get attention, rewarding me with headbutts and purring. I went into my study and looked at the drawing of the case I'd made earlier. I'd written Fabrice and Therese's names on the left-hand side of the page and the family's names on the right. That right-hand side was where Thomas thought the murderer came from.

My mother might think I could just tell my colleagues to let Arjen go, but in reality, the only way was to find another suspect who was more plausible. One who was actually guilty, I corrected myself. I could try to show why Arjen couldn't possibly have done it, but that would also really annoy Thomas and the CI, and in this situation it would be best not to annoy anybody.

I needed to look at the case with fresh eyes. I drew large circles around Patrick's name in the centre of the sheet of paper. Was it possible that he had just run into the wrong person at the wrong time? Arjen had said that he had been belligerent and drunk. He could have had an argument with a complete stranger on his walk home. It hadn't been a mugging, because nothing had been stolen. His wallet had been still secure in the inside pocket of his coat. Water-damaged, but not stolen.

At this stage, there were two clear motives for someone to have killed him: first, his behaviour towards women; and second, his company possibly going bust and the financial repercussions of that. I wrote down the names of the other people in Linde Lights underneath those of Therese and Fabrice. Karin. Nico. I drew a dotted line between the two sets of names. Above the line I wrote *women*; below the line I wrote *money*.

My eye was drawn to Fabrice's name, as if my division into two groups was really there to highlight him. He was my main suspect. It wasn't that hard to picture him hitting Patrick, and Therese pushing him into the canal. In fact, it was very easy to imagine that.

I knew that Therese and Fabrice had left the Clipper whilst Patrick was still alive. Therese might well have told Fabrice why she was so upset. She could have told him that while they were still in the car. If she had, Fabrice could have insisted on turning around and driving back to the restaurant. In my head, they parked their car out front, knowing only too well that Patrick would be having a final smoke at the back, because he always did that. Then what?

Arjen was there, of course, talking to Patrick. Arguing with him about his behaviour.

Patrick had said that it was an affair. That Therese had wanted it. That she was only embarrassed and upset because Nico had walked in on them.

Of course. This could have had a major impact.

If Therese had heard that, she would be doubly upset at this perfect example of victim-blaming. *She really wanted it, Your Honour.* She would have been livid. She would have told Fabrice that this was absolutely not what had happened. That Patrick had been pestering her for months. That he'd pushed her up against the wall and forced himself on her. She might even have started to cry again at this point. Arjen left, Patrick set off towards home and then Fabrice attacked him. To teach him a lesson maybe.

No, that was wrong. I had to remember that Patrick wasn't some stranger; he was their boss. They would have wanted to talk to him. Maybe they'd asked him for money. They probably both wanted to leave their jobs at this point. If he paid them off, gave them some cash, they wouldn't go to the police. Only there was no money.

Also, Patrick probably thought there was no problem with what he'd done. He might even have said that to Therese: that she hadn't been so reluctant before she started sleeping with Fabrice, and that she was a hypocrite.

At that, Fabrice punched him in the face, and Patrick fell and hit the back of his head. Or no, Patrick turned to walk away and Fabrice smacked him with something: a brick, a rock.

Now they had a problem. Best roll him into the canal. He was unconscious anyway. They hated him. They would have had no qualms about killing him.

Did I even need the rest of this drawing? This made so much sense.

Now came the tricky part: I needed to prove it. I chewed the end of my pen. Without any CCTV footage, this was going to be very hard.

Pippi jumped on top of my drawing, meowing for attention. I scratched her behind the ear, then checked my watch. What was keeping Stefanie? Immediately, as if she could hear my thoughts, the doorbell rang.

As I went down the stairs to join her, I was thinking how my mother had tried to keep quiet about why she was babysitting because she thought I'd be upset. Therese hadn't initially told Fabrice about what had happened with Patrick because she thought he'd be upset. I hadn't told Mark that my current case involved my ex-husband because I thought he'd be upset.

How would I have reacted if my mother had told me from the beginning that she was babysitting purely for the money, and not because she wanted to have a grandchild and was lonely? I would have been annoyed with her, but I wouldn't have been hurt. Not like I'd been hurt when I'd discovered that she was seeing this perfect little family on the sly, behind my back.

Fabrice had found out anyway. It had seemed to me that he and Nico hadn't got on well in the past. Was Fabrice annoyed with Therese for not letting him play the part of the hero? For allowing Nico to get the plaudits by taking the role of the rescuer, a role that he might have thought should have been his by rights. Was that why he'd resorted to murder? It was a stretch, but one I was willing to consider.

Stefanie insisted we drive. This was the downside of work-ing with her – she refused to cycle anywhere. I'd called Therese to see if she was going to be at work, but she'd told me that nobody was coming into work any more. The com-pany would probably fold within the next couple of days. I felt sorry for the people who would lose their jobs, but at least she and Fabrice were both at home. This was perfect, because it allowed me to talk to them at the same time with-out tipping off Fabrice that he was the person we actually wanted to interrogate.

'I hope you're proud of me,' Stefanie said as soon as I'd fastened my seat belt. 'I didn't call you earlier to ask what the hell was going on, but waited until now.' She pushed the car into gear and moved off.

'You waited until you had me locked up in your car,' I said.

'It was my cunning plan. I think it's working out well. So now tell me.'

'I think Fabrice killed Patrick van der Linde and that's why we're going to interview him and Therese.'

'Not that. Tell me about meeting up with your ex the night before he was arrested.'

'He called me and said he wanted to talk to me. That's all.'

'Why did you go?'

'I thought he wanted to tell me something about the case.'

'And you went by yourself? He made it sound as if you met up for a drink.'

'I recorded our conversation. But it wasn't about the case. It was about something else.'

'You don't trust him then. If you recorded him.'

'Of course I don't trust him. He lied to me and cheated on me. Why would I trust him? But,' I said quickly before she could open her mouth, 'that doesn't make him a murderer.'

'That's fair. I looked into Fabrice Timmer after you called, and I like your thinking. We'd be fools not to at least question him.'

'Right. I've come to realise that my team should never have taken this case. Arjen being my ex doesn't just colour my thinking, but Thomas's and Charlie's too. They look at him differently because of it.'

'I think the issue isn't that they look at him differently,' Stefanie said, 'but that they look at *you* differently. They no longer trust your judgement, and I get that. I think I'm the same, especially after hearing you'd met him by yourself the other day.' She stopped at a traffic light and looked at me. 'If Fabrice hadn't had prior, I wouldn't have come with you this morning. I think you should know that.'

Stefanie parked outside the houseboat where Fabrice and Therese lived. Across the wide water of the Schinkel was the Olympic stadium, which had originally been built for the 1928 Olympics. On the other side of the road was a little drawbridge over the Olympia Canal. This was Amsterdam's outskirts. The centre of town, full of tourists, felt a million miles away. Here, it was as if you were halfway to the countryside. It was a false feeling, of course, as it was only a twenty-minute bike ride to Centraal station, but for anybody who wanted to see green around them, Schinkel

Island with its numerous houseboats was the perfect place to live. If you liked living on a boat, that was, with water your close neighbour.

I didn't think Margreet could live in a place like this any more. For her, water had become an enemy.

Hidden behind the trees were the towers of a business park. It shouldn't be too hard for Fabrice, with his IT knowledge, to find a job right around the corner.

Therese greeted us by the walkway that linked the safety of the shore to their houseboat. I had to duck to go in, but once inside, it was very spacious. She asked if Stefanie wouldn't mind taking her shoes off, because the heels might make dents in the wooden floor. Stefanie grudgingly agreed. Her feet looked vulnerable covered by nothing other than tights. I was happy with my boots and equally happy that I wasn't asked to take them off.

They had decorated the boat in such a way that outside and inside fitted seamlessly together. It was filled with house plants of a similar type to the ones on the water's edge, so that it seemed the park was an extension of the interior. The large window on one side was entirely filled with the view over the canal. It was soothing. The sound of the water washed against the boat, the kind of noise that would send you to sleep in an instant.

'You have a lovely home,' I said.

'Thank you.'

Fabrice was sitting on the sofa, a mug of coffee in his hand.

'We were just going to have breakfast when you called,' Therese said. 'We were told not to go into work anymore.'

'Thanks for taking the time,' I said. 'I hope you won't mind if I record our conversation.' At their nods, I took my phone out and switched the recorder on. 'I'm really looking to get all the facts right about the company party. I'm particularly interested in who saw what.'

'What do you mean?' Fabrice's voice was sharp.

'Can we talk about this without Fabrice here?' Therese asked. She thought I wanted her to retell the story of the assault.

'I'd just like to know what time you called him and what time he came to pick you up,' I said, to set her mind at ease. I was interested in the aftermath, not the sexual assault itself.

'Okay.' She seemed to relax.

'I'll be able to tell you exactly,' Fabrice said.

Stefanie shot me a look. People who knew exactly what they'd done and at what time always seemed suspicious. Normally people had a vague idea of what they'd been up to, maybe linked to whatever programme they'd watched on TV. 'Exactly' implied that Fabrice might have had a reason to watch the clock.

But my suspicions were unfounded when he got his phone out and scrolled through. He didn't seem nervous. He didn't look as if he had something to hide.

'Nico called me at 21.45.' He held the phone out to me and I took a note of the time.

'How long would it have taken you to get to the Clipper?' Stefanie asked.

'There was hardly any traffic. I don't think it was much more than fifteen minutes, twenty at most.'

Therese nodded. 'I think you were there just after ten.'

'You were outside with Nico all that time?' I asked.

'Yes, we sat outside on the steps.'

'Did anybody see you?'

'I'm sure some people walked past, but nobody I recognised.'

'I mean from inside the restaurant. Did anybody from your company come out?'

'Oh gosh, not that I noticed. You should ask Nico, I wasn't paying attention.'

Arjen had said that he had seen the two of them outside; that he had listened to their conversation. Was it possible that Therese hadn't noticed him? She could have been too upset to be aware of what was going on around her, of course.

'What did you talk about?'

'Nothing special, I don't think. I really can't remember. Is this important?'

'It might be.'

'We just chatted. I was upset and Nico was trying to calm me down. We didn't talk about Patrick, as far as I can remember.'

'Did you leave straight away?' I asked Fabrice. 'Or did you stay and talk to Nico?'

'I didn't stay,' he said. 'To be honest, Nico and I have never really got on. I feel bad about that now, but he was always agreeing with Patrick. His little lapdog. Or maybe I should say his rather big lapdog.'

'Fabrice!' Therese said.

'Sorry, but it's true. I'm grateful to him for helping you, of course, but that doesn't mean I shouldn't say what I think.'

'Nico had worked with Patrick a long time,' Therese said. 'He was used to doing things Patrick's way. I don't think there's anything wrong with that.'

'Sure, but he was never going to change. Nothing at the company was ever going to change. It's no wonder we ended up closing down.'

'Why do you say that?' Stefanie asked.

'It was hard to win new business,' Therese said. 'Other companies were doing similar things to us but at a much lower cost. It hadn't always been like that. We used to have the edge, or so Nico kept telling us.'

'He should have designed something new,' Fabrice said. 'Instead, he just sat in the corner, sulking.'

'A couple of years ago, we were at a trade show and there was another company who were doing exactly the kind of T-shirts we were selling, only at a fraction of the cost. Nico went over to talk to them, all casual, and they told him it was their bestselling item. But it was his design. They had ripped it off.'

That was interesting, but not what I was after. 'What time were you back here?'

'It must have been around ten thirty. We can check with your mum,' Fabrice said.

'Your mum?'

'Therese's mother was over for dinner that night,' he said.

'That's why it was so annoying that I had to go to that company do.' Therese put her hand on his knee. 'Patrick would never accept that anybody might have had other plans. I knew you'd be upset.'

He covered her hand with his. 'I know. It's okay.'

This was all lovely, of course, but it put a spanner in the works of my theory. 'Your mother was with you all evening?'

'Yes.' Fabrice looked away from Therese, suspicion suddenly looming on his face. 'Why are you asking that?'

'As I said, I want to get the timeline right. Can you give me her details? I want to follow up with her.' If there had been a third person here and she could provide Fabrice and Therese with an alibi for the rest of the evening, that killed my theory. We knew Patrick had still been alive at 11 p.m., when he paid the restaurant bill. It ruined my idea of presenting Fabrice as a more plausible suspect than Arjen.

Therese gave me her mother's phone number without hesitation. I would call her later.

'Tell me more about those ripped-off designs,' Stefanie said, much more interested in the workings of the company than I was.

'It's been a nightmare,' Therese said. 'They're still at it. That's why I lost my latest deal. They use our own products to compete against us.'

'And nobody has done anything about it?' Stefanie leaned forward, either fascinated or frustrated by the company's lack of action.

'Patrick asked me why we didn't get the contract, and I explained it to him, of course. I think he went to talk to the other company. He was livid.' She looked at Fabrice. 'He could be useful sometimes.' Her voice was softer, as if she didn't like admitting this in front of her boyfriend. 'When things like this happened, he had your back. He never doubted that it was a product problem.'

'He only helped you,' Fabrice said. 'I don't think he would have done it for anybody else.'

'That's not true.'

'You're still defending him?'

'The man's dead, Fabrice. I can talk about the things he did right as well, can't I?' Her voice rose.

I watched with interest, intrigued by how Therese had this apparent need to still think positively about Patrick, regardless of what he'd done to her. It made me wonder about their relationship in the past. Not that it justified what I still believed had been a sexual assault, but it meant Arjen had told the truth about how Patrick had seen the incident.

'When was this?' Stefanie was taking notes as she asked the questions.

'When was what?'

'When did he go and talk to that other company?'

'Two weeks ago, I think.'

'And you first noticed that they were plagiarising your products when?' Now that she was talking about financial things, Stefanie sounded totally in control, despite the fact that she was sitting here in stockinged feet. The waves might give the houseboat just a hint of a rocking motion, but she was on solid ground. For me, this interview had been a disaster. For Stefanie, it seemed to be fascinating, giving her insight into why the company had gone under. I wanted to tell her we were investigating a murder and not a financial fraud, but I'd dragged her along to help me, so I felt obliged to let her ask her questions, however pointless they were.

'It was a while ago,' Therese said. 'When was that Stockholm trade show? Do you remember?' She looked at Fabrice. 'You were there to help set up the booth.'

'The one where Nico completely lost it? At least two years ago, I think.' Fabrice made an effort to sound amenable. He knew better than to get angry in front of two police officers.

'He lost it?' Stefanie asked.

'Yeah, when he saw that they were selling his stuff. I didn't think it was identical at all, to be honest. It looked different to me, but what do I know?'

'True,' Therese said. 'It looked different to me as well, but Nico said there was something in the underlying design that infringed on our patent.'

The couple were in harmony again, the moment of argument past. I was annoyed with Stefanie that she'd started a topic they agreed on.

'Did Patrick take them to court?' she asked.

'No, nothing came of it,' Therese said. 'But it kept happening, and then we lost the deal the other week. The client said the products were very similar but our competitor's was slightly better, and cheaper. So I told Patrick.'

'And he was going to meet with them?'

'That's right.'

'What's the name of the other company?'

'Ozone. They're called Ozone.'

I didn't know what to think as we drove back from the houseboat. After observing Fabrice and Therese, seeing the way they were together and how calmly and openly they'd answered my questions, I had a hard time believing that my theory of how they'd killed Patrick had been correct. This was a nuisance. There was no doubt in my mind that the mother would back up their story.

'We need to check with that other company,' Stefanie said. 'I don't think the timelines quite match up, but for the last three years the sales at Linde Lights have been very bad. It's as if they fell off a cliff. I wondered what had happened, but if another company was making the same products at a lower cost, that could be the reason.'

'But did you see Fabrice's temper flare up as soon as Therese said something good about Patrick?' Even though I knew I was grasping at straws, I still couldn't quite let go of my favourite theory.

'Annoyed that there was something good about him more than guilt over having killed him, I thought.'

She was probably right. 'I'm still going to follow up with the mother,' I said.

'Sure, because her mother would be a perfectly fine alibi.' Sarcasm was heavy in her voice. 'Mothers are as objective as ex-wives.'

'Give it a rest.'

'You want those two to be guilty so that your ex is off the hook. They didn't look all that guilty to me.'

'You just stick to your numbers.' I hated it when she was right.

I called Therese's mother and she sounded delighted to hear from me. It was quite an unnerving experience. We drove over to her house. 'You know this is pointless, right?' Stefanie said.

Deep down, I agreed, but I was also aware that I needed to double-check Fabrice's alibi, otherwise I would think I hadn't done enough and hadn't tried my hardest for Arjen.

'This is about that guy, isn't it?' Therese's mother said as soon as she opened the door. I didn't even have time to get a question out. 'Come in, come in.'

I tried to remember if I'd ever been so warmly welcomed before. If this woman was covering for her daughter and her daughter's boyfriend, she was a very good actress.

'I popped out and bought biscuits after you called. I'm Sally Kroese. Call me Sally.'

Stefanie shot me a glance that clearly said: not guilty, I told you so. Guilty people didn't buy biscuits for police officers.

'This is so exciting,' Sally said. 'Just like one of those police shows. I love those, don't you?'

'Did you ever meet Patrick van der Linde?' I asked.

She grimaced. 'No, but I heard a lot about him. Therese worked closely with him, and it seems he could be quite difficult. There's no hiding in a small company, is there?'

'Can you tell us about the evening you were with Fabrice and Therese?'

'I was annoyed with her, to be honest. I'd come over to have dinner with them and then she went to the work do. I get that work is important, but being forced to spend the evening with your colleagues when you have other plans is really too much.' She handed round the plate of biscuits and poured tea out of a pot that had obviously been brewing for a while. 'Fabrice had left work early to cook for us, I was already at their place, and then Therese rang to say that she had to go to the drinks. Apparently Nico had called to tell her it was important that she was sociable with this Arjen guy. Patrick's son-in-law. It's always the ones with the connections that get the good jobs, isn't it?'

'Nico called?' I said. 'I thought Patrick called her.'

'Yes, he called her as she was on the phone to me. I remember that. She said, oh God, now my boss is calling me as well.'

'That's interesting,' I said. 'I had no idea Nico had spoken to her.'

'Yeah, she told me he'd promised to keep an eye out. Nico knew what Patrick was like when he was drunk.' Sally grimaced again. 'Dirty old man. That guy was older than I am, for goodness' sake. Not that it's fine to harass people when you're younger, that's not what I'm saying, but Patrick was revolting. Seriously. So yes, I was glad Nico was looking out for her.'

'Therese told you what happened that night?'

Sally nodded. 'She was very upset when she got home, I could tell. When Fabrice popped out for a cigarette, she told me. She didn't want me to tell Fabrice.' She lowered her voice to a confidential whisper. 'He's got a bit of a temper and she was concerned about what he was going to do. I like him well enough now, but when she first moved in with him I wasn't that happy. I like Nico much more.'

'Nico? You know him?'

'Yes, he worked with my husband for a bit before he moved to Linde Lights. He got Therese the job there. I thought maybe they'd end up together – he always had a bit of a crush on her – but, well, he wasn't her type. She said they were just friends and would never be more than that.' Sally took another biscuit. 'I'm sure it was awkward, all of them working together. I think Nico would have liked to be more than friends.'

Now I totally understood why Fabrice and Nico had never got on, and why Fabrice wasn't happy about being in Nico's debt. It also explained why Nico, the man described as Patrick's lapdog, had stepped in. That he'd known Therese, that he liked her, was probably why he'd been willing to confront his boss over this, especially if he'd told Therese beforehand that he'd keep an eye out for her.

'Nico nearly got what he wanted,' Sally said.

'What he wanted?'

'To get closer to Therese. It's just like one of those rom-com movies where the guy sets up a plan to save the girl so that he can look like a hero. He did end up looking like a hero, didn't he?'

I shook my head. This woman had watched too many movies. 'Nico called Fabrice to come and pick her up.'

'Yes. She could have asked Nico to drop her off here instead, but I think he'd been drinking. It was lucky that Fabrice and I had decided we were going to wait to open the wine until after Therese had got home. I'd brought a nice bottle, and Fabrice said we shouldn't have it without her. So yes, he picked her up and they came back here. She had a bit of food but was just picking at it. Fabrice was annoyed with her for having drunk so much, but I could tell she wasn't drunk. She was upset about something.'

'Did either Fabrice or Therese leave again after they'd come back?'

'Fabrice had a smoke on the deck of the boat, that's all. That's when Therese told me what had happened, and then she was sick. I felt so sorry for her. That bastard.'

'How long was Fabrice gone?'

'He wasn't really gone; he was right outside. He saw that Therese wasn't well and came rushing back in.'

'You could see him the whole time.'

Sally nodded enthusiastically. 'The whole time. This really is just like a detective show, isn't it? Have you got any ideas about the suspect yet? I guess it's just like an Agatha Christie, where really everybody had a reason to want the guy dead.'

Maybe everybody did have a reason, but I could tick one suspect off my list at least.

'It was interesting what Sally said.' Stefanie pulled out onto the main street.

'Which bit?'

'About Nico being the hero for Therese.'

I remembered. I also remembered Fabrice saying how much he would have liked to have been the one to have saved Therese. His comment that it was nice that Nico got to be the hero. 'What's your point?' I said, because I didn't like where this was going. 'Do you think Nico planned this? Got Patrick to assault Therese so that he could rescue her?'

'Sally was right: it's what happens in the movies.'

'Movies written by some guy, I'm sure. Movies where borderline stalking is seen as a romantic gesture and obsession is confused with love.'

'Love can feel like obsession, can't it?' she said. 'When you want to see that person all the time. It's only bad when it isn't reciprocated.'

'But you wouldn't want anything bad to happen to someone you're in love with. You wouldn't want them to be at risk, even if that means you can rescue them.'

'Oh my God, I've just realised something!' Her voice was all fake-excited, like a schoolgirl spotting a member of her favourite boy band. 'It's what you're doing at the moment. You're trying to rescue Arjen. So romantic. Is that how you're going to win him back?'

I'd known there was going to be a price to pay for having Stefanie help me. I'd known when I walked into her office to ask for her assistance that she would irritate the hell out of me at some point. That I knew she was doing it on purpose didn't stop me from responding. 'I'm not trying to get him back. I don't want him back. I'm trying to keep an innocent person out of prison. That's not really romantic.'

'I think you're protesting too much.' She winked at me. 'What does Mark have to say about all this?'

'How do you know about Mark?' I had no idea she knew anything about my personal life.

We stopped at a red light. There was no escape when you were in a car with someone. I should have cycled. I would cycle next time, regardless of how far it was or what the weather was like. Getting soaked in the rain would be less aggravating than talking to Stefanie.

'Charlie told me you've got a new guy,' she said.

'When did you talk to Charlie about my private life?'

'Is your new guy jealous? Just like Fabrice is?'

I shook my head at the ridiculous idea. 'So in the rom-com movie that's taking place in your head right now, I would have arrested Arjen just so that I could get him out again?' I didn't want to think about the fact that I hadn't told Mark about any of this. And I obviously wasn't going to confess that to Stefanie.

She pursed her lips as she waited for the traffic light to turn green. 'No, I don't think that would have worked. I don't think you could have arrested him yourself. You would have someone else do it, make it look as if you had nothing to do with it, and then go all out to save him.' She whipped her head round, sending her hair flying. 'Oh, wait, is that what actually happened? Did you whisper in Thomas's ear to arrest Arjen? Tut tut, Lotte, you're much more devious than I thought.'

'Shut up,' I said. Later, probably as I was lying in bed tonight, I would come up with a much better retort than that one. For now I resorted to sulky silence and switched on the radio.

Stefanie parked in the basement of the police station and I was back at my desk before I remembered that I was supposed to stay out of the office as much as possible. Thomas and Charlie weren't there, and I took my coat off and sat down. Stefanie's words came back to me. However much I'd hated what she'd said, there was something about it that niggled at the back of my mind, though I couldn't quite put my finger on what it was.

While I was there, I should have another look at the CCTV footage from the Clipper. If nothing else, I could prove that Stefanie had been talking garbage, and remind her there was a reason why she was in the financial fraud department and I was in CID. I'd watched it a few times already, to see who had been aware of what had gone on with Therese. Previously I'd wanted to check what people's reaction had been when Patrick returned to the table afterwards. Now I looked at the beginning, when the group first turned up.

Four people arrived together: Patrick, Arjen, Nico and Gerry. I knew that it was forty-five minutes later when three more people came. It would be almost two hours before Therese arrived to take her seat at the far end of the table.

I started from when they sat down. Nico took the seat diagonally opposite Patrick. I sped up the footage and it became clear that the two of them didn't talk to each other at all, but Nico did continue to ply Patrick with wine. The footage wasn't sharp enough to allow me to see it exactly, but it seemed to me that he was keeping Patrick's glass full. They finished one bottle and then another. Most of it went into Patrick's glass. The others hardly drank. My guess was that he had had the best part of a bottle in the forty-five minutes before the next guests arrived. Then a couple more bottles were ordered. I didn't know how much he usually drank – it could well be that a bottle of red made no impression on him – but seeing Nico topping up his glass over and over again made me wonder if he'd had a reason for doing that. It was as if he wanted Patrick to get really drunk.

Even Therese's mother had known how Patrick was going to act under the influence. She'd called him a dirty old man. He wouldn't be able to keep his hands to himself. Had Nico got Patrick drunk, then called Therese to come to the restaurant? As Sally had said, if this had been his plan, it had almost worked.

But surely that was just something people did in movies? Surely nobody would think it was a good idea to do it in real life? Had it got out of control? Had he thought that Patrick might just put his hand on Therese's knee, for example, and he would be able to say something about it and be the good guy? Instead, Patrick had pinned her up against the wall, a sexual assault instead of the mild annoyance that Nico might have expected to happen.

I closed my computer and got my coat, ready to leave the police station again. It was silly to work from home or away from the office, but if that was what the boss wanted, that was what I'd do. The alternative was to join Stefanie in her office, and I really didn't fancy that. With a bit of luck, they'd release Arjen at the end of the twenty-four-hour period and I could return to my desk without any qualms.

As I walked down the stairs, I couldn't stop thinking about the footage I'd watched. What if Nico had tried to get Patrick drunk for other reasons? Not to get in Therese's good books, but to make him behave in the kind of way that would force him to step down as managing director. As long as Patrick was the head of the company, nothing was going to change. That was what Fabrice had said. Had this been a strategy to remove him from the helm?

A thought popped into my head that I didn't particularly like: was that why Arjen and Patrick had been arguing? Because Patrick had behaved in a way that could lose him control of the company and put Arjen's future in jeopardy?

I remembered thinking as I'd watched Arjen being questioned that there was probably one more layer of truth to unpeel. Was this it? That he had been pissed off with Patrick for his own sake? His own job? Would this have made him more or less likely to start a physical fight?

I hated the direction my thoughts were going in; that whenever I tried to do something to prove Arjen's innocence, I kept wondering about the possibility of his guilt.

With those doubts in my head, I left the police station.

I saw her as soon as I'd crossed the little garden by the exit. I had no idea how long she'd been waiting for me. There was a list of people I really didn't want to see right now, and she was at the very top of it. Because nothing good could come of meeting my ex-husband's second wife.

Chapter 30

I sped up and tried to walk past her, but she grabbed my arm.

'I need to talk to you,' she said.

I wanted to say something snarky, like: get a number, there's a queue. But instead I decided to be polite and professional. This was work, after all. 'If it's about your husband, I don't think it's a good idea for us to talk.'

'Not a good idea? You locked him up. I know we've done things that hurt you, but this is taking it too far.'

'We pulled him in for questioning,' I said. 'We haven't locked him up, as you call it.'

'This is ridiculous. You can't possibly think he killed my father.'

'Please talk to his lawyer.'

'I already did that. I know why you called him in for questioning, as you call it. I hope you understand that you're responsible for all of this.'

'I am?' I stuffed my hands deep into my pockets. 'Enlighten me.'

'You made it personal. Don't you see? I don't think Arjen would have lied if you hadn't been involved.'

My mother had said something similar, but that didn't surprise me. Nadia had called her to fire her as their baby-sitter. She had probably also given this same explanation as to why it was all my fault.

'I could have accepted that if he'd lied only to me, but he was giving evidence to my colleagues. He lied to them,' I said. I wanted to be fair. I really did.

Nadia shook her head. 'You might not have been in the room, but you were involved from the start. You came to our house that first time. You met with my mother.'

'Can I point out that you came to me first? You asked me to look into your father's disappearance, remember?'

'Only too well.'

'If you hadn't done that, I would never have been part of the investigation. I'm sorry Arjen felt the need to lie to the police. He's made everything that much harder.'

'I know that. But there's no way he murdered my father. I would have known if he had.'

It wasn't the first time I'd heard a family member say those words: *I would have known.* 'Did you know what your father got up to?' I said.

Nadia sighed. 'Let's talk. Not here in the middle of the street. My mother said you took her to a café around the corner. Let's go there.'

I shook my head. 'Not just the two of us. That would be a bad idea. Wait for a second. I'll get one of my colleagues to join us.'

At Nadia's nod, I called Stefanie. I didn't think I'd ever heard her quite this excited before. That Nadia was okay with it made me feel marginally better.

We waited for Stefanie in silence It would probably have been better to have this chat inside the police station, but the boss had said I should stay away. The fact that I wouldn't want to be seen by Thomas and Charlie talking to Nadia was something I pushed to the back of my mind. When Stefanie came out, still putting her coat on, we set off across the bridge to the café.

And that was how I ended up having a coffee with the woman my husband had cheated on me with, and the woman who thought my ex-husband could so easily have murdered someone.

'I'm not your enemy,' Nadia said to me across the table.

I pulled my hair away from my face and laughed. The whole situation was too ridiculous. Here was this young woman trying to make friends with me because she desperately needed my help. How the tables had turned.

'You know as well as I do that Arjen didn't kill anybody.' She fell silent as the waitress approached and put our coffees in front of us.

'If you want to help him,' I said, 'you can answer our questions.' I put my phone on the table between us and pressed the record button.

'Sure,' she said, giving me a challenging look. 'Ask away.'

'Did Arjen tell you what happened that night at the restaurant?'

'Not as such, but he did tell me afterwards that we weren't going to put any money into the company. That pretty much told me enough.'

'What do you mean?' Stefanie said. Her face lit up with

pleasure that this talk was going to be all about finance after all.

'I worked there for a couple of years and hated how he behaved. He even did it when I was there. Can you imagine having to watch that? Your father flirting with the women in the company, always going that little bit too far. It's why we argued all the time.'

'Your mother said the arguments were about the direction the firm was taking,' Stefanie said.

'What do you think I was going to say to my mother? Mum, I hate watching my father put his hand on the admin girl's knee? Mum, the girl asked me if I could talk to my dad and get him to stop? That's not really something you can tell your mother. It's much easier to make up a business reason.'

'So that's why you left?' I asked.

'I couldn't stand it any longer. I told him why I couldn't work there any more. He said something really annoying, like how he was just weak. Or the girls were just too pretty. Or whatever. Some lousy excuse. I got so angry, I broke off all contact with him after that.'

'Your mother told us he'd had counselling and that he'd stopped drinking.'

'It was easy, wasn't it? To accept that the cheating was only down to the fact that he drank too much. As I said: some lousy excuse. I guess part of it was my fault. I never told my mother the extent of how he behaved at work. I met with her, of course, and after Arjen and I got married and . . .' She stopped. 'Whatever.'

I knew what she'd been about to say. 'And after your daughter was born,' I said, 'you got back in touch.'

'Yes. We would go round there for lunch every other weekend. I felt bad for my mother not seeing her grandchild as much as she wanted, but I just couldn't stand being in the same room as him.' She tore the top off a sugar packet and stirred it into her coffee. 'I avoided him, but then I felt guilty for being a bad daughter. You can't win, can you?'

'And Arjen knew about this?' I asked.

'I told him I was embarrassed about the money. Two years ago, my father got in touch. The firm was in need of money and he asked us if we were willing to put some in. He'd sold the house a couple of years before that, and I'd suspected he needed to release the equity to prop the company up. I confronted him about it at the time and he was pretty evasive. Said that they were downsizing, nothing to do with Linde Lights. My mother has no idea; she still thinks there's a lot of money left.'

'You haven't told her?'

'I don't know for sure what's there and what isn't. A solicitor is going through it all; it's a total mess. I prefer to wait until I actually have some facts, then I'll sit down with her and discuss the situation.'

I nodded. I understood that. 'Did you not have the money back then?'

'No, we could have given him what he wanted,' Nadia said. Her voice was sharp. 'But he wasn't changing anything about the way he was running the company. He wasn't going to give us any say in return. He thought it could be a loan – which would have ended up as a gift – without any interest. I told him to go to hell.' She looked at me over her coffee cup. 'Those were the words I actually used.'

'What changed between then and now? You were going to bail him out this time.'

'He must have been desperate. He offered to give us half the company in return for the cash. He was willing to modify the way they were working. He would take my opinions into account – no, he would be legally bound to do what I wanted, as he was going to make me a co-director with the same number of shares in the firm as he had.'

'But it wasn't just about a say in the company,' I said. 'That's not what you argued about in the past.'

'Exactly. Our falling-out was about how he behaved. I told Arjen to look around for a bit, to see if he really had changed.' She raised her eyebrows. 'And of course my father insisted on throwing that company do, getting horrendously drunk and snogging Therese Klein.'

'Arjen had an argument with your father about that.'

'I'm sure he did. He was pretty pissed off when he got home. But when my father went missing, we decided not to tell my mother about what had happened at the drinks. At first we thought that maybe he'd spent the night with Therese. That he'd decided to divorce my mother.'

'Therese has a boyfriend. She says he sexually assaulted her.'

'Whatever.'

Nadia's dismissive response annoyed me. 'Both Therese and Nico said that Nico had to drag your father off her. Do you think he would have done that if they were just making out?'

'Nico did?' Nadia laughed. 'That's a surprise. He only ever does what my father tells him to do.'

'Someone called him your father's lapdog.'

'Yeah, that's about right. He was already working with my father when I joined. I didn't see him stand up to him once.'

'But now he has.'

'Wow. Okay, but we didn't know that at the time. My mother called me, distraught because my father hadn't come home, and Arjen told me about their argument and that he'd been kissing this girl, and we decided that it was probably best to go to the police before my mother went insane. We expected him to turn up the next day with his tail between his legs.' She paused, a grim smile on her face. 'No, actually we expected that he would have disappeared with whatever cash he still had. He knew the company was beyond rescuing and it wouldn't have surprised me if he'd cut his losses. There were no other assets left: the house was sold, the new flat was rented. He could have run away from his responsibilities. I wouldn't have put it past him.'

'But he didn't run,' I said.

'No. He was murdered. But it would have made no sense whatsoever for Arjen to have done that; you see that, don't you?'

'I'm trying to prove it,' I said. 'I'm in a tough situation where I have to be seen to be objective when I'm clearly not. I had nothing to do with his arrest. For once, I think we're on the same side. Just one last question: the investment two years ago, where did that come from?' Part of me hoped there was some shady moneylender in the background, or that Patrick had been smuggling drugs in the shipments from abroad.

'He never said. I think he might have got some of his friends to put money in.'

'Money that they were going to lose unless you bailed them out,' Stefanie said. 'Did anybody know about the ultimatum you'd given your father? Or maybe I should say the conditions you attached to the loan?'

I could see where her thinking was going. Conditions that he had clearly broken that evening.

'I'm not sure he told anybody he'd asked us for money. Keeping stakeholders informed wasn't my father's strong point. Some of the old-timers had a pretty shrewd idea why I'd left the company, of course. They might have put two and two together when Arjen showed up.' She shrugged.

'Or maybe not,' Stefanie said. 'Maybe they thought you no longer cared about your father's behaviour.'

'Sure, they could have thought all kinds of things. I don't know.'

Would any of the people who'd given Patrick money all those years ago be annoyed enough at his behaviour to murder him? Maybe they knew his daughter wasn't going to bail him out after the way he'd acted in front of his son-in-law. If they were going to lose a lot of money, who knew?

'Did your father tell you anything about their products being plagiarised?' Stefanie asked.

'Plagiarised?'

'Therese Klein told us that there's another firm out there that copied Linde Lights' products and made them more cheaply. That was why they were having a tough time gaining new business.'

'I wouldn't believe anything that girl says. She's probably just terrible at her job and only kept it because my father fancied her.'

'Do you know her?' I asked. Any sympathy I'd felt for Nadia over the last ten minutes had quickly ebbed away.

'Never met her, but I know her type.' She abruptly put her cup back on its saucer. 'I didn't come here to argue with you,' she said. 'Actually, I want to apologise.'

'Apologise?'

Nadia shot Stefanie a look.

'Don't worry,' I said. 'She knows what happened between you and my ex-husband. I'm guessing that's what you were planning to apologise for?'

'Yes,' Nadia said. 'I know it was wrong. I shouldn't have gone after him.'

'It's funny,' I said. 'Arjen apologised too. He did it just before he asked me not to tell your mother that your father was cheating on her. You're doing it because you want me to help your husband out, aren't you?'

'Yes. Don't be angry with us. I'm sorry about—'

I cut her short. 'Why does your apology seem so much like an insult? You both appear to think that I won't do my job properly unless you apologise to me.' I looked over at Stefanie. 'She's actually insulting you too, now that I think about it.'

'You're right,' Stefanie said. 'She must think I only do what you tell me to.'

'But I really am sorry.' Nadia tried again.

'No you're not,' I said. 'Well, you might be sorry that your husband isn't coming home tonight, but I don't think you're sorry you slept with him, got pregnant and married him. You're only apologising because you want something from me. That's not an apology, it's a bribe.'

'No,' Stefanie said. 'I actually think you were right first time. It's an insult.'

Nadia pushed her chair back and walked off.

Stefanie and I watched her storm out, then grinned at each other.

'That went better than I expected,' she said.

'Are you working on this case or are you laughing at me?'

'I can do both at the same time, can't I?'

I shook my head and took a sip of coffee. The air had become more breathable now that Nadia was no longer there. I had to laugh at the thought that both mother and daughter had stormed out on me in this café, leaving me to pay.

'Still, that plagiarism case interests me,' Stefanie said. 'And even more so because Patrick didn't mention it to Nadia, a possible investor.'

'What do you mean?'

'Well, you would, wouldn't you? You'd say: give me money to sue these people; they'll have to pay damages and you'll get your investment back with interest. If there's a structural reason for why the company is in financial difficulties, you would mention that.'

'Unless it's something that's hard to prove,' I said.

'Right. Or unless it isn't actually true.'

'You think Therese was lying about it?'

'We should check it out. Confirm it either way.'

Chapter 31

Stefanie and I met with Nico Verhoef at the Clipper. After talking to Therese and Fabrice earlier, I had known none of the Linde Lights staff was going to work any more, but the fact that the doors of the office were locked came as a surprise. Nico told us that now that the bank had refused to extend their line of credit, there was no longer enough money to keep the heating or the lights on; more to the point, the rent on the premises hadn't been paid and the landlord had kicked them out.

'That happened quickly,' I said.

'Yes. It's come as a huge shock to all of us. Another huge shock, I should say. After Patrick's death.' He sat with his arms folded and his legs crossed. I could see from the hang-dog expression on his face that the events of the last week had taken their toll. He looked as if he hadn't slept in days.

I felt sorry for him. 'I understand. You'd been here for a long time,' I said. 'Nadia told me you were one of the early employees.'

'Patrick hired me away from the company where I

288

worked,' Nico said. 'He wanted my designs, said they were perfect for what Linde Lights was trying to become.'

'Where had he seen them?' I wanted to give him time to reminisce about the early days before asking him about the topic that had made it all fall apart. I didn't do it purely to make him feel better, but also to make him relaxed enough that he'd be open about what had gone wrong. Thinking about it earlier, it seemed to me that everybody had been defensive all the time: of Patrick's behaviour or the company's strategy.

'I worked for one of the large design companies that Patrick used in the early stages to create the specs for him. He would do the sales part and organise the production.'

'That's interesting,' Stefanie said. 'So he outsourced the design initially.'

'Yes, but we worked so well together that he decided to bring it in-house.'

'That was a huge gamble,' Stefanie said. 'For you, I mean, to take that job.'

He unfolded his arms. 'Oh, I wouldn't say huge. It was fun to see the process from beginning to end, and being in a small firm gave me freedom. I was no longer just a cog in the machine.'

'But also you were working closely with one person,' she said. 'If for some reason you fell out with him, it would be a problem.'

'I'd worked with Patrick before, of course, so I knew we got on.' A defensive note crept into his voice. It must have seemed to him that Stefanie was questioning his judgement.

I tried to smooth things over. 'It makes it even more impressive that you decided to step in to rescue Therese.'

Nico shook his head. 'It wasn't a big deal. It really wasn't. He would have appreciated it the next day. I'd saved him from a tricky situation.'

'A tricky situation? He told his son-in-law that it was consensual,' Stefanie said.

I wanted to kick her under the table. She needed to stop attacking him.

'Yeah, well,' he said, 'whatever he might have told Arjen, it really wasn't. And there's a huge difference between having your staff pissed off at you and having to talk to the police. After the last time, Therese said she would press charges if he tried anything like that again.'

'She told you that?'

'Yes. She said she'd get him somewhere with CCTV or record him. I couldn't have Patrick being arrested. It would have been the end of us. Of the company, I mean.'

It was quite ironic that what his colleagues saw as his bravery in standing up to the boss had actually been an attempt to protect him and stop him from being arrested. 'Patrick didn't know that, though, did he? He was angry with you.' I made it sound as if Patrick's anger was misplaced.

'He would have done the next day, when he'd sobered up. I'd never seen him drink that much before. He was plastered before the food even turned up.'

I remembered watching the CCTV footage of the dinner table and seeing Nico fill up Patrick's glass again and again. If he'd been concerned about his boss's drinking, he hadn't done anything to stop it. I had noticed that Nico was spinning everything to do with Patrick in a positive light. I wasn't sure if it was because he didn't want to speak ill of the dead, or if this was what he liked to think had happened now that Patrick was no longer alive to contradict him.

'We talked to Therese yesterday and she told me that one of your products had been plagiarised,' Stefanie said.

Now the barrier of his body posture finally came down and Nico leaned forward, suddenly keen to talk. 'I told Patrick that we should take those people to court, but he was reluctant. I think he was just too nice. Or maybe he didn't have the money for it.'

'When did you first notice what they were doing?' Stefanie asked.

'When we lost our first sale to them around this time two years ago.' He took a sip of his tea, getting ready to tell us the full story. 'When we asked the client why, they said that our competitor had something very similar but at a much lower cost. They said their quality was better. We were very upset to have lost the sale, but I was even more upset to see my design being used by someone else. I knew we had a patent on it, so I don't know how that could have happened.'

'You saw them at a conference too?'

'Yes, they were exhibiting there. They had the nerve to tell me it was their bestselling product. I was so angry, I called Patrick and told him to fly out to Stockholm, where the conference was, and take them to court.'

'You talked to Patrick about it?' I asked.

'Of course. But he didn't want to do anything about it. They were making huge amounts and we were going under. It was so unfair. He refused to come.'

'Why?'

'I think he was worried about the legal fees.'

'You were in financial trouble already then?' Stefanie asked.

'I'm only saying this with hindsight. I can't think of any other reason. Patrick wanted me to come up with new ideas all the time, but at the same time he pushed me to produce the existing ones at a lower cost so that we could compete, and that took up all my time. It was that real dilemma between keeping existing clients happy and getting new ones. In an ideal world, we would have hired someone to run production so that I could concentrate on design. But it's a far from ideal world.'

Stefanie nodded. 'I'm sure you addressed this with Patrick.'

'Plenty of times, but the answer was always the same: there was no money. It was a real chicken-and-egg situation. We should have spent the money then and gone under fighting. Now we've gone under anyway.'

'You must have been very angry with him,' I said.

'I felt bad, sure. But I was much angrier with Ozone.'

'Patrick went there two weeks ago.'

'Yes, I heard. Therese losing that deal was the final straw for him.' He shrugged. 'She was the one who finally made him act. I'm just sad that it happened too late.'

'We're going to meet with them,' Stefanie said. 'To hear what Patrick told them.'

'Why do that?' Nico asked. 'It's too late now. Too late to save the firm.'

The fact that he didn't want to take action against them made me wonder if he was going to apply for a job with them.

Chapter 32

I checked my watch and noticed with a shock that it was ten to seven already. Mark was coming over for dinner tonight. I called the Chinese takeaway place and said I'd come to pick up the food in fifteen minutes. They were always very quick, and half an hour later I was walking back along the canal with a white plastic bag in my hand, thoughts running through my head.

All of us were keeping quiet to protect someone else, or maybe from self-preservation. We didn't want to deal with how the other person would react when they were told the truth. I tried to keep certain things about my job from Mark. He didn't need a bucket of unhappiness chucked over his head as soon as he got home. I had no doubt that this was the right thing to do.

But this case was different somehow.

Not telling him about talking to my ex was not the same as not telling him about what Patrick's body had looked like when he'd been dragged out of the water after many days. One of these things I could justify; the other was me stepping away from confrontation.

It was me being a coward.

That was also why I hadn't been working on this case properly. I had been a coward. I had wanted to stay away from the victim's family. I hadn't wanted to see the little girl, the new wife, my ex. I had told the son-in-law information I hadn't told the daughter. I hadn't wanted to talk to the daughter about the money situation because I didn't want to meet with her. I hadn't spoken to the widow because she was asking me questions about my divorce.

In any other case, I would have done these things. In this case, I was staying in the background, I was sitting behind my desk, I wasn't asking the questions I should be asking.

And maybe that had led to Arjen being arrested for murder.

I opened the door to my flat and saw that Mark was already inside. I loved that he had a key and would let himself in. Pippi was sitting on his lap and opened one eye to check who was coming through the door. She was ungrateful like that. Surely she should show more excitement about her owner coming home. But no. As long as she had a nice warm lap to snooze on, she was perfectly content. I bet he'd fed her as well, otherwise I would have been greeted by dramatic meowing rather than this ongoing snooze-fest.

I held up the plastic bag. 'I brought food,' I said. 'Couldn't be bothered to cook.'

'You should have called me; I would have cooked,' Mark said. 'I'm sure I could have made something edible out of whatever you've got in the house. How's your hand?'

'My mother told me I'd been overly dramatic for something that was covered by such a small plaster.'

Mark laughed. 'That sounds like her.'

'I went to Elise's to pick up my bike and we had a nice chat and a cup of tea. At least I didn't ruin their kitchen floor. There were no bloodstains left behind.'

'That's good. Even though it would be like your personal graffiti: Lotte was here, there are even bloodstains to prove it.'

I put the bag on the table and started opening the boxes. Pippi woke up properly and jumped off Mark's lap. She probably thought there was going to be some food for her too. She thought wrong. It was all ours.

I scratched her head. 'Nothing for you, puss,' I said, and she meowed in return.

'I hope nobody gave you a hard time for coming in late after the accident.'

'I don't think anybody cares about that,' I said. 'Plus I actually did some work whilst talking to Elise. You were talking about strategy and I was curious how that worked.'

'Is your latest case the murder of a strategist? I had no idea that was such a dangerous job.'

'No, it's the murder of a company director. He'd hired a strategist and was introducing the guy at a company do. He was murdered that evening.'

'You think there's a link?'

'I just wondered if that meant there was something going wrong at the company. Elise told me very kindly that I knew nothing about how business works, so I got someone from the financial fraud department to work with me. To help me,' I corrected. 'But I think I was right after all, as the guy's corporate credit card bounced.' The thought I'd had while walking back here came to me again. I shouldn't be a coward; I should tell Mark what had been going on.

'It all got a bit trickier,' I said, 'because the strategist is my ex-husband.'

'Wait . . . what?'

'The man who's been murdered is Patrick van der Linde. Arjen is his son-in-law. Patrick seemed to have brought him into the firm.'

'Just don't arrest him. Nobody will believe you didn't have an ulterior motive.'

'Too late. He's already been arrested. Though not by me.'

'Oh shit.' Mark put his fork down. 'Are you okay?'

The moment I'd been worried about had turned out to be a non-issue. All Mark cared about was me. 'It's been hard.' I didn't know why I said that, other than as a reaction to how lightly he was taking this. 'Talking to him and his new wife. Seeing their kid. It hasn't been easy.'

'In what way?'

'It brought back a lot of bad stuff. Things I hadn't thought about for years. Our daughter dying, the cheating, the divorce. It's not good to have your face rubbed in that.'

'He talked about those things?'

'No, the wife's mother did. She thought I was Nadia's friend at first so was taking me into her confidence in an uncomfortable way. Then, when she found out who I actually was, she wanted to know if I'd been aware of what had been going on.'

'Why would she want to know that?'

'I think it was because her husband had been murdered. She was asking herself if he'd done something to get himself killed. She wanted to know if it was possible to be totally ignorant of what was going on around you.'

'Is it?'

'Her husband hadn't been the nice, caring, faithful man she'd thought he was. I didn't tell her that, of course. It's difficult, because it's all become quite personal. I'm second-guessing myself, trying to figure out what I would have done if it hadn't been Arjen's father-in-law. I see parallels everywhere between his behaviour at work and his daughter's with Arjen. The widow and me.' I started ladling rice onto my plate.

'You'll figure it out. Or you could take some time off. We could go on a trip, if you like.'

'Now's not a good time.' There was no way I could stop working on this case now. 'We've got my mum's wedding coming up in a few weeks too.'

'Is she okay?'

'She's no longer angry with me for bleeding over her stepdaughter-to-be's kitchen floor. Now she's angry with me for arresting Arjen. Which I didn't do.'

'Do you want to tell me about the case without all the personal stuff? Would that be helpful?'

'Linde Lights. Have you heard of them?'

'It's them? I pitched for redesigning their office a few years ago. We didn't get the business, but the guy who did told me it took forever to get paid. He thought he was going to have to take them to court, but it all worked out in the end.'

'How long ago was this?'

'Oh, maybe three years ago?'

Thinking about when Patrick had sold his house to put

money into the firm, that didn't surprise me at all. 'There were money issues already, then.'

'I'm not sure there were issues; it could be that they're just slow with paying. Some companies do that: try to delay for as long as they can. They were probably just like that.'

I helped myself to a portion of beef rendang.

'I did hear about some other problems.' He seemed reluctant to tell me.

'Let me guess: was it about female employees?'

'Yeah, that's it. It wasn't a pleasant working environment, apparently.'

'That's what I've been hearing as well,' I said. 'It seems it was common knowledge then.'

'I don't know. But the guy who got the deal wished he'd never landed it. He ended up having to replace the female project manager because she refused to go on site. He had to put a guy on the job instead.'

Chapter 33

Regardless of what Nico might have wanted us to do, Stefanie and I made the trip to Ozone. I was excited. The fact that Patrick had come here a week before his death felt significant. I didn't know how this would tie in with his murder, but it seemed important not to leave a single stone unturned. Plus talking to this company was better than staying in the office and brooding. Or no, staying *away* from the office and worrying. Stefanie was intrigued by the lack of action on the plagiarism issue, and this way I might actually be helping her do her job for once rather than the other way around.

We drove into the business park on Amsterdam's outskirts. I had expected something shabby. 'These are nice offices for a company that stole someone else's designs,' I said.

'What? Taking another firm's bestselling products is a very handy short cut to profitability. See it as an extreme form of product research. Big companies just do it on a larger scale. The same way rich people steal on a different scale.'

My mother would call that a very cynical point of view. I could only accept the truth in what Stefanie was saying.

Ilse Regen, the director of Ozone, was about our age. She showed us into a meeting room. 'I was sad to hear of Patrick's death,' she said. 'It's not that I liked the man, but it's still a shock when someone you know gets killed.'

That was honest.

'I'd heard stories about him,' she continued. 'A couple of people who used to work there joined us over the last years. The way he worked, the way he treated people . . . I don't know, I don't think you should behave like that.'

It didn't seem right for this woman who had plagiarised Patrick's products, who had helped his firm to go under, to talk like that. 'But you used their designs,' I said. 'We were told that Patrick came here a week before his death because you'd won a deal with products that he had a patent on.'

'I was quite shocked when he came here,' Ilse said.

'Because he'd found out?' Stefanie asked.

'There was nothing *to* find out. We won that deal fair and square. I didn't appreciate him coming here and shouting at me. I mean, I knew the man wasn't professional, but that was going too far.'

'Too far? What did he say?' Maybe he had threatened her with physical violence, but I understood why he'd been angry.

'At first he just ranted. He kept asking how we dared do it. I thought I might have to call the police. He was very aggressive.'

'With good reason,' Stefanie said.

'No,' Ilse said. 'There was no reason whatsoever.' She sounded like a school teacher telling a pupil that there was no excuse for smoking behind the bicycle shed.

'I don't understand,' I said. 'You used his designs to win a deal against his company.' I turned to Stefanie in case I'd misunderstood something, but she nodded to show I'd got it right.

'It wasn't our fault we were better at producing the goods. He kept chasing the lowest cost, swapping manufacturers all the time, and the quality of his items was rock bottom. We worked with one trusted factory. We could make the product at a better quality and still cut a good deal for our clients. I think he was pissed off that he'd sold us the rights.'

'Hold on a second,' Stefanie said. 'He sold you the rights?'

'Yes. Two years ago, we bought a licence. They had accused us at a trade show of plagiarising their product. I didn't agree, there were distinct differences, but when the opportunity came up to buy a licence at a good price, we decided that we should do that and make it all above board. Their design was better than ours and it's worked out very well.'

'That was a bad business decision,' Stefanie muttered as she made a note.

'Yeah, well, I got the impression Linde Lights was in financial difficulties, and I had no qualms about taking advantage of that. They needed the money and I thought we'd be able to do a better job than them at producing and selling those goods.'

'So why did Patrick come here?' I asked.

'My guess is that he was the kind of person to blame his failures on everybody else. That he came here to shout at me instead of trying to improve his own sales process and

302

production workflow didn't surprise me at all.' She shrugged. 'I've seen it before.'

'I talked to Therese Klein,' I said. 'She said that Patrick was upset because you plagiarised the lights.'

Ilse sniffed. 'He should have been upset with her. The client went with us because she never followed up with them. But yes, that was one of the things he accused me of.'

'Can I see the paperwork?' Stefanie asked. 'I'd like to see the licensing contract.' She wasn't just going to take Ilse's word for it.

'Sure,' Ilse said. 'Just wait one second, I'll get our lawyer to dig it out for you.'

She left the room.

'Do you believe her?' I asked Stefanie as soon as the door closed.

'People don't normally get their lawyers to find paperwork that doesn't exist. She seems very confident.'

'So what happened? Patrick signed away the rights to their bestselling product and then forgot all about it?' This made no sense to me. Though if he had sold the rights to get the money he needed, that explained why he'd refused to take Ozone to court. He obviously hadn't told Nico or any of his other staff about the deal.

'We need to read the contract,' Stefanie said. 'The devil is in the detail with those things. There could be a clause that says they can use the product but not in direct competition with Linde Lights. That's what I would have insisted on if I were Patrick. Or it might exclude a certain market segment or order size. Unless you were going to go bust without this cash, you wouldn't do a deal like this.'

'Why not?' I had to acknowledge that it was a good thing Stefanie was here to help me with these details.

'Allow your competitor to sell your product in what seems to be a small market space? It's financial suicide.'

'It must have been where the money from the second cash injection came from.'

'Yes, and you've seen what happened to the sales figures since.'

'Because Ozone did a better job producing the lights than Linde themselves.'

'I think Ilse was right: chasing the lowest cost didn't work out for them. You heard what Nico said about being pulled in different directions.'

'So maybe Patrick was angry because he'd done a lousy business deal.'

'We'll see,' Stefanie said. 'Let's wait until we can read through the contract.'

Ilse came back five minutes later with the corporate lawyer, who introduced himself as Jan Smits.

'I had the paperwork to hand,' he said with a smile. 'You're not the first to ask me for it.'

'Who else?' I said.

'Oh, Patrick van der Linde contacted me about two weeks ago. Said something about having lost a deal and that it was plagiarism. He'd been here that morning and met with Ilse.'

'I had no idea he contacted you,' Ilse said.

'I sent him a copy of the contract and didn't hear anything subsequently.'

'Tell us exactly what he said,' Stefanie said impatiently.

'He called me, said he was going to sue us; that he had irrevocable proof we'd done a deal with one of their clients using a plagiarised version of their design.'

'Did he sound as if he was serious?'

'Deadly.' He leaned forward. 'I was very surprised. We'd only signed the contract for the licence two years before. I'd worked on it myself, and there were no exclusions, so I had no idea why he would think he could sue us.'

'Can you show me a copy?'

'I'll email you the electronic scanned version.'

'That would be great. Can you also send me the details of the account you wired the money to? And the total amount?'

'Of course,' Ilse said. 'We paid the money to Linde Lights directly. We've got nothing to hide. It was all above board.'

Stefanie nodded. 'I think we're finally getting somewhere,' she said softly.

'Leave it with me,' Stefanie said as we stood outside the police station. 'I'll go through the contract and call you with what I find.' She swiped her entry card and went inside.

I was left on the pavement. Her claim that we were getting somewhere didn't sit well with me at all. Were we really? Sure, we'd found evidence of Patrick's erratic and maybe desperate behaviour. We were getting somewhere if we were only interested in why Linde Lights had gone bankrupt, but that wasn't my priority.

Right now, Arjen was still locked up – though the twenty-four hours we could question him for would run out in six hours – and there was a seemingly unbridgeable gap between me and the rest of my team. I knew that if I waited it out, Arjen would walk out mid afternoon, but there would be damaged relationships that I might never be able to repair. On the one hand, my mother would hold a grudge against me for not having done enough to help him; on the other hand, my team would resent me for having interfered.

I'd never enjoyed just waiting around. If I was in the wrong either way, why not do something? I paused for a few seconds, decided I had nothing to lose, then put my swipe card against the reader.

Chapter 34

I was surprised to find Thomas and Charlie in our office. They must be taking a break from interrogating Arjen.

Thomas looked up. 'What are you doing here? Trying to convince us to let your ex go?'

'This is ridiculous,' I said. 'We're not competitors. We're working together on closing this case. If Arjen murdered Patrick, we should keep him locked him up.' It didn't bother me all that much now to say those words. 'It's crazy that I'm running around trying to prove you wrong. That's not how things should work.'

Thomas grinned. 'Does this mean you realise I'm right and are giving up?'

'Not funny,' I said. 'I can accept that something happened between the two of them; that they argued, that Arjen hit Patrick and Patrick fell and bashed his head. All of this I can picture without any problem.'

'Good,' Thomas said. 'You're halfway there then.'

'But I have a massive problem with the thought of Arjen pushing him into the water afterwards.' This was what I'd decided yesterday, and I hadn't changed my mind. 'The place is wrong too,' I said. 'It's much more likely that the body went into the canal further down; not at the back of the Clipper, but along the path.'

'They were arguing behind the Clipper, that's what the manager said.'

'Sure. I know that. They argued there, but that doesn't mean Patrick was murdered there.'

'Is that what you've been doing? Looking for a more convenient place for the murder?'

'I talked to Fabrice.' I sat down. 'Remember that I said he had prior? I checked that out, but he's got an alibi for the night of the dinner. He had Therese's mother with him the whole time.'

'So that's why you didn't get in touch. I wondered. Makes sense if your big hunch didn't go anywhere.'

'Don't be like that.' I was tired. 'Let's stop playing these stupid games. If Arjen did it, I'll help you put him away. Convicting the right person is more important than my personal feelings. All day long people have been attacking me because they think I'm trying to lock him up out of revenge. Now you're being stupid because you think I'm trying to keep him out of prison. Maybe you should all just accept that I want justice to be done.'

Thomas looked at me thoughtfully.

'There are a few things you need to know,' I said. 'I talked to Arjen's wife. She used to work at Linde Lights but couldn't stand it because of the way her father treated his female staff: the affairs, touching them up. She said she told him to stop and he continued, so she got pissed off with him and went to work somewhere else. Two years ago, he asked her for money and she refused. Then he asked her again recently, said he'd alter the way the company was run and give her a fifty per cent stake. They decided that Arjen should work there for a bit, look into the strategy but also Patrick's behaviour.' I shrugged. 'That evening at the Clipper pretty much proved he hadn't changed at all. Arjen came home, told Nadia he'd argued with her father over Therese.'

'They didn't give him money two years ago?'

'No, Patrick sold the patents to their top-selling product to another company. It solved the short-term financial issues but only got them further into problems.'

'Did everybody know that?'

'I don't think so. Therese told me she and Nico saw the other company at a trade show and he went nuts. Said they were plagiarising the designs, even though the other company denies that. He tried to get Patrick to sue them, but I'm guessing Patrick subsequently met with them and signed a deal to keep Linde afloat.'

'We'd been wondering where that other payment came from,' Charlie said.

'It was all above board, just not very smart from a business point of view.' I had learned something from Stefanie at least. I'd even started to sound like her.

'He probably thought Nico would just come up with something new.'

'He put huge pressure on him to do just that.'

'And Nico failed. So that's why Patrick wanted to fire him,' Thomas said.

'He wanted to do what?' This was news to me.

'Arjen said it was what he and Patrick talked about before the argument.'

I thought about Nico telling me how Patrick would have realised he'd intervened with Therese for his own good. It now seemed more likely that Nico would have been sacked.

I was still trying to figure out if that meant that he had deliberately lied to us, or if he hadn't known about Patrick's intentions, when Stefanie burst into our office. 'I got the document from the lawyer,' she said. 'He just emailed it to me. Look at this last page.'

I wondered how she'd known I was in the office and hadn't gone home.

She opened the printout and flipped to the end. 'This wasn't signed by Patrick van der Linde.'

'Who signed it then?'

'Nico Verhoef.'

'What? Could he do that?'

Stefanie sat down at the desk next to mine. 'I looked into that. He was a director of the company. He was legally allowed to sign.'

'Patrick probably didn't know about it.'

'Right. That's why he went to Ozone. That's why he was so angry. He probably wasn't aware of the licence agreement at all; even if Verhoef had told him about it, he might not have realised the impact.'

'That's all well and good,' Thomas said, 'but it doesn't mean Verhoef killed Patrick. I'm not going to let your ex off the hook just because of this.'

'You're right,' I said. 'We need to keep Boogaard locked up. Carry on interviewing him.' I looked at Stefanie. 'He'll be the perfect decoy while we investigate Nico Verhoef.'

310

Chapter 35

Stefanie and I walked to Nico's house. I'd convinced her that it would be quicker than driving. I had a lot of questions about him and I wanted to see where he lived.

His flat was in Amsterdam East, upstairs from what seemed to be a museum for bric-a-brac but was probably just a shop. He buzzed us in and we went up two flights of steep steps. The building was on a busy road, rather than along a canal like mine.

He opened the door and stepped back to let us in. There were no signs of anybody else living here; no photos of family. It was sparsely decorated, as if he needed all the space himself.

'We met with the people from Ozone,' I said. 'We've seen a copy of the contract you signed giving them the licence for your design.'

'Your decision single-handedly bankrupted the company,' Stefanie said.

Nico flinched. 'It wasn't like that.'

'You sold the rights and Ozone produced your stuff at a higher quality for less money.'

'I wasn't to know that. We needed the money. Patrick told me we were going bankrupt if we couldn't come up with half a million euros.'

'But you didn't tell him where the money came from.'

'After the trade show, I'd told him we should sue Ozone, but he didn't have the cash to do that. He said he couldn't afford the lawyers. He wouldn't sue them, he wouldn't sell the rights. He was sitting there doing nothing, panicking about going bankrupt. That fear seemed to have paralysed him, and I had no other way of raising the capital. I saved the company. Whatever you might think, I saved it. I didn't bankrupt it.'

I realised that Nico hadn't lied to us yesterday; he'd just omitted what had happened after he'd been frustrated by Patrick's lack of action. I remembered thinking that he was keen for us not to talk to Ozone. Now I understood why: not because he wanted a job there, but because the part he'd played in destroying his own company would come out.

'You signed the contract behind Patrick's back,' Stefanie said.

'They were my designs. I had the rights to them. I'd patented them before joining Linde. It was a large part of why Patrick wanted me to work with him.'

'But when you started working for Linde, your designs became their intellectual property?' Stefanie asked.

'Yes, that was part of my employment contract. But I was also a director of Linde Lights. So even if they weren't my designs, I was legally allowed to sign the documents.'

'What happened when Patrick found out?' I asked. 'He went to Ozone after Therese lost that deal, and the lawyer showed him the document. That's when he knew you'd signed it.'

'He was angry, of course. He said I shouldn't have done it. Even after I explained that we'd had no choice, he was still livid. Said I hadn't had the right to do it. I told him I had.' His voice was calm, but I could see that his hands were shaking. 'But when Patrick was in that kind of mood, there was no talking to him.'

'When was this?' I asked.

'Three days before he died.'

He'd gone to Ozone a week before his death and asked for the contract. He must have waited a few days to think about how he was going to react.

'But we talked again the day after,' Nico continued. 'And then we went to the Clipper. He still wasn't happy about it, but at least he was no longer quite as angry. He said that what was done was done. I felt really bad. Maybe I hadn't thought it through. I'm not saying I'm a business genius, but at least I bought the company two years' grace. Otherwise we would have gone bankrupt sooner. And I still think that if Patrick hadn't died, we would have weathered this storm too.'

'Patrick said he was going to fire you and get in a new lead designer.'

Nico shook his head. 'That was just something he said on the spur of the moment. He was angry with me. He was angry over the contract with Ozone and he was angry about the Therese situation, but I don't think he would have fired me. We would have talked the next day and he would have understood why I'd done what I did. I signed the deal with

Ozone so we would survive. Because Patrick refused to take them to court, we had no other option. I interfered in the situation with Therese because the last thing he needed was for her to call the police. So yes, that night he was angry with me, and he might well have told someone he was going to fire me. He used to say that all the time. But there was no way he would have actually done it. He would have called me into his office and apologised, as he'd done a number of times before.' He smiled. 'He was like that: his temper flared up and then he calmed down again.'

'But this time he was murdered after you argued.'

'I know. I'm distraught that we can never put things right again.'

Back outside, Stefanie said, 'I'll go through the company records. There must be something there. I just can't believe that this was all done above board.'

'Was that a crime? Going behind Patrick's back like that?'

'If Nico personally got nothing in return, then no. It was a bad business move, but if – and this is a big if – he was a signatory for the company and Ozone paid Linde directly for the rights, then no crime has been committed. I just can't imagine that Patrick accepted such a large sum of money without asking questions. And from a competitor, of all people. Surely he must have wondered why they'd paid him, unless he was so relieved that he didn't stop to think. It just doesn't seem right.'

'I can't see it as a motive for murder,' I said.

'I could see that Patrick would have wanted to kill Nico, not the other way round.'

'Maybe they got into a physical fight.'

Stefanie threw me a look. 'You're grasping at straws,' she said. 'This could well have been all above board.'

Back in the office, I called Nadia. I'd never thought I'd voluntarily dial those digits, but work was more important than my personal dislike and she was the only one who could answer my question. If she was surprised to hear from me, it didn't show in her voice.

'Did you know Nico Verhoef was a director in Linde Lights?'

'Yeah,' she said, 'I knew that. My father didn't tell me at the time, but he told Arjen recently. I was pissed off, of course.'

'Why?'

'If he'd offered Nico that deal, why not give us better terms two years ago? I might have made the investment then in return for a directorship. A say in the company. But my father only asked me for a loan, while making his mate a director. Just typical.'

I wished that Stefanie was here to help me make sense of what Nadia was saying. Instead, I was going to have to show my ignorance in front of my ex's new wife, like I'd shown it in front of my stepsister-to-be the other day.

'What do you mean?' I asked through gritted teeth. 'Wasn't Nico a director from the start?' That was what I'd assumed when he'd first told us he was one.

'Oh God, no. My father made him one in return for money. That was where the financial injection came from.'

'He made him a director because they got the money from Ozone?'

'Ozone? No, it was money from Nico himself.'

'The money came from Nico personally?' I was obviously being dim, because I didn't get this at all. I had thought that the financial injection had been from Ozone, when they bought the rights to Linde's bestselling product.

'Yes, he made a large investment in the firm when I refused, and my father made him a director in return.'

'And this was two years ago?'

'Yes. I'd say he must have gone begging to Nico the day after I turned him down. And with terms I might have accepted, too. But then Nico never questioned my father's morals or his business sense, so my father probably thought he would be easier to deal with than me.' She sighed. 'I'm not supposed to speak ill of the dead, am I? Do you want me to come and make a statement about this? Are you going to let my husband go now?'

'Just a little longer,' I said. 'Please be patient.'

Stefanie called me as soon as I'd put the phone down, before I could even tell her what I'd heard from Nadia. 'I've got a present for you,' she said. 'Come on up. I think you were right after all.'

I went upstairs to her office. 'What is it?'

'Look at the dates,' she said. 'I pulled the records from Company House. Nico Verhoef is indeed a director at Linde Lights.'

'Right, so there's no problem?'

'Check these dates,' she said. 'I'll make it clear for you.' She drew a long horizontal line on her office whiteboard.

I should be annoyed that she thought I wouldn't be able to understand it without a drawing, but in fact I was grateful that she was using my favourite technique to explain an important point to me.

'Nico Verhoef makes a payment of half a million euros on the twenty-third of September. Two days later, Patrick makes Nico a director. And here's the interesting bit: he also transfers a quarter of the shares in the company to Nico.'

'Nadia told me that Nico became a director in return for that money. So he wasn't a director when he signed the agreement with Ozone?'

'I thought you'd think that,' Stefanie smiled, 'but he was. He signed the deal with Ozone a month later.' She drew a spot on the timeline. 'But here's the interesting bit: Ozone then paid Linde Lights half a million euros.'

'Hold on. So there were two payments? One from Nico and one from Ozone? Did you see that when you looked into Linde's finances? I thought there was only one payment.'

'Exactly. There was only one payment to that reserve account, and it came from Nico. That's when I double-checked the details of the account Ozone paid that money into. It was a third Linde Lights account.'

My head was spinning. 'Wait, there was a third account?'

'At least there was another account under that name. I didn't think there was any point in asking Karin, She was in charge of invoices but wouldn't have known anything about this. So I called the bank.'

'What did they say?'

'This was a business account with a completely different bank. Not the one the two main accounts were with. It was opened by a company director of Linde in late September. Guess who that was.'

'The new director, Nico Verhoef.'

'We'll make a financial expert out of you yet, Lotte. Nico, with all the proper paperwork, perfectly legally opens another business account. Ozone pays the money into it and Nico personally withdraws the funds a few days later. He never uses that account again.'

I shook my head. 'That's crazy.'

'No, it's smart,' Stefanie said. 'Very hard to trace, and no statement would ever have reached Patrick or Karin. Without Patrick's murder, we'd never have found out about it.'

'If Patrick hadn't gone to talk to Ozone after Therese's deal fell through, he wouldn't have noticed any of this.'

'Actually, I'm surprised he didn't contact them sooner if he thought they were plagiarising Linde's designs.'

'That's the inaction that annoyed Nico so much, I guess.'

'Yeah, well, he still shouldn't have done what he did. If he wanted to sell the rights, he should have put that money in the reserve account and told Patrick about the deal he'd struck.'

I still didn't quite get what had happened. 'But Nico paid money to Patrick, to Linde Lights, before he became a director. Where did that money come from?'

'If I had to guess, I would say a loan. He probably took out a second mortgage on his flat. No bank would have lent him that amount without collateral.'

'So Nico takes out a mortgage, gives Patrick the money, becomes a director and major shareholder, signs the deal with Ozone, gets the money back and pays off his mortgage?'

'In a nutshell, that's exactly it.'

'But what if Ozone refused to sign? What if they hadn't paid the money?'

'Those negotiations probably took a long time. To be honest, Ozone got a sweet deal, probably because Nico couldn't raise more capital on his flat.'

I shook my head. 'Then Patrick found out and went crazy.'

'He probably threatened to take Nico to court over it. Not just fire him, but send him to prison.'

'It's the perfect motive for murder.' No longer a reason for Patrick to want to kill Nico, but for Nico to want to murder Patrick to keep him quiet.

I thought about the CCTV footage from inside the Clipper. 'Look at this and tell me what you think.'

'You want my opinion now?'

'Just watch.' I pulled it up on Stefanie's PC and pressed play. Together we stared at the screen. The last time I'd looked, I had been focusing on Nico filling up Patrick's glass. Now I also saw that Patrick seemed angry with Nico. His body language told me at least that much. He was sitting turned away from him, and as I'd noticed before, the two men didn't speak to each other at all, even as Nico kept pouring the wine. Was he doing that because it was easier to dump a man into the canal if he was drunk? Make it seem like an accident? That would mean the attack hadn't been a spur-of-the-moment thing, but carefully planned. When had

Nico first known that Arjen was going to come to the office and that there would be an evening do? He had known exactly how Patrick was going to behave after he'd had a few too many. Get him drunk, get Therese to come to the Clipper, and it was an accident waiting to happen.

Why, though?

So that Nico could be the hero and no suspicion would attach to him? Or so that he could explain away any argument with Patrick as being about the sexual assault?

Another thought came to mind. What if he'd wanted to set up Fabrice? Had he planned to create a scenario where someone with a record of violence would have a reason to attack Patrick? It could have worked; if Therese's mother hadn't been there to give him a solid alibi, I would have continued to investigate him. Instead, Thomas had focused on Arjen. Nico couldn't have seen that coming – that Arjen and Patrick would argue over Nico's behaviour – but it had worked out very well for him. He had seemed like a hero and he was in the clear.

I sat back. 'I need you to explain this to Thomas and Charlie. You need to convince them.'

'There's nothing to convince them of. These are facts.'

'Convince them that Nico murdered Patrick.'

'We have no evidence for that.'

Nico had filled Patrick's glass again and again. He was a tall man who could easily have bashed Patrick's head in and then tipped him into the canal. Maybe he'd even overheard Patrick and Arjen's argument and couldn't believe his luck.

'I'll tell them about the fraud,' she said. 'You can try to

get them to switch their main focus from your ex to your suspect.'

'You're so frustrating,' I said.

'I do the financial part. Remember? You wanted me to find the money problems; I found them. That's what I do.'

I didn't have to make a drawing to get a picture of what must have been going on inside Nico's head, and why he'd killed Patrick. Not only would it mean he'd get away with his fraud; he was also going to keep the company as the sole director. It was very possible that he hadn't appreciated what Patrick's death would mean financially, only thinking that if Patrick was dead, his way would be clear and his crime of two years ago would be covered up. He probably wasn't all that fussed about what he put Therese through. If she hadn't gone running to the boss after she'd lost her latest deal, Patrick wouldn't have gone to Ozone and none of this would have happened.

An unpleasant lesson for Therese: her boyfriend arrested and Nico seen as the big hero. That could have been his plan. It had so nearly worked.

'After all this,' I said, 'you don't want to see it through to the end? You don't want to help close the case?'

Stefanie looked down at her high-heeled shoes. 'I thought you were going to kick me out at this point.'

'Don't be an idiot. Let's do this.'

She smiled. 'Okay.'

I should check with Charlie whether he'd seen Nico anywhere on CCTV that night. I knew he'd checked the public transport footage. That would at least show that Nico hadn't gone straight home. It wouldn't be evidence of him killing Patrick, of course. For that we needed more. We should plan before confronting him. As of now, he thought we were still focusing on Arjen. He had no idea he'd become a suspect.

Chapter 36

I sat back as Stefanie ran through the fraud again. I'd called Thomas and Charlie out of their interview. She told them exactly what Nico had done, and how. How he'd basically swindled Patrick out of a quarter of his company by selling the rights to their main product behind his back. How this had eventually made the company go bankrupt as Ozone did a better job of producing the lights than Linde. They were being outcompeted by their own product, as she phrased it.

'So what do you want us to do?' Thomas said. 'Drop our investigation into Arjen Boogaard and switch to Nico Verhoef?'

'One of these men has a motive for murder,' I said. 'We haven't looked into Nico's movements for the rest of that evening. He said he got on the tram and went home. He would have known that Patrick was likely to smoke a cigarette after the drinks, as he'd gone with him to so many of these events before. That's what you guys said about Arjen and it's just as true for Nico. Even more so, probably.'

'So, what, he waited until Arjen left and then bashed Patrick's head in?'

'To be honest,' I said, 'I think he waited for Patrick somewhere along the path. I never liked the patio behind the Clipper as the place for the murder. I think he did it somewhere further down, where it's much easier to roll the body into the water. He just had to wait longer than he'd expected, because Patrick had an argument with his son-in-law first.'

'We were getting nowhere with Boogaard anyway,' Charlie said. 'We pulled his mobile records and found he called his wife to tell her he was on his way. We could pinpoint him en route to Haarlem twenty minutes after Patrick paid the bill, according to the Clipper's till.'

'Twenty minutes? He argued with Patrick, hit him over the head and dumped his body in the canal, then got into his car and drove off, all in twenty minutes?'

'Fifteen, actually,' Charlie said. 'It would have taken at least five minutes to drive to where the GPS pinpointed him.'

'Seriously? Why did you arrest him, then?'

'Purely to piss you off, Lotte,' Thomas snapped. Then he calmed himself down. 'Because fifteen minutes is plenty of time. You know that.'

'But you had nothing on him. There's no motive, just the location and opportunity. And if the opportunity now looks dubious—'

'Plus he lied to the police.'

'He lied because it was me,' I said. 'He felt he needed to protect his father-in-law's reputation. If I had been nowhere near this case, he probably wouldn't have lied, but because I came to his house with you that first time, he didn't want to make Patrick look bad. It was stupid, I warned him about it twice, but there you go.'

'You should have stayed away.'

'Yes, remember I told you the same thing? This time it wasn't because it influenced my behaviour, but because it influenced his.'

'It influenced yours too,' Stefanie said. 'Look how you've been running around to prove he's innocent.'

'Because he *is* innocent,' I said. 'I've been running around to make sure an innocent man doesn't get charged with something he didn't do. That he's my ex-husband just means I'm more certain he couldn't have done it.'

'We were going to release him anyway,' Thomas said. 'Even without your running around.'

'How long have you got left?' I said.

'Another hour.'

'Let's arrest Nico Verhoef first. As long as Arjen is locked up, Nico won't feel the need to run.'

'We haven't got enough to arrest Verhoef for Patrick's murder,' Thomas said.

I shook my head. 'We won't arrest him for murder.' I turned to Stefanie. 'We'll arrest him for financial fraud.'

Chapter 37

We were outside Nico's flat again. Even if there was still a full-scale terror investigation going on, that didn't mean there weren't enough officers to support us as we were about to arrest a murderer. I knocked on the door to the flat, my gun ready. There was no response. I waited. Nothing. On my signal, one of my colleagues bashed the door in.

The flat was empty. When I looked in the bedroom, the wardrobes were half empty too. I'd been wrong: even having Arjen in custody didn't make Nico feel safe. He had run after all.

'Call in his licence plate,' I said to Stefanie. 'We need to trace his car and stop him.' She didn't even say anything snarky like suggesting I do it myself. I called the Schiphol police and asked them to run the passenger list for a Nico Verhoef.

'Singapore.' The answer came back quickly. 'He's booked on a flight to Singapore in an hour.'

'Whereabouts is he? There's an arrest warrant out for him,' I said.

'He's airside. He's gone through security already.' The man's voice was calm. 'Leave it with us.'

Nothing like an airport full of armed police to make a nice clean arrest. I wasn't even nervous.

'See,' Stefanie said. 'If it wasn't for fraud, you would never have been on time.'

'You're right,' I said. 'If it hadn't been for you, we wouldn't have been able to arrest him.'

'Let's go to Schiphol,' she suggested.

'No,' I said. 'We should leave that to the airport police. We'll stay here and do our job.'

I put on my nitrile gloves and began to search the flat to see if I could find something that linked Nico to Patrick's murder. I only stopped to answer a call fifteen minutes later. The Schiphol police had picked Nico up and detained him.

I thanked the officer and went back to my search.

I found what I needed stashed in a corner of the wardrobe, hidden underneath a pile of jumpers. It was as if he'd kept it as a souvenir of what he'd done. Maybe he needed this reminder. I might not have thought anything of what I was holding in my hands if I hadn't known the exact shape of what I was looking for. Even though it was washed clean, forensics would be able to find blood traces.

What made someone do something like this? Why leave this behind when you were leaving the country? Had he forgotten it was there?

Either way, here was the evidence we required.

He'd kept the brick.

Chapter 38

My mother looked beautiful in her pink dress – which she insisted on calling red. I had to admit that this wedding ceremony was rather sweet. I sat next to Mark and held his hand. It helped me not to cry. The registrar looked just as happy as the couple.

They had decided not to get married in church and I was pleased about that. Instead, it was just a small affair in the town hall. Elise and I were the witnesses. Richard had joked that we could be flower girls or maids of honour, but luckily Elise had been as little enamoured with that idea as I was. Instead, we signed the register as our parents got married.

The reception afterwards was an informal affair. There was no official line for congratulations; people just milled around. My mother and her new husband were doing the rounds. I saw them go up to Arjen and Nadia. I didn't join her on their tour of the room. I stayed behind and chatted with Mark, Elise and Michael.

A few minutes later, Arjen came over. I made the introductions. 'Michael you've met before,' I said.

Michael grinned. Arjen didn't get what we were laughing about, but I didn't bother explaining.

'Thanks, Lotte,' he said, 'for getting me out.'

I shrugged. 'You didn't do it. It wasn't a big deal.'

'We didn't bring Iris.'

'Iris?'

'Our daughter.'

'Lovely name. It's a shame you didn't,' I said. 'My mother would have liked to have her here.'

I wasn't being magnanimous, just honest. My mother would have liked it, and I realised it didn't hurt any more. Instead of the man I used to love, I now saw the current man in Arjen's face. The thinning hair, the skin that sagged around his jawline. I'd successfully severed the ties to the past.

We talked amicably, like acquaintances at parties do, but quickly ran out of things to say.

'Anyway,' Arjen said after we'd fallen silent, 'Margreet said hi.'

'How's she doing?'

'Better now she's finally arranged the funeral. Also we were relieved that Patrick had some life insurance so she can stay in the flat.'

'I hope there'll be a good turn-out.'

'Will you come?'

'I don't think so,' I said. 'I have no reason to be there.'

Arjen nodded, and when I didn't say anything more, he said goodbye and strolled over to Nadia.

The old part of my life walked away, and I turned away from him to go back to talking to Mark, Elise and Michael.

My new life.

Acknowledgements

I want to thank everybody who helped me with this book. I'm fortunate to work with a great team of people. In Allan Guthrie from The North Literary Agency, I have a fantastic writer as my agent. My editor Krystyna Green, editorial manager Amanda Keats, copyeditor Jane Selley and all at Constable and Little, Brown have worked hard to make this book the best it could possibly be.

Finally, I want to thank all the readers who continue to enjoy my books.